lily@lilywhitebooks.com
http://www.facebook.com/authorlilywhite
www.lilywhitebooks.com

FEAR THE WICKED

Illusions Duet – Book Two
A Dark Thriller by Lily White

LILY WHITE
BESTSELLING AUTHOR

If you are interested in reading additional books by Lily White or would like to know when new books are being released, Lily White can be found on:
Facebook, Instagram and
Twitter

Join the Mailing List!
If you are interested in receiving email updates regarding additional books by Lily White or would like to know when new books are announced or being released, join the mailing list via this link.
http://eepurl.com/Onoeb

Join the Facebook Fan Group!
If you are interested in receiving exclusive previews for upcoming novels, or to participate in giveaways, join the fan group for Lily White Books.
FAN GROUP LINK

Follow Lily on BookBub!
https://www.bookbub.com/profile/lily-white

OTHER BOOKS BY LILY WHITE

MASTERS SERIES:

Her Master's Courtesan
(Book 1 of the Masters Series)
(Available on Smashwords and lilywhitebooks.com)

Her Master's Teacher
(Book 2 of the Masters Series)

Her Master's Christmas
(Novella in the Masters Series)

Her Master's Redemption
(Book 3 of the Masters Series)

Her Master's Reckoning
(Book 4 of the Masters Series)

STANDALONE NOVELS:

Target This
Hard Roads
Asylum
Wake to Dream
Four Crows
Crazy Madly Deeply
Rules of Engagement
Wishing Well
The Five

Sin & Discipline

ILLUSIONS DUET

Illusions of Evil
(Book 1 of the Illusions Duet)

Fear the Wicked
(Book 2 of the Illusions Duet)

DARK EXCLUSIVE - Available only on LilyWhiteBooks.com:

The Director

Author Note and Disclaimer:

This book is intended for entertainment purposes solely. This novel discusses sensitive subject matters. Readers who sensitive to triggers are advised to proceed with caution.

The opinions given by the characters in this novel do not reflect those of the author. They are fictional characters with minds of their own.

Table of Contents

1

ELIJAH

It would take some finesse on my part to bend the morality of the citizens of the small town I'd inherited.

Every Sunday, they showed up faithfully. And every Sunday, I eased them into the violence I knew lay just beneath their skin. It was right there, an electric current just waiting for the proper outlet to be expressed. Time would pull them all into my mind, would set them on the path of salvation that the family had already begun to walk.

Most were readily pliant, others more difficult. My twin brother, Jacob, had done an impressive job losing the trust of his parishioners. During the week he went mad, he was rude to them, he'd distanced himself from them, and he'd insulted them.

Especially the father of Annabelle Prete.

Just thinking about that poor girl had my shoulders shaking with soft laughter against the cheap, secretarial chair in Jacob's prior office.

Richard walked in and I tracked his short journey across the room, my eyes meeting his when he dropped

1

his weight into a chair facing my desk. I pulled the clerical collar from my neck and threw it on the wood surface.

"How much longer, boss? The family is getting antsy."

"A few minutes at most. Eve is ready. The martyr that she is." More soft laughter was a vibration over my chest.

Grinning, Richard glanced over my shoulder toward the window at my back. "Joshua may have an issue with the example being made of his sister."

"Joshua knows," I explained, little concern in my voice for how the family members would react to the show.

Three months wasn't a long time in the grand scheme of things, but it was enough time to isolate the town. With the small farms and bevy of blue collar talents, it wasn't difficult to become a community without much need of outside assistance.

In response to my sermons, the citizens had slowly closed themselves off, had turned away from the televisions and internet, had burned whatever cultural items their children had acquired in an effort to blend in with the youth of the larger cities hundreds of miles outside our borders.

Isolation was key and to accomplish that, I'd spoken to the Diocese regarding the threat against the Mother and remaining Sisters at the convent following the discovery of Sister Joyce's body. There wasn't much left of her. It appeared she'd been abducted by the same psychopath that stole Eunice from the convent's doors, but rather than returning her to the parish, he must have left her to the wild animals along the lonely dirt road where she was discovered.

2

A smile had stretched my lips during that particular phone call, but fortunately they could only hear the feigned regret and sorrow in my voice.

The Diocese agreed that the remaining nuns should be removed to another convent far from our sleepy mountain, at least until the killer was caught. They'd left me in charge of the small congregation, alone and unsupervised, and then thanked me for the foresight to see to the nuns' safety.

Oh, yes, Father Hayle, you are so wise...

I'd laughed at the compliment. They were nothing but slack-jaws, all of them.

Richard's meaty hand ran through his brown hair. Shoulder length, it framed the parts of his face that his thick, long beard didn't hide. With broad shoulders and a rotund stomach bulging over the large buckle of his belt, Richard leaned back in his chair, kicked his legs out and crossed them at the ankles.

Unlike him, I was the sleek rural priest with black hair and blue eyes, shoulders as broad as Richard's, but a stature standing a few inches taller. Built to seduce, my body was a weapon of deception as opposed to Richard's brute strength.

It was no surprise to me that the younger female parishioners - those girls that had come to an age where childhood was far behind - batted their eyes when I looked in their direction. In truth, they were flirting with Jacob, not realizing I'd taken his place.

"Five minutes," Richard finally said, his voice as gruff as his appearance. "You should get in your robe and get out there." He paused, considering. "Not many people showed up from town."

"I didn't invite many," I explained as I pushed to my feet. "And the cassock won't be necessary. This isn't

3

Mass or anything formal, just a gathering of the family and the men from town that I think will be ready for this little treat. Once we have them convinced that it's normal, they'll help convince the other men. Once we have the men, we'll have the women, and once we have the women, we'll have the town." I winked at him. "Baby steps, Richard."

Nodding, he smiled and stood to walk with me into the hall, our booted steps heavy and in no hurry against the ground.

Turning the corner, we looked across the nave toward the sanctuary. Eve sat in a single, small chair to the left of the pulpit. Covered by a hooded black robe, she angled her head down so you couldn't see her face.

Silent. Motionless. Both fearful and excited, Eve proved her worth to me every single day.

Anticipation was the tension across our shoulders.

"You think she'll scream?" Richard asked, a touch of humor in his question, his eyes darting between Eve and me.

My lips curled at the corners, desire crawling inside me as electric sparks beneath the skin.

"I know she will," I answered, "in both pain and perverse pleasure. And I can promise you, Richard, there is no other music like it."

2

EVE

The ceremony would begin in a few minutes.

I listened to the people who gathered, felt compelled to peek out from beneath the hood just to know who would stand in attendance of the first *true* cleansing. But no matter how badly I wanted to know who would stand in witness, I kept my head bowed and out of sight, just as I'd been instructed.

Elijah warned me that it would hurt. Not as bad as the brand I wore on my shoulder, but more than what he did to me in bed. Yet, I didn't fear what was coming. Only because I knew that what would follow would be a release of pressure like I'd never known.

Wickedness is only relieved with pain. And pain is a balm to the sinner's soul. It flays you open, settles inside, and shreds you until there is nothing left.

You're meat, pulled open and tenderized while the pain whistles across you. But once you're clean, once every last ounce of the sin you carry is lifted and banished into the ether, you're free. A bird flying high. A dolphin gliding through water. You are lost in a moment of pure bliss that is a comforting hug in the warm morning sun.

Only Elijah could give that to me.

Created. Molded. Shaped and formed, I was what he wanted. I was what he alone knew existed inside me. But for all his power, all his wisdom and his strength, he was never able to remove the doubt I carried.

I loved him and feared him. Worshipped him and despised him. I couldn't live without him, even while knowing he would one day kill me.

The shuffling of feet quieted, the soft thud of bodies settling over the pews, and the sharp clatter of keys slapping against the wood from where the rings hung on the parishioners' belts.

Only one set of footsteps could be heard. Low and rhythmic, they approached the altar and pulpit, beats measured by a steady gait, the powerful and seductive walk of a predator.

"Good afternoon, gentlemen. I thank you for gathering together with me today."

Elijah's voice was a low hum across the room, a soothing melody in a rich tenor, a tone that was as soft as it was fierce. My heart sped at the sound of it.

"I'll start off this meeting with an explanation to those few who were invited. You'll notice there are no women or children in attendance, and the only people here tonight are the few men who I didn't doubt were ready to protect the serenity of their small town."

Grumbles of understanding and murmurs of approval were the harmony accompanying Elijah's words.

His manner of speaking was casual, a group of men discussing simple politics. There was no rush to the point, no emotions beyond the soothing laziness of a well-trained voice. I fell easily into the hypnotic lull of a peaceful summer afternoon just like the others.

6

Silence for only a moment. Broken when Elijah spoke again.

"I had a female parishioner approach me this week, gentlemen. She came to confess, came to speak in earnest about the sins she'd committed outside of town. I know this woman well, as do many of you. And it pains me to find that she's fallen for the Devil's seductive temptation."

He paused, his voice deepening. "She's possessed, it appears. Possessed by a demon that could infect your children...your wives."

More murmurs erupted, a few sharp inhalations of breath that betrayed the shock felt by a few of the men in attendance.

"We owe it to this woman to help her. More than that, we owe it to ourselves to protect our families from the threat staring us in the face." Another drawn out pause before, "May I speak frankly, Mr. Prete?"

The man's response wasn't oral, but he must have given some indication that Elijah could go on.

"We haven't always seen eye to eye have we, Mr. Prete?"

Another silent answer.

"And I think most of the people in this room know why. But for those who don't, I'll state the facts of the situation as delicately as possible. Annabelle Prete was a good girl. She was a believer in the Almighty, a young woman with a bright future ahead of her. She made her father proud and the town right alongside him. She was going somewhere."

I could hear Elijah pacing slowly to my right, his steps the only sound breaking apart the silence pregnant with trepidation and hesitant interest. It

7

would have smothered me beneath its heavy weight if not for Elijah moving around.

"Annabelle is dead, and between what was said to me in her last confession and what was sent to me by an unknown person outside of town, I'm concerned that the spirit infecting the woman seated next to me was the same one that infected Annabelle."

His steps stopped.

"I won't show the pictures, but I can tell you they were indecent, immoral, and utterly shocking. They were porn, images of a young girl who didn't know she'd lost her way. Disturbing as they were, they only verified what the young woman said to me before she died. More disturbing than that was my behavior toward Mr. Prete following the death of his daughter. I was so full of righteous fury and intolerable regret following Annabelle's death that I'd forgotten the discussion I'd had with Mr. Prete. At least until he reminded me."

I remembered the girl's death, recalled that it changed Elijah in a way I couldn't understand. While I'd always feared the power inside him, I'd been shown a softness I never knew existed. The first few days in the parish, he'd tended to me with a gentle hand. Resisted me until I'd cried believing I'd been rejected.

When he resumed his attentions on me, the first few times had been a caress of healing hands and sensual teeth. But after that girl died, after he witnessed a woman lost to the demons that plagued her, his attentions on me had changed.

The pain was exquisite, yet agonizing. His fear that I'd be lost as well driving him to exhaustion as he worked his magic inside me, as he battled and fought the sin that filled me until I was practically screaming.

8

Elijah had changed from one man into another. I couldn't understand why that change frightened me. Perhaps I was coming to life for once in my life, or perhaps I was being dragged back into the veil of ignorance and doubt that had always consumed me.

"I want to apologize to you, Mr. Prete. For both my weakness and my cruelty. I'm sure having lost one of your daughters, you can understand the pain I was feeling."

Mr. Prete wasn't much of a talker and it drove me a little mad that I couldn't see what was happening in the room.

"I was unable to save that young woman from whatever sickness plagued her. I was unable to guide her away from whatever monster it was that stole her virtue and took pictures of the crime he committed against her - the pictures he thought necessary to send to me."

My breath caught. I knew what was coming. Elijah's voice grew in strength as he spoke his next words.

"I couldn't save Annabelle, but I can save this woman. However, I'll need a strong body around me, a group of men whose faith in the Lord is without doubt. I need prayers, gentlemen, while I exorcise the demon ensnaring this young woman. Can you offer that to me despite what you see? Can you bless me and this suffering child of God with your participation and understanding?"

The men in attendance spoke, each acknowledging that they would give Elijah whatever help he needed. Faceless voices in different pitches and tones, each one resolute in their agreement that my sin needed to be cleansed.

9

"We'll begin," Elijah announced. "Eve. Please walk to me."

My legs barely held me as I stood, but I managed to cross the distance between us, was able to remain on my feet at Elijah's side. I wondered if the pain would be excruciating.

"This may shock you, gentlemen, but I believe desperate times call for desperate measures. She has the demon of lust inside her. Its sharp claws are entangled in her heart, its razor sharp teeth embedded in her soul. It's stolen her virtue and sanity, her ability to think clearly in the face of temptation."

His hand touched my shoulder. I lifted my eyes to see the men sitting in attendance. My gaze stilled when it locked on the faces of my father and brother. There was no fighting the tears that fell.

"Eve," Elijah said, "We'll need you to confess before we can drive the demon from you." His voice softened. "Can you do that for me?"

I almost laughed. He'd never asked me that question before. Normally he demanded a confession out of me.

"Yes," I finally answered.

The fabric of the hood slid from my head as he removed it, the cloth sash tying the robe around my body loosened until the robe itself was pulled from my shoulders. When they witnessed my nudity, some murmured in surprise, while others stared at the parts of me that brought on my shame.

Fully exposed, I was the spectacle of a woman's deception.

"Calm down, gentlemen, I know this is uncomfortable. But if we are to help this woman we need to stand in witness of her shame and degradation.

We need to believe in the Father who will lend us His strength in casting out the evil that holds her captive. We need to look upon her with an eye of pity rather than that of lust. It is just a naked body, one with a natural purpose that has been used to the Devil's advantage."

The hum of conversation grew quiet and I was directed to stand between two large posts, my face turned to the stained glass window, my arms bound above my head and to the sides of my body - cuffs attached to the posts that would secure me in place.

A shudder of doubt rolled through me, most likely the demon shaking beneath the knowledge that it would be expelled.

My head fell forward.

"Confess, Eve. Tell God your sins so that your penance will cleanse them from your body."

More murmurs of surprise erupted just before the strike of a whip cut into my back. The scream that burst from me was unholy, my tears hot and steadily flowing as I forced myself to speak.

"I've had disgusting thoughts," I breathed out, trying and failing to add any strength to my voice. The burning line across my back felt like it seeped beneath my skin to set my lungs on fire. I couldn't draw in air, could barely think past the sting of purification. "Thoughts that no person should have."

Another strike and I screamed again, my throat torn by the sheer volume, my jaw aching from how wide I stretched my lips. My wrists shook in the cuffs that held them, my legs giving out until I couldn't find the ability to push to my feet again. Tears dropped to the floor beneath me, small, wet puddles of evidence that could be used against me. Those same tears soaked

11

into my lips, the salt flavor of my agony a coating over my tongue.

Through sobs, I called out, "I've wanted immorality, craved sensuality, exposed my body and tempted men. I let one touch me. Let him press his naked body against mine." A terribly deep sob racked me. "He wasn't my husband."

The next strike of the whip cut through the cries of surprise and grunts of disapproval from the audience. Voices picked up, prayers being repeated as the men witnessed my shame. I wasn't sure my knees would hold me much longer.

Memory took me back to that night on the road, the night I'd willfully shown my body to a man who wasn't Elijah. For months, I'd believed he'd forgiven me, but in a state of panic about my eternal soul, Elijah had remembered within the last few days, all because I'd confessed what happened that night had become a fantasy.

Not the man. Never him. Just the way he'd controlled me.

"I invited the man to look at me," I breathed out before the whip came down again. The crack of leather caused my body to jump. The burning strike against my skin driving the breath from my lungs. My voice cracked and splintered beneath the strain of pure torture.

Euphoria settled in as I hung limp from the cuffs that bound me, and I felt free once again, slickness evident between my thighs.

The whip stopped, its weight dropped to the floor at my feet.

Elijah stood silent for only a few seconds before turning to the audience and claiming, "Gentlemen, the purge of evil has begun."

3

JACOB

Darkness doesn't settle, it consumes.

Flames of burning onyx, smoke full of mortal dread. Talons that tear you limb from limb until you're only a shadow of what you once had been.

I know darkness, and darkness knows me. I'd stared into its eyes and breathed its noxious poison. I'd supped on the sensual torment of every girl who'd crossed my bed. They scream until the night is cut through by the violence in their voice, but they keep coming back, one by one, begging to do it again.

They weren't her, though - weren't Cassandra or Eve. Sure, they begged and cried like the other two, but not for me to keep going. They wanted me to stop. Fear overtook them, the pain unsettling, but I never listened, never cared, never fell for the pathetic pleas and moans.

They knew what they were walking into when they climbed into my bed.

My heart was absent after the loss of Eve, but I hadn't been knocked down by her death. I was brought to life. I was charged by vengeance and the patience of biding my time.

Because if the monster inside couldn't be glutted by the sadism in bed - if I could no longer grow hard over the trembling bodies of the weak and desirous, the temptresses who keep me enraptured - then that vengeance I needed would be the only escape, the only balm, the last wicked act that would console me.

It was only a matter of time...

4

ELIJAH

"Shhhhh, my girl, shhh. It wasn't that bad. I didn't lose control like I feared I would. Don't worry."

After the building had emptied and the men returned home to think over what they witnessed, I stood behind Eve spreading ointment over her wounds. Her arms were still bound to the posts at her sides, blood seeping down her back where the thin lashes had broken the skin.

"You're tired. You should rest when I pull you down. You're limp."

"I could sleep for days," she answered, her voice haggard and breathless.

Soft laughter was a rumble in my chest. "Not that I'd let you."

Stepping closer, I ran my lips across her shoulder, enjoyed the shudder of her body as my hand reached around to take possessive hold of her breast. "You make me hungry in ways no man should hunger. I can't look at you without wanting to taste your decadent sin."

"Then I'll destroy you."

"No, my sweet girl. You'll never be powerful enough for that."

I fought not to laugh at how confused she was - had always been since the day her parents brought her to live with the family. Tiny and shy, she'd stared at me with distrustful eyes, her body angled so that she was partially hidden behind her mother's legs.

I'd smiled down at her and hadn't known at that moment just how much potential existed inside her.

As the years passed and as she grew into the woman she now was, that potential revealed itself to me until I was no longer able to deny it.

She was everything I needed, everything that Jacob needed to lose himself once again.

Raising her, training her, molding her, had been so damn sweet.

Reaching to unbuckle her cuffs, I released one wrist to watch her arm slap down to the side. Every ounce of strength in her body was gone. She was malleable and pliant, weak willed and distraught.

"You were a good example today, Eve. A testament to what I've made of you. You'll help me lead them to the light."

Her other wrist released, she would have fallen to the floor had I not caught her. "We'll get you cleaned up. Let you sleep."

Cradling her to my chest, I made my way to the rectory and placed her on a chair in the bedroom, reminding her not to lean back against her wounds as I drew a bath.

Eve's identity remained a mystery to the residents of the small town. They neither knew she was my *wife* nor that she stayed at the parish with me as entertainment for the long nights I spent within the dismal confines of a rural building.

I missed the energy of the city where I was raised, missed the constant stimulation to be had from the myriad of faces.

The family had been a distraction for as long as it took Richard and me to gather them and cure them of the morality they'd learned from the world. Our games had been amusing, an experiment that kept boredom at bay over the years I created my small army.

Now, however, confined to a parish that meant nothing more to me than what it would offer within the town, my tastes delved into deeper darkness, my mind screaming for sensation within the shell of a life my brother had left behind.

How he hadn't gone mad prior to my delicate prodding, I wasn't sure. The lack of light, the absence of activity, the hours of solitude were enough to push any sane person over the edge.

Water filled the tub, a sheen of steam rolling over its surface before I turned it off and returned to Eve. Her wounds weren't as bad as they would one day become, a web of striated scars over her skin telling the tale of the abuses she'd endured for her faith.

I'd feel wrong for taking such full advantage if I didn't loathe the easily deceived, the pathetic minded majority that clung to a story told for over two thousand years.

She trembled as I carried her to the tub, her hair draped over my arm and her hands clinging weakly to my body. Dropping her into the water crossed my mind. She wouldn't be able to stop her fall.

But it would break her too much, too soon, and too badly for the games I wanted to play.

Lowering her beneath the surface, I closed my eyes in response to the painful cry that burst from her lips.

"Shhhhh," I reminded her. "It will all be over soon."

Tears streamed down her cheeks to mingle with the water, her body's quiver becoming still as the heat soothed the wounds.

"Is that better?" I whispered.

Her head nodded, the ends of her hair trailing in the water. Like dark silk, it floated on top, the pale tone of her skin blurred beneath the ripples. My gaze dragged across to where her collarbone broke the surface of the water, down farther to where the tight peak of her breast was just beneath, the soft rose color teasing me until I had to force myself to look away.

I couldn't fuck her after what I put her through. I couldn't use her body even more just to gratify mine. That would be cruelty beyond bounds, the hunger of a monster.

Or could I?

Did I really care if it hurt her or not?

Balancing an arm over the lip of the tub, I skimmed the tips of my fingers over the water. Eve's breathing was slow and rhythmic, a soothing sound against my ear as I dipped my fingers down beneath to trace them over the soft curve of her abdomen.

Her lips parted on a sigh, her chest arching up just enough to tell me she would accept the pain of my body against her wounds just to linger within the pleasure I could give her.

So perfectly trained.

"Do you still think about the man on the side of the road, my love? The man who saw the parts of you that

20

should have only been for me? Who touched you when you belonged to a man of God?"

Eyes blinking open, she stared at me from beneath waterlogged lashes. My hand traveled lower over her body, my fingers brushing down between her legs, not to torment but to tease. Her breath rattled from her lungs.

"Yes. I've told you the story so many times. And you've punished me each time I've told it, but still, when I close my eyes, I see him touching himself, feel his eyes on my body while he-"

Her words cut off when my finger dipped inside her body to massage around the entrance, to tantalize the muscles into expanding for my intrusion.

I tsked my tongue against the roof of my mouth, smiled down at a living doll who was created to house my spirit. The girl she'd been before the week in my cabin was no longer staring out from behind green eyes, she was locked away and caged, a phantom that should have never existed.

A steady rhythm in and out, my hand worked to push her to that edge. Studying her the way a cat would watch a wounded bird, I noted every shiver across her skin, every flicker of her eyelashes, and the heavy breath pulsing across her lips. I watched as a faint pink blush colored her skin, listened as the soft moans of a woman seeking her seductive release crawled up her slender throat.

I'd give her what she sought, send her careening over that edge into ecstasy, but not without a price.

Leaning closer, I kept my lips a teasing distance from her ear. My free hand pressed to her forehead, I gave her only one warning. "Hold your breath."

21

Her eyes opened and rounded just as her head sank beneath the water, my palm pressed against her forehead as if I were baptizing her all over again.

Still working her body, I held her down, watched as small bubbles of air escaped her lips to float to the surface. She writhed beneath the touch, fought against being held in place, her terrified eyes still staring up at me despite the water between us.

"Don't be scared," I said softly, unsure whether she could hear me. "Just let go. Trust me, Eve. Turn your life over into my hands."

It was the undiluted panic that fascinated me, the sound of splashing water against the porcelain tub and tile floor, the way her body shifted and moved as she struggled against my hold. It was the knowledge that, despite her fear, a climax had burst through her body, the sound of it woven into her breath as it rose in large chaotic bubbles through the water.

When she stilled, when the light behind her eyes faded until I knew she was close to unconsciousness, I lifted her head above the surface of the water, my voice a soft hum against her weary senses.

She gasped for breath as I smiled.

"Always trust me, Eve. And I will be sure to take care of you."

5

JACOB

"You should get out more, Jacob. Do something besides sulk in your room. I thought you wanted to leave the priesthood. Why do you seem so bummed about it?"

Alan Ross stared across the small bar-top table at me as he traced his fingers over the condensation of his mug. Inside the glass, his beer had settled into a golden liquid, the white froth that topped it off all but gone now that he'd taken two large swallows.

I wrapped my hand around the shot glass of whiskey, my eyes glancing up at the bartender before I motioned her for one more. I drank the shot in one quick swallow. The burn down my throat reminded me of when Alan and I would hang out like this in college.

"I'm not sulking in my room," I answered.

A bark of laughter escaped his lungs. "Yeah, I've heard what you're doing in there. You scared the crap out of Tracy's friend."

I didn't know who Tracy was, and I didn't know the name of her friend. But I could say that if either of them had been in my room since the time I moved in with Alan, they were just more woman within a sea of faces.

He must have picked up on my thoughts. "Elena? Blonde with big-" He held his hands up to his chest, his lips stretched into a grin. "If she wasn't Tracy's best pal, I would have dragged her into my bed a long time ago."

A brow arched over my eye. "I'm surprised you're sticking to one woman at a time. That wasn't like you in college."

"And I'm surprised you became a priest," he responded, his hand running through his shaggy blond hair as he leaned back in his seat. After taking another swallow of his beer, he dropped the weight of the glass onto the table. The beer sloshed up to spill over the rim.

Without looking at me, he lowered his voice and asked, "Was it because of Cassandra?"

Hearing the name drove a spike of anger down my spine. Cassandra was one of the last people I wanted to discuss. "Tell your friend if she has an issue with me than she should stay the fuck away."

Another burst of laughter shook his shoulders. "I'm not saying she's complaining. Just that you scared her."

"I have to piss," I said, not concerned with the pathetic concerns of a prissy bitch who liked to dabble with a man such as me.

Alan watched as I walked away, his face blending into the crowded bar as I wove my way around different groups standing between our table and the back hallway. I'd almost made it into the dimly, lit space leading to the bathroom when a hand landed on my shoulder.

Pivoting on my heel, I clenched my fist before meeting the stare of a red headed woman.

"Hey," she called out over the loud music. Playing it off, she feigned surprise, her green eyes widening subtly. "Oh, I'm sorry. I thought you were someone else."

She was lying.

But even still, the room spun around me, memories creeping in that dragged me back to a small parish in the middle of nowhere - to green eyes that had mistaken me for someone else and had ended up flat and lifeless as a result.

I fought to push them away.

"No problem," I answered before brushing her hold off my shoulder and stepping toward the hall.

Before I could go far, she called out, "My name is Kristen, by the way."

Like I gave a damn about her name.

The shadows of the hall wrapped around me as soon as I turned the corner. I'd almost reached the men's room door, when the same voice called out again. "You know, it's polite to tell a person your name when they tell you theirs."

I stopped, not bothering to turn back and look at the woman. "I didn't ask you for your name."

"But I gave it to you anyway. How does that make you feel?"

She was just flirting, just toying with a man she found attractive on her night out. It was only fair to warn her.

"You don't want to know me. I can promise you that."

"Yet, here I am."

Glancing at her from over my shoulder, I cocked a brow and looked her up and down. Beneath the long red hair, her face was unmarked by lines of age. I

25

guessed her for twenty-one, twenty-three at most. Not as young as Eve, but still just as stupid.

Narrow shoulders led down to a decent sized chest, the upper swells peeking out from above the tiny blue shirt that hid nothing. Her stomach was flat, her hips rounded, her shapely legs sculpted by the tight jeans she wore. It was obvious she hadn't worn a bra. I wondered if she'd even bothered with panties.

Regardless of the tight body that called to the carnal parts of any man, it was her hair that caught my attention. The same color as Annabelle's, it had more of a wave, but the length was just the same. I smiled at the whispered thoughts running through my head.

"You should be careful of who you tease, Kristen. You never know what kind of man you're facing."

I gave her the warning nobody had ever thought to give Annabelle.

Her gaze studied my body as thoroughly as mine had studied hers. "You look like the type I'm after."

A grin stretched my lips. "What kind is that?"

A full mouth parted, white teeth barely visible beneath the scarlet lipstick she wore. "The kind that can show a girl a good time."

Turning fully, I checked the hall to ensure we were alone. Not another soul existed within the shadowed interior. With one measured step toward the woman staring me down, I was damn close to being on top of her. She had as much intelligence as she did sense of personal space.

Maybe it was the look in my eyes, or maybe it was the malicious energy rolling off me, but she understood then that she was locked down by the attention of a predator. Taking a step back, she smiled hesitantly.

I closed the distance and laughed softly when her back hit a wall.

Canting my head to the side, I kept my eyes trained on hers.

Speckled within the soft green were flecks of brown. Not exactly like Eve's had been, but close enough. My voice was a bare whisper, just loud enough to be heard over the echo of music rolling down the hall. "What do you consider a good time?"

My fingers trailed up her arm. Goosebumps broke over her flesh, her wide eyes rounding. Brushing my thumb over the side of her breast, I looked down to see her nipple beading beneath her shirt.

Like every other bitch I'd had beneath me, she shivered when my lips touched her ear. "Do you like being bound and helpless, Kristen? Do you like it when a strange man takes control of your body to do whatever wicked thing he dreams up?"

Breath rushed from her lungs, hot and heavy. Our hips were pressed together, her breasts tight to my chest. I ran my free hand up the inside of her thigh, stopping just before reaching the apex. "Do you want me to just strip you down right here, or were you looking for something a little more private?"

It was no longer a question of whether I'd given in to the beast inside me. Darkness was always a ring around my vision, death a possibility that hung in the air each time I let go to my desires.

They'd complained about the marks being in visible places, but once I was seated within the heat of their bodies, those complaints fell away on sated voices, quieted down as sensual moans crawled up to flow from their mouths.

If I wasn't careful, I would break another before too long.

And this one reminded me of precious Annabelle.

"I was hoping you would buy me a drink first," she answered, breathless.

My laughter was a beat against her ear. "I don't buy drinks for sluts. Don't buy them dinner and I don't buy them jewelry. All I do is show them the good time they're after."

She tried to move away, tried to shuffle out from beneath my weight, but I caged her against the wall when my hand slammed against the plaster at the side of her head. My other hand gripped over her hip. "Where are you going? I thought you wanted to play?"

Our chests collided together with the force of her breathing. No longer turned on, the little thing was now frightened. But wasn't that what happens when you approach strange men? Wasn't that the consequence of following them into shadows where no other person can see if he's stolen you away?

"I want to leave," she said, her voice choked off by the very thing that fed my monster. I ran the tip of my nose along her jawline, my body hard against hers, demanding and strong.

"That's too bad," I crooned. "Guess you should have listened when you were told not to talk to strangers."

"Jacob! Man, come on! Go take that fucking piss you're after and let's go! This place is bullshit."

Alan's voice rolled through the narrow hall, his steps down the interior growing louder as he rounded the corner. The little bitch beneath me screamed.

"Let me go!"

She fought, her hands pressed to my chest, but she wasn't anywhere near strong enough to push me away. "Get the hell off of me."

"Jacob?"

My head spun to my right, a smile tugging at the corners of my lips to see Alan approaching.

He paused mid-step. "Let her go, man. She asked nicely."

"Did she?" I turned my head back to where she was pressed against the wall. "I don't remember hearing you say please."

A tear slipped down her cheek, her fingernails embedding themselves into my t-shirt where she was still trying to claw at me and force me away. "Let me go," she begged.

"I only asked for one word."

"Jacob," Alan warned, "seriously. Let the nice lady walk away. We need to leave."

Ignoring him, I pressed my chest tighter against her hands, my breath ragged at the drag of her claws over my shirt. Those nails would feel like heaven down my back.

Keeping my voice low enough that only she could hear, I spoke to her with humor and disgust weaved within my tone. "There were two women in this world that wouldn't cower and cry when my attention was on them. They understood a man like me. Craved me until it ended them. They were everything and nothing at all, and with them I could have fun. I could play and bask in the beauty of their bodies. But you? You are so fucking boring to a man like me. Quite frankly, taking a piss will be more fulfilling and memorable. Now take the fuck off, sweetheart, and be careful about the next man you approach for a good time."

29

Pushing away from the wall, I didn't bother tracking her path as she ran. My hand was pushing open the bathroom door when Alan's voice sounded at my back. "Was that really necessary? What the hell did you do to her?"

"She asked me to buy her a drink," I answered, pulling myself out to relieve my bladder into the urinal. The stream had just hit the porcelain when I added, "and I was teaching her not to talk to strangers."

"Seriously, Jacob. You're scaring the shit out of me. I understand a little slap and tickle in the bedroom like we used to do to the chicks in college, but you've gone over the edge. What if she runs to the cops?"

Shrugging a shoulder, I drip dried and shoved myself back into my pants. The zipper pulled up easily as I turned. "I didn't do anything illegal."

He rolled his eyes and threw an arm around my shoulder. Opening the door, he led me into the hall, his hold tight like he was concerned I'd run away. Laughter was a soft edge to his voice. "I don't know what happened in that church of yours, but you've lost your damn mind. We're going to a new place. Hopefully we can get out without the authorities chasing after us."

6

EVE

Dreams plagued me the night after the ceremony. Elijah's face rippling above the surface of turbulent water. The soft touch of his hand as he bathed me after finding me collapsed over a sprawling lawn. His voice a seductive song whispering to me of beauty and goodness, until it slipped back again into the shadows that crawled across my skin.

One man and then the other. The same face but different personalities, all wrapped up into one beautiful body so full of power that it burned me sometimes just to look at him.

The images kept spinning. A tumultuous storm raging across still waters. Left and then right, up and then down, I was tossed every direction as I fought to grasp on to one simple truth I knew I'd missed.

Jacob or Elijah.
A soft hand or a heavy fist.

I didn't understand the names or my purpose. It made me feel even weaker to be so confused all the time. The doubts were circling sharks surrounding a small island only large enough to hold me above water.

He told me I would grow into the perfect wife for him. Was I even strong enough to help lead people into the light?

I didn't know, and when the storm raged inside me, when I opened my mouth to scream just to relieve myself of the pain, I opened my eyes to see the birth of sunlight over a distant horizon, the ephemeral glow of a new day sitting just outside the window.

His body heat was beside me, but I couldn't turn to him, couldn't move because of the manner in which I'd been bound. There was no telling how long he'd hold me here, how long he'd deny me food, how hard he'd laugh at me when I asked to go to the bathroom.

He wasn't the same person. Not this man. Not him.

And yet, I never wanted him to go away.

"Go back to sleep, Eve."

"I had a nightmare," I admitted on a weak, sleepy voice.

"I'm not worried about your nightmare. Go back to sleep."

"You were two different people."

The mattress moved beneath me then, his weight crushing it down at my side so low that my body shifted and the bindings tightened over my wrists. I didn't understand why he insisted on keeping me bound now that I was brought back here. He'd never insisted on it before.

I braced for whatever he intended to do, but it wasn't necessary. He simply reached up to undo my binds. Once I was free, he turned me to him and tucked my cheek against his chest.

For the first time in what felt like weeks, my body relaxed against him.

"Tell me about the dream," he asked, his voice soft but for the hint of concern.

Shifting through what I could remember, I shook my head against his chest. "It's all just bits and pieces. There's a storm and then there's you ... but it's not you. I don't know how else to explain it."

"How am I different?"

He was using the soothing voice, a sultry pure that pulled all those in the room into his orbit. It was like he was singing, a ballad or the slow beat of blues. It was a perfectly timed rhythm, a low pitch used just right that connected you to him just by the vibration it caused inside you. It was the voice he'd used on me the first night we spent in his cabin.

"You're -" My voice died off, my thoughts a jumble except for that one nagging whisper telling me something wasn't right. "I don't know, Elijah. I'm sorry."

"It's all right. You'll figure it out, and as soon as you do you'll tell me, right?"

When I nodded, he kissed me on the head. "Just be sure you do, sweet girl. We wouldn't want the demons getting to you."

JACOB
(Six months later)

There's nothing quite like the wind blowing against your face. A blanket of tranquility, it wraps over every dip and angle, settles into the hollows of your cheeks, leaves a gentle kiss on the forehead and chin just like my mom used to do when I was young.

She always kissed my brother and I after our father was done forcing our repentance. Never stepping in because the man was in charge of the castle, she'd sat back and watched him purge us of sin.

The memories had come back to me slowly, a small piece of the puzzle that explained Eve and what Jericho had made of her.

But I knew there had to be more, only because I hadn't become the same kind of monster.

Sitting twenty-two stories high, on a ledge overlooking the frenetic rush of life beneath my feet, I watched the city where I grew up. Obscured by shadow, I doubted anybody could see where I sat. Had I been a kid, I would have felt like a super hero standing guard against evil. But I was an adult, and in the years I'd lived, I realized the evil I should be worried about was me.

Two lives. Two beautiful souls that were bright stars among a constellation of the mean-spirited and ordinary, they were a rarity. In my life before this hell, I would have called them a blessing.

Two streets south of me, and three buildings to the left stood the cathedral I'd attended my entire life. With a peaked roof and large, ornate stairways leading directly from the street to God's door, it was a bastion of light, a spectacle that must have cost the Diocese a fortune. Its bells played short hymns every hour, its bevy of large wooden front doors a welcome mat for the weak and weary.

In the years that Jericho and I had attended it, the parish managed to become our Hell.

I'd watched it all day from so high up the parishioners resembled ants.

After spending nine months at Alan's place, I'd run through as many women as it took to get past Eve's death. And although I was no longer reliving it every time I closed my eyes, a slow montage of destruction that chased me from my bed, I was just barely balanced.

Any strong gust could come along and blow me right over, any sweet sprinkle of rain could wash me down into whatever churning river would ferry me straight to Satan's gates.

There was no place for me to run this time, no escape that could protect me from the world, or protect the world from me. God himself couldn't save me now. He'd tried. He'd failed. And all because of one person.

Sex could no longer appease me. Ravaging some woman as she screamed and moaned could no longer

36

let me pretend that everything would be okay. Vengeance was the steady pulse inside my heart, the black shadow over my eyes and the caustic veil that smothered me day in and day out until I promised myself to take it.

But first, I needed to understand *why*.

Yes, Jericho had laughed at the repeated question. He'd mocked me and scorned me, told me to enjoy the ride I never wanted. But for as much hatred as I held for him, for as much I wanted to throw my hands up and sink into oblivion without ever thinking of that small, rural town again, *why* was the question ceaselessly whispering in my head.

What had I done to make my twin brother want to destroy me so thoroughly? Why had it brought him so much pleasure to sacrifice Eve's life to me?

The only trail I had to follow was our past, the only breadcrumbs left behind were those rooted in the city where we had parted ways as brothers, only to come back together in life as enemies.

The first question I needed answered wasn't *why* my brother had set out to hurt me, it was *why* had he gone mad?

The answers wouldn't be found in the small town where he was known as Elijah, they would be found in a large, turbulent city where he was raised as Jericho Hayle, a devout Catholic boy who, for reasons I didn't yet know, had been scorned by the faith he'd once held so dearly.

I would have those answers, but first I had to gather the courage to walk in through the parish's doors, to humble the beast inside me just long enough to pretend like I had any faith left at all.

A large cross lifted into the sky above a building designed to express the glory of the Almighty, and behind it shone the lights of a city in which Jericho and I had once thrived.

Would the good little girls recognize me now that they were mothers and wives?

Would I be able to control the violence inside me just long enough to get what I needed before heading back to that small town in the heart of the Appalachians?

I wasn't sure of any of those answers. The only thing I knew was I had to try.

Hopping off the ledge – toward the roof and not the streets below – I angled my head into the breeze that was blowing and tried to steady the beat of my heart for where I knew I had to go.

Back to the city. Back to parish that I'd once run from screaming. And back to a family home that now stood bleak and empty after my parents both died without either of their children giving enough of a damn to return in time to say goodbye.

8

ELIJAH

Dull. Boring. Quiet and so antagonizingly slow. Life as rural priest was the epitome of living Hell. The parish was deafening in its silence, a low static hum of white noise filtered through my ears, the whir of ceilings fans in small rooms, the tranquility of a mortuary that was full of the dead.

Several times, I'd considered returning to the compound just to entertain the family with my sermons and healings. Several times, I'd inflicted pain on the only companion I had, just to appease my curious mind. And several times, I'd been met with Eve's insistence that I wasn't one man, but two.

No matter how I tried to prod her, she couldn't give me more than that simple statement.

The recognition inside her was unsettling, to say the least, but it wasn't yet dangerous. I had ways of clouding her mind.

Leaning back in a scuffed wooden pew, I lifted my feet to rest atop the pew in front of me. The altar and pulpit were in my direct line of sight, the large stained glass windows a beautiful wash of color to behold on a cool, spring morning. The day was still young, and I sat in wait wondering if any of the men I'd invited to witness Eve's cleansings would return today to discuss their final opinions of what they'd seen.

Richard wouldn't arrive from the compound until early afternoon and I reclined back with my hand behind my head, contemplating how long it would take to have the entire town under my wing.

Word had gotten around about the poor woman possessed by the demon of lust. But it hadn't crawled far, only a few men knew what occurred during the meetings, and they've kept their mouths shut, save for the friends they knew would remain silent as well.

Farmers could be a bloodthirsty lot when you threatened the livelihood of their families. In the time that I'd become Father Jacob Hayle, two foreclosures had been filed, two banks opening their wide mouths ready to swallow the land and small profits of two families that had nothing left to give.

The head of those families came to the meetings, witnessed the lust that couldn't be driven out of a woman despite the pain she suffered, and within the stress addled state of their weary minds, they'd believed Eve was infected with something we couldn't see or name.

A door opened at my back, the hinges creaking ever so slightly in warning. I lowered my legs and twisted in my seat to find Gentry Holmes walking toward me.

Silver hair speckled with black pepper, he wasn't yet fully grey, but was getting closer, day by day. Gentry was a proud man, that fact evident in his strong shoulders, stick straight posture, and a swagger that spoke of hard work in Mother Nature's harshest weather. He had a steely gaze, the dark brown of his eyes focused and attentive, but today a shadow crossed his face. Gentry's lips were pulled into a taut line, his large, callused hands gripped into fists at his sides.

Either I was in a bit of trouble for what he witnessed last night, or something else was brewing on the horizon that he felt it necessary for God's intervention.

What he didn't know is that the God he'd always prayed to had left the building, and I'd replaced Him with every intention of finally seeing to the needs of His forgotten people.

On my feet, I offered a hand in greeting. "Mr. Holmes. It's a pleasure to see you again. What brings you out so early in the morning?"

"Bank called," he announced gruffly.

Ah, I thought, *another land owner in need.*

"Let's take a seat, Mr. Holmes, and discuss your problem." Giving him a sympathetic smile, I fought not to let my expression reveal my true thoughts. Once a man's livelihood is challenged, he's much more receptive to intervention - even if such intervention goes against what he would normally do in his life. Gentry was an esteemed member of the community, but it was his brother - Sheriff James Holmes - that interested me more.

Seating himself in a pew, Gentry's expression shadowed with concern. I leaned on the back of the pew in front of him, my legs crossed at the ankles, my hands clasped loosely over my thighs. "Tell me the trouble you're facing."

"Crops have been low," he mumbled, his eyes not meeting mine due to the shame he felt to face losing his farm. It wasn't easy on a man's pride to accept failure, to believe that his ability to care for his family has been lost to him. "I fell behind in mortgage payments, did

41

everything I could to catch up, but without the proper weather-"

His voice trailed off, his palms scrubbing over his face as he pondered what he could do to save not only his farm but his pride. "That property has been in my family for generations. All the way back to my great grandfather. The only reason I had to mortgage it was to pay for several failed seasons." Glancing up at me, his normally sharp gaze was dulled by worry. "I can't let the property go. It's my son's future."

Patience, Elijah...Don't jump too quickly.

"Tell me what the parish can do to help. Is it prayers you're seeking? Comfort, perhaps, that God has a plan?"

Gentry's forehead wrinkled, his eyes glaring up at me in part question, part anger. "I want to know about what you showed us last night with that woman. Are there really-"

He scrubbed his hand over his face again, modern day reality warring with his spiritual beliefs. "Are there really demons, Father?"

My lips lifted at one corner before I could force my expression back to neutral. Keeping my voice at a low whisper, I answered, "I believe so, yes. Unfortunately, the way this country has gone, the lack of belief in the Almighty brought about by atheism, other religions and this innate need for progressive thinking, has made it difficult for the Church to fight the battles that need to be fought."

Eyes lifting to me once again, he settled back in his seat, relaxing more with the topic of conversation. "Doesn't God take care of that evil? Isn't our belief strong enough for him to help us?"

"Have you read your Bible?" I asked. A question for a question, it was the best method to make a person believe that the ideas you're feeding them are their own.

"Of course, I have," he answered indignantly.

"Then you know the answer to that question. It is through our belief that God grants us the tools to combat evil. We have many tools, some of which have been lost to the modern world."

"What are you saying, Father?"

Gripping my fingers over each other, I dropped my gaze to my shoes, gave the question time to linger before offering an answer. "I'm saying that, as a whole, we no longer actively combat the evil that plagues this world. We've become complacent, have forgotten the violence implicit in the assault against that which attacks us. If you know history, you know that not all battles have been fought with prayer alone."

He nodded his head, silently considering my words, struggling to make sense of them. "In a situation like mine, where does the evil exist? Is it in my family? Myself? The bank?"

I smiled, not one that reached my eyes denoting happiness, but one that was sad, resigning to the truth of our discussion. "The bank, perhaps. Money is the root of all evil, is it not? But then, our society runs on money, making everything evil to a certain extent. I don't think there's much to be done about that."

"What can be done, then?"

Edging him closer and closer, I was careful with my words, both their meaning and the speed with which I delivered them. Conversion wasn't a hatchet job, it was more precise than that, the use of a fine scalpel sometimes necessary in order to gain what was needed. "You said the crops have failed repeatedly. Despite your prayers, I assume."

"Despite everything," he grunted.

"Perhaps," I offered, "it has nothing to do with you personally, but the town. The evil that infects it. Look what happened to poor Annabelle Prete. What could have happened to the woman you saw last night during my demonstration."

"How do we stop it, Father? How do we fight against it?"

His sharp gaze was pinned on me, his hands wringing over his lap. Desperation oozed from his pores, his mind ripe and open, waiting for the answers that would relieve him of the problems in his life. I needed him to find those answers, while I simply walked beside him to the conclusion.

Lifting my gaze to meet his, my lips pulled into a tight line. "How do *you* suppose we should handle it?"

Shaking his head, he cast his eyes toward the altar, the sun shining through the stained glass window bathing his face in reds and golds. "We fight it with any means necessary. We bring God back to this town. But we're only a few people in a world of billions. What power do we really have?"

On the outside, I was without expression, my posture contemplative and morose. But inside, I was beaming, a brilliant light blistering out through the fissures of my innermost shadows. "We have God's power, do we not?"

His eyes snapped to mine. "Yes. Yes, we do."

I canted my head to the side. "His power is greater than anything in this world, is it not?"

"It is," he answered, the worry written across his features sharpening until resolve set into the creases of his face.

"However," I acquiesced, "there is one slight issue we cannot control, one small problem that would prevent us from achieving what we need to survive."

Waiting silently, he didn't move a muscle. So focused and attentive that he appeared frozen in place, he was a tightly spun ball of need just waiting to be unfurled. I had to be careful which string I plucked. "The law, as it stands, would not agree with our methods - the old methods - of dealing with such a threat. Without God in our government, what can be done?"

I shrugged a shoulder, breaking our stare to cast my gaze toward the front doors. So full of anticipation that it had become a vibration beneath my skin, I forced my breath into a steady rhythm.

"My brother is the law around here," he said, drawing a smile from my lips. Finally, he'd said exactly what I needed him to suggest.

Schooling my features, I returned my attention to him. "Your brother is the Sheriff, correct?"

He nodded in response.

"Why do you bring that up?"

"Perhaps he could turn a blind eye. Keep our activities off the radar, so to speak."

It was difficult - damn near impossible - not to clap my hands together and praise God for the direction this conversation had turned. Well, not God so much, but myself. I had been the one to lead Gentry to this point. Divine guidance was isolated to my hand alone.

"Your brother is a Godly man?"

"You know that to be the truth, Father Hayle. He attends your parish every Sunday when he isn't working. He's as attached to the family farm as me. If there is a solution, he'd be willing."

Taking a deep breath, I blew it out, pausing just long enough for the thought to settle in. "He wasn't here last night," I pointed out. "He hasn't seen the truth of what's infecting this town."

"So, we'll show him. If he sees it with his own eyes, I can guarantee he'll do whatever is necessary to save this town. We've been here for generations. Our blood is tied to this land, our fathers, our grandfathers. I have no doubt at all that he'll understand once he sees the truth of it."

Tapping my fingers against my thigh, I met his stare for several seconds before inclining my head.

"I believe I can set up a demonstration. But not here. I tell you what: why don't you come out to a special place I've acquired, a secret place I've been using to help the town? It's hidden away, tucked discreetly behind walls to keep out prying eyes. I believe you should see it before we bring your brother into the mix."

Bringing Gentry to the compound was a risk - one I was willing to take, if for nothing else but to gain his utmost alliance with my mission. He was the only man to approach me after witnessing the demonstration with Eve and, through him, I knew I could gain the compliance of the town.

Slowly but surely.
Baby steps.

"I'm willing to see whatever you need me to see, Father. I'm done with being blind."

My smile reached my eyes this time. "Good, Gentry, that's very good. You should come tonight. I'll ensure that the family is ready to meet you."

9

EVE

Left in Elijah's room once again, I sat on the bed. My dreams eluded me every time I attempted to remember them, a feeling inside me that something wasn't right. The days blended into the nights, the hours passing quickly and so slowly at the same time. Elijah was angry with me, but I didn't know why.

My stomach churned as I thought of food, my eyes blinded to whether the sun was high in the sky or setting over the horizon. I couldn't see past the black cloth tied over my face, couldn't move due to the restraints used to keep me in bed. Elijah hadn't offered me breakfast, hadn't worried for my needs after allowing me to use the bathroom just once before he left to tend to his *duties*.

Drifting through what felt like molasses, I shook my head when sleep escaped me, casting me out into some dreamless state where I was floating within clouds of consciousness, lost to everything around me. The room was deathly quiet, the darkness invading me until I was hovering above myself looking inward until I questioned whether I was dead or alive.

Kicking my foot every so often, I brought myself back to the present, but as time passed, I slipped again into the ether, my mind conjuring images that I wasn't sure were fake or true. My arms yanked at the ropes binding my wrists, the burn of the twine pulling me from the abyss to remind me I was here on this bed awaiting his judgment.

He'd been angry when we woke this morning, untrusting, uncaring, and for the life of me, I didn't know why. Didn't I give him everything he asked of me? Hadn't I helped him in every way he needed? What had I done to deserve the restrictions he placed on me now that we lived in this new place?

A shuffle sounded in the distance, the bang of a door, the light rhythm of unhurried footsteps approaching. My heart raced to hear something - anything - in this dark, quiet room and I prayed that he wouldn't turn away before releasing me from these restraints. Another door creaked open, the footsteps a beat against the floor of the bedroom. I turned my head in the direction of the sound, my arms shaking against the ropes holding them in place.

Something clattered on the table near me, the mattress dipping beneath my body where Elijah sat to my side. He yanked the blindfold from my eyes and I squinted against the shock of sunlight streaming in through the window.

"I've brought you tea," he said, his normally booming voice soft and careful. It reminded me of who he'd been when I first arrived here. The tenderness he'd shown me over the course of the week I'd spent secluded inside his room. Despite the games he'd played, the lies he told, the back and forth, those days had been an awakening of sorts, moments crafted by the side of him I'd never known before.

His hands were working to untangle the ropes binding my wrists. Ignoring the burn of air colliding against flesh rubbed raw, I breathed in the scent of him. "Will you be kind again, Elijah? Sweet, like you used to be?"

The tick of his jaw drew my gaze, the sharp line of his cheekbones pushing out until shadows fell across his smooth skin. "I've never been sweet." Blue eyes finding mine, heat rolled behind them. "You should drink your tea and stop telling stories. It bothers me that you believe them."

He hadn't lifted a finger toward me and still I felt slapped. "What stories?" I asked, the covers rustling beneath me as I pushed into a sitting position.

Pulling the teacup from its saucer, he handed it to me. I wrapped my fingers around the warm ceramic, enjoying the warmth of it against my palms. Heat always helped the blood flow again, and my fingers were numb from having remained bound to the bed.

"The one you told me last night was interesting." His head canted to the side just slightly. "Or do you not remember what you said?"

I'd spent the majority of the day trying to remember *something* from last night. Like a hummingbird hovering over the open mouth of a flower, the recognition that an important moment had happened - a truth had been revealed - stayed just out of reach.

He tipped the rim of the cup to my lips, his eyes commanding me to drink before I could answer. Each time we stopped talking, the silence would settle between us as an unsettling white noise. I became lost

51

in it, dragged back to the same abyss of being blindfolded and bound. It's lonely living a life like mine since marrying Elijah, but even more so when your senses are stripped away. That's what the white noise does to you. It fills yours ears with a constant vibration, seducing your mind into compliance. You drift from the world that exists around you and find yourself stuck in place. I needed something to pull me back, so I slurped from the cup just for the sound.

"Drink deeper," he demanded, voice gritty and curt.

I did, the sound of my throat working the liquid down replacing the slurping and white noise. Shoving my tongue against my lips to stop the flow of tea, I took a quick breath through my nose. His gaze darted up, eyes narrowing. "Drink."

I can't breathe, I thought, unable to speak without dribbling tea down my chin. My head spun from the lack of oxygen, but still I drank, only because he wanted it.

The last drop fell past my lips and Elijah pulled the cup away to place it on the saucer. Light clatter overcame the white noise that kept creeping back no matter what.

A sense of weightlessness overcame me. Not heavy and imposing but just a hint of the ether I fought against all day. Why now when I was no longer bound and blind?

"What do you remember, Eve? Of last night?"

He was always asking me questions. Always. Even without answering mine, he tosses another my way, somehow digging deeper inside me without concern that I'd become hollow because he'd stolen all there was to know. He couldn't get to that one hidden place

I'd managed to protect, the one so guarded not even I could penetrate its walls.

"Nothing."

"Nothing?" He repeated as a question. Always questions.

Something was hidden in that place, but I was never strong enough to reach it.

My throat swelled suddenly, my tongue overfilling my mouth. The room spun and tossed, my stomach quivering with the need to heave. Parting my lips, I struggled to make it stop, drawing in wisps of air in the hopes they'd clear the clouds of confusion. "Nothing," I managed to answer, unsure if the word made sense to his ears.

"I don't feel so good." I may have spoken the words aloud, but I wasn't entirely sure. Three of Elijah stared back, four then two. Shaking my head, I blinked several times to find one of him smirking at me.

"You're sick again, my love. Sick like you were in the cabin after we married. It took me days to relieve you of your demons."

Even my memory of those days was blurry. Unable to sleep when I should, so damn tired when I walked beneath sunlight, I only came alive when he worked to free me of my sins. I didn't remember ever sleeping, and eating was impossible with how badly my stomach always hurt. I should have known when I saw the teacup, should have realized the demons had returned. I could only hold down the tea he'd given me in the week we'd spent in the cabin.

"Again?"

He'd worked so hard. I remembered that much. Sweat would drip from his skin and his lips would pull into an unforgiving line. His eyes would go wide, anger and fierce resolve beaming behind the silver-blue. He chased the diseased spirit from my body, only proclaiming me saved when all I knew was him. Then I'd run off. That must have been when the demon found me again.

Smoothing his palm over my forehead, he smiled. Sure that it was beautiful as always, I couldn't tell with how blurry his image had become. "I don't know when Satan corrupted you again, but I'll rid you of him. Starting tonight, we'll begin again. And this time, I'll have the backing of the family to watch me. Now that they know we're married."

10

JACOB

I was invisible where I stood. Surrounded by the city, people milling around me, they made wide circles to remain out of my sphere. My boots were planted to the newly powerwashed sidewalk, my eyes glaring up at the intricate carvings on wood doors that were polished to a gleaming shine. Six broad steps rose up before me, a silver handrail running up their middle promising safety and a helping hand to the unsteady who climbed. I didn't need that damn rail, didn't care whether the doors were polished or rough, because, inside, the parish would still be ugly.

Not ugly in sight, but ugly in spirit. No. I knew the treasures that awaited the weary inside. I knew the serenity of the stained glass, the flicker of candles. The artwork that stole the breath from the lungs of the faithful. Every damn image would be more depressing than the next as we were blamed for the pain of our Savior.

Even though I was standing there as people moved around, in front, in back, to my sides, I was really falling down a long, black tunnel leading me closer and closer to the truth of my life.

The serpent had always been so sneaky.

It spoke to me within shadow, slithering back just enough to let me think I could be saved. And here again, it waited patiently for me to go inside, walk between the pews, find a seat and stare at the symbols of a God who had never listened. I knew while I sat there and regretted each action, each thought, each hidden desire that was another lash of the whip across Christ's body, evil would sit beside me and laugh.

Only this time, I had a different mission. I wasn't running to God for salvation, I was running to him for revenge. The serpent was welcome to tag along, welcome to coil himself languorously around me.

I moved forward, and like a school of fish parting for a shark, the people around me changed their paths to avoid being anywhere near me. The mindless sheep going about their day knowing better than to approach a man doomed to the fires of Hell.

Taking the steps two at a time, my hand wrapped around the large handle of the door, my forearm clenching and releasing as I turned it. The well-oiled hinges gave no indication I was walking inside, the serenity and silence finding me instantly. A faint scent of incense lingered in the air, the flicker of candles just barely noticeable in the distance. I walked forward until I was standing at another doorway, my eyes wide and staring at the large open space before me.

One man sat in a pew to my left, his head bowed and shoulders hunched. I watched him for several seconds, followed his movement as he swung a hand down to lower the kneeling bench, lowering his body as he held his posture in silent prayer. Pitying him for his ignorance, for the desolation he would feel when he realized the being to which he prayed didn't care, I stepped farther inside to see if any other person existed in the room.

Just one. The priest. Father Timothy Simmons from what the plaque said near the front doors. The name wasn't familiar to me.

Cutting a hard right, I weaved between the pews until I was close to where he stood. Watching him light certain candles and blow out others, I knew he was lighting new prayers and extinguishing old ones. The practice wasn't maintained in every modern day parish, but some still held to the older ways.

Clearing my throat, I drew his attention in my direction. His eyes widened almost instantly. "Are you Jacob or Jericho?" he asked. I may not have known him, but he certainly recognized me.

"Jacob. How did you-?"

"You bear a striking resemblance to your father," he answered before I could even finish the question. "Have you left your own parish to come visit mine?"

"I'm not a priest anymore."

His brows pulled together. "Let's sit and talk. I happen to know you're a long way from home."

Long way from home? Hardly. More like I'd returned to it, even if I had no desire to stay. This city had been my home for the first eighteen years of my life. I'd spent twelve at the parish in the Appalachians, and all the time in between I was lost. I was lost at that moment once again, floating on some turbulent breeze that ensnared me and dragged me back here.

The priest sat in an empty pew at the front, twisting his body around to face me when I lowered down next to him. His dark brown hair was cut short to the skull, hints of grey peeking through to denote his age. His tan skin was unlined, however, unmarred by age or time, his brown eyes observant and focused. I assumed he was of Hispanic descent, possibly Italian, but I couldn't be sure. Most striking was his demeanor. Although calm and collected, he had a fire about him that was obvious in the manner in which he moved, a purpose that I could only conclude came from the God he worshipped. Not all priests were as conflicted as I had been, and his purity of character was a blatant truth in the manner in which he spoke and moved. Unhurried, this man knew without doubt it was his task to lead the weary to what he believed was the light.

"Your father was quite proud of you," he said without giving me even a second to remind myself why I was there, without giving me the opportunity to collect my thoughts. "He told me you'd been ordained, but couldn't remember the name of your parish."

My lips tipped up to think that this man believed giving me information about my father would ease me into a sense of trust. That's what priests do: open you up and calm you down so you can dump out all your sin for their naked eyes to inspect. Too bad for Timothy my father was one of the worst demons of all. Nothing about him would soothe me into trusting this conversation.

"Our Lady of Serenity. Not that it matters. And I didn't come to talk about my father."

"Maybe you should," he answered, pinning me with his brown gaze, the flecks of gold in his stare highlighted by flickering candles. "You never returned to see him before he died. Didn't even bother showing up for his funeral. You or your brother."

This is not how I envisioned our conversation going. I was losing control - wondering if I'd ever had it in the first place. "I'm came to talk about Jericho."

His expression softened, his eyes glimmering with knowledge. "Ah. Well, then I was right to say we should discuss your father. It was through him that I learned of Jericho's failings."

Failings? I scoured my thoughts for what little information Jericho had told me during the days he'd played and won his game. There was no failing during our small battle and I highly doubted he'd failed against my father before running out of town. Curiosity sat up to slap me across the face and I found myself asking a question that should have been left alone.

"What did my father tell you?"

"Too much, I'm afraid." He looked away, his round face sharpening as he mulled over what to say. I could see the indecision popping out in the tic of his jaw, the furrow of his brow. "You're a priest-"

"Was a priest," I corrected before he could finish whatever thought he wanted to voice.

"Why did you leave the Church again, Jacob?" his voice softened to a whisper, "After finding your way back?"

His question smacked me across the face. What was I supposed to tell him? That my brother was a cult leader? That I'd killed a woman while fucking her in the ass? That I'd berated a grieving father by telling him his daughter was a whore? There were too many things to say, so I chose a blanket statement to cover them all. "I figured out that no matter how hard I prayed, God wasn't listening."

His eyes darted to mine, pinning me in a gaze that was as intense as it was angry. "You know better than that."

"Do I?" It was a bad idea coming to this parish, returning to a place where they would berate me as thoroughly as my father had. He had been the reason for my departure as a young adult, and this priest was reminding me of the hours I'd spent repenting for every sin my father believed I'd committed. I wouldn't regret the dark side of me, wouldn't spend the next twenty years doubting whether I could be redeemed. There was nothing left to redeem, nothing left to do but give in to the creature God had created in His image – if any of that could be believed.

"You attended seminary. You grew up under the watchful eyes of God, and now you sit here questioning Him. A man like you should know better."

Laughing, I settled back against the pew, my eyes scanning the altar and pulpit in front of us. So much glitter and gold infected this place, the cost must have been astronomical. How many starving people could be fed if these treasures were given to God's creatures rather than being hoarded by the very place that should have been an example of God's love for His people?

If I'd been ordained and assigned to a parish such as this one, I would have left the service within the first year. Something didn't sit right with telling a person to pray for God's assistance when that very assistance could be given by the Church. How many had been denied the help they needed? How many had sat in prayer, starving while they spoke to a being that cared little to help?

"I'm not here to discuss God, Timothy. I'm here for answers regarding Jericho." My voice was rough was anger, gritty with the truth I carried inside. The organized religion to which I'd once been devoted was nothing more than a farce – a lie told to appease the masses while their livelihoods were sacrificed to men using God as a power play and tool of building their own wealth.

It wasn't the Faith I condemned, it was what had been done with it when left in the hands of man.

Timothy settled back, taking the same relaxed posture as me. Neither of us looked at each other, our eyes trained to the symbolism arranged before us in the candles and stained glass, the relics and glimmering gold.

"Your father," he stated, his voice careful, hesitant, "he told me that between the two of you, Jericho had always been the most faithful. Often he described a set of twins standing on opposite sides – one light, one dark. He was the hardest on you, was he not?"

A grunt escaped me, my lips curling with disgust to remember just how *hard* my father had been on me. Although, it wasn't me alone. Often, though, I was blamed for the sins committed by Jericho. Our father assumed it was by my influence that Jericho partook in any act considered unclean or foolish. That may have been true when we were young, but by the time we were teenagers, Jericho was just as culpable as me.

"What do you know of my father?"

The parish priest when I lived in this town was an older man with silver hair. Father John Clarke was short of stature and had one foot in the grave the entire time I attended the parish. I'd always hated confessing to him because I could never tell whether he understood the issues and problems faced by youth. He

61

was too old – too far on the side of the past that the present I experienced in the Church was lost to him.

"Your father confessed much to me in the weeks before his death. He didn't blame you or your brother for not coming to say goodbye. He'd expected such a rejection. However, prior to dying he wanted the weight of his actions off his shoulders. He wanted to walk through Heaven's gates having no secrets or burdens to carry. I know of the abuse, Jacob. Of the standards to which he held his children, and I don't agree with what he did to either of you."

I didn't comment on his response, didn't so much as look at him. My mind was trapped back in that house, in the rooms where I'd been locked away listening to my brother cry out in pain for the punishments he'd received. Father never punished us in front of each other, especially not after we were old enough to defend one another. Even though childhood abuse could explain why Jericho became the man he did, I highly doubted that was the true reason. We both endured it and yet, my anger and hatred had been with myself more than the religion jammed down our throats at every opportunity.

No. Something else warped my brother, it was like pulling teeth trying to find the answers.

"What my father did," I finally said, "was wrong. I still carry the scars of his lessons and punishments, but it's not the reason Jericho was cast from the Church."

Timothy's head swiveled in my direction, the speed so quick I assumed he must have pulled a muscle in the act. "Have you spoken to your brother recently? Your father assumed that not even the two of you communicated any longer."

Laughter barked over my lips. "He was right to assume that. Jericho only reached out to me recently."

"How is he?"

Turning to stare at a man who was a practical stranger, I hated the manner in which he acted as if he personally knew my brother and me. "He's changed." Leaving it at that, I waited for Timothy to finally get to the point of the run around we were playing in this conversation.

Timothy nodded his head, his eyes searching my face for more information than I was willing to give him. I wouldn't turn Jericho in, wouldn't call out the cult he was running, nor lead the police to the town in which I'd once been priest. Revenge was mine and I wasn't willing to give it up easily. It was better if nobody knew.

Letting out a deep sigh, Timothy flicked a piece of lint off his pants, turned his head to see how many other people sat in the parish around us. Once he returned his attention to me, his expression was tight, hard with the truth of what he knew about my family.

"You need answers, Jacob. That I can see easily in your eyes. But I'm not the one to give them all to you. I have duties to which I must attend this afternoon, but I'm available for a more thorough conversation in the morning. I can't give you the answers you seek, not without the right questions being asked first. You should return to your old home, dig for the answers there first and then come back. If you ask the right questions, I can fill in the details without breaking my vows as a priest to hold my tongue."

I knew my childhood home had stood exactly as my parents left it after death. Left to both Jericho and I, the house hadn't been touched for many years. My father's estate had managed the taxes and other such tasks to maintain the inheritance left behind. I didn't want it, and had never responded to any of their correspondence or phone calls. But perhaps, the answers could be found lingering behind the walls of the place I'd once called home.

"Tomorrow morning, then. I'll be here at nine."

He nodded again and reached out to lay a hand over my shoulder. It took effort not to shrug off the contact, but I didn't want to distance the only person so far who seemed to know more than I realized.

"I'll see you then. Have a good night, Jacob. Hopefully, God can lead you to the answers you seek."

11

ELIJAH

Eve passed out within minutes of drinking the tea I'd given her. Like an angel, she slept peacefully, lost to whatever dreams floated through her consciousness. I took the opportunity to pack her up and drive her to the compound, delivering her to the cabin situated discreetly in the woods out of sight of the family. Only a few knew of this place, Richard being one, and it didn't take long for him to meet me inside, his broad shoulders filling the doorway as he stepped through.

"You needed me?"

Sitting on the platform to the side of where I'd laid Eve's resting body, I brushed my hand over her hair as my gaze tracked Richard's movement through the cabin.

"We may have a slight problem," I mentioned casually and without too much concern.

Despite the calm tone of voice I'd used, Richard's attention snapped to me. "Such as?"

"Eve said something to me last night. She wasn't fully awake, still somewhat trapped in a dream, but her words were clear enough." Locking my eyes to his, I arched a brow. "She's remembering bits and pieces of her time with my brother."

Leaning back against a wooden wall, Richard tucked his hands into his pockets, his bulging belly challenging his shirt to stay tucked into the waistband of his navy blue pants. The buttons of the white shirt were equally as challenged, the material straining to remain closed. "I thought you said you'd screwed her up enough. That the drugs you'd given her had clouded her mind so thoroughly that a week away from our control wouldn't matter."

"They should have," I remarked, turning my eyes back to the small girl silently sleeping. "She's stronger than I thought."

For the week I kept Eve confined to the cabin, the week that I took an innocent, hopeful girl and turned her into exactly what she needed to be to pull my brother out from beneath the lies he told himself about his faith, I'd used every means to my disposal.

She was already so close when I chased her out here, already so conflicted that it was easy enough to get inside her head, but keeping her there was another story altogether. Whereas other women in the family were blind in their devotion, this particular woman still had questions, still harbored doubts. I could read them as clearly as if they'd been written on a billboard and I knew that warping her enough would take more than a few carefully spoken words.

Sedatives during the day while I kept her awake. Amphetamines at night while I left her alone to pace inside her cage. Always keeping an eye on her, I never let her wander far enough outside of my sphere that she would become lost, but just far enough that she became lost to her insanity, that she truly believed nothing else besides me existed in her world.

The sex - fuck - the sex was phenomenal. She gave as much as she took after a while. Shy at first, Eve developed a hunger that almost eclipsed my own. A few more drugs had her writhing and begging, just the feel of my fingertips sliding across her skin enough to send her careening into an orgasm that screamed from between her full, soft lips. The cocktails and blends of the drugs would have altered any sane person to the point of utter insanity. But not her. Not as much as I'd believed.

Although the effects would have worn off hours after her last dose, the damage should have lasted through the week she spent with Jacob.

The brain can only take so much. Lack of sleep, lack of food, hallucinogens, and the pleasure that comes with pain, she'd been immersed in it all, walking out of this place as the perfect specimen, the perfect tool of submission and empty thought. I'd fried her mind with the concoctions, stealing her questions and doubts and replacing them with everything I needed her to believe.

And yet, she still saw the difference between Jacob and me, and somewhere, trapped deep inside her subconscious, the girl she'd been before that week peeked out, whispering truth and perceptions to the woman I created. I had to kill that girl once and for all, and do it in a way that didn't alter the woman she'd become.

"What will you do with her now?" Weaved within Richard's voice was a rancid hunger that made my skin crawl. In ways, his thirst for violence sickened the civilized beast inside me. There was no art to his darkness, no polished surfaces to the acts he committed against women powerless to fight him off - and Eve, he'd wanted her for so long. "Leave her here and I'll take care of her."

"The rules haven't changed, Richard. She's still off limits." Twisting so I could pin him with the seriousness of my words, I reminded him, "She is my wife, after all."

Rolling his eyes, he fidgeted in place, scuffing the toe of his boot over the worn floorboard beneath him. "You let your brother have a taste. That's all I'm asking."

Violence slithered through me, just beneath the skin. Although I'd known Richard for many years, could rely on him to keep his mouth shut and do as he was told, there were still aspects of him that drove me to a killing edge, moments when the satisfaction of jamming a blade into that fat belly of his was just out of reach.

"She was created for that purpose. Or have you forgotten? The moment I saw her face, saw what it would become and how it could be used, I knew what I would do with her. But that doesn't mean she'll be passed around from man to man. What has she done to deserve such a fate?"

He would have been smart to hear the warning in my tone, but Richard was too much of a brute to understand subtlety. "Why do you even care? She served her purpose. Why keep her around?"

Now that was a question I wouldn't answer him only because I didn't want to admit it to myself. Leading him down a different path of conversation, I changed the subject. "You've had plenty of *tastes* of many women. If I'm not mistaken you've made good use of our arrangement for your idea of a good time."

"Yeah, except, lately, you've been the only one having fun. I'm bored. You promised me more than this bullshit when we originally agreed to starting the family."

My eyes narrowed. "Haven't you had that fun? For years if I'm not mistaken?"

"Not for the last few months. Not while you've been shacked up with Sedra in the church pretending to be a fucking priest. When does shit get good again?"

Breathing out in order to maintain my cool, I smiled. "Well, now you've brought me to the reason I called you out here. We have a show to put on tonight. An important one."

Expression brightening with the excitement of the tasks he knew I'd assign him, Richard straightened his posture. "Tell me."

"Gentry Holmes is coming out to the compound tonight. He's important because his brother is the sheriff, and thus the law around these parts. If I can convince them both to take part in the war we're starting, I'll have no concerns about any person reporting what occurs in this sleepy town."

"What do you need me to do?"

Eve stirred beneath me, a small moan escaping her lips that told me she was returning to consciousness. The tea I'd given her worked well to knock her out, but would have made her sick with no food in her stomach. The pain must have been immense to cause her to groan in sleep. It was too bad I wouldn't be able to feed her before the next special brew - one that would have her crawling up me like a cat in heat, presenting every bit of herself and mewling to feel fingers brush her skin.

Petting her hair with one long stroke, I answered Richard. "I need you to go a few towns over and acquire a businessman for my demonstration. Make sure he's as clean cut as possible. Someone that, by sight alone, people would assume was responsible and focused."

Richard huffed. "How is that fun for me?"

"Because you'll also be acquiring a woman at the same time. One you can amuse yourself with at the cabin after the demonstration." My lips tipped up at the corners. "If you can find a pair that are husband and wife, that'll be preferred."

His eyes blazed with anticipation. "I think I can figure it out." He paused for a moment, his expression twisted with contemplation. "You sure this Gentry guy is ready for whatever you have planned? What if he runs to squeal to his brother? We haven't exactly introduced him to the family yet."

My voice dropped in tone, anger at being questioned sharpening the edges. "He was at the demonstration last night and came to me this morning seeking help. The seeds have been planted, Richard, now it's up to us to help them sprout and grow. I believe we should offer Mr. Holmes some special refreshments prior to the demonstration. Bend his mind a little. Make him more receptive to the truth we give him."

Richard laughed. "You're going to drug him?"

Grinning, I crooned, "That's a rough way of putting it, Richard. I only plan on tipping the scales in our favor. Not enough for him to know anything's different, just enough to make him feel more involved in the demonstration he witnesses. You catch my drift, I'm sure."

My fingers brushed through Eve's hair. She stirred just a bit beneath my touch, her eyes moving beneath the closed lids, her lips parting just slightly. "Give him a water downed version of the initiate brew. Enough to make him believe he's seen God, but not so much he can't drive home. I want him suggestible, not stoned out of his mind."

Grunting his approval, Richard couldn't hide a grin. "What are the two people for? The man and woman?"

"The man is for the demonstration. The woman is to prepare the man for the demonstration. I need to expose the demons in our world tonight, and I'd like to have several for Mr. Holmes to witness. They can't all be sexual demons, can they? I think rage is another one that needs to be strung up and destroyed in order to lead Mr. Holmes to our side. Which is why I would prefer to pick up an intimate couple, husband and wife, boyfriend and girlfriend. Hell, even mother and son would do as long as that son is a grown man. Can you take care of that for me? Have them back here within a few hours?"

Pushing his considerable weight off the wall, Richard ran a meaty palm down his beard. "Of course, I can."

I smiled. "Excellent, Richard. Trust me when I say you'll be having fun in no time."

12

JACOB

Returning home was just as hard as I'd imagined it would be. Driving into the city hadn't been so bad. With large glass towers and busy streets, the city had changed through time. The population was denser, the landscape constantly shifting as buildings were demolished and modernized. Creeping down the road through thick traffic hadn't clogged up my throat with memories and long faded emotions, but the same can't be said for the sleepy neighborhood where my childhood home sat empty, for the lazy sway of tree branches and winding streets that had stayed the same despite the amount of time that had passed since I last traveled this path.

Not even the parish, in all its holy glory, had affected me as much as the driveway I was now pulling into.

A semi-circle, the driveway took me up one side of the property, curving me around through the lawns and landscaping that had been meticulously maintained by the men managing my father's estate, right past the front door that sat deep inside a large, shaded portico. Slowing down as I approached the front, I stared at the driveway that kept going, that would lead me away from a place to which I'd never thought I'd return.

My hands gripped over the steering wheel, my eyes glaring at the house as I pulled to a stop. Even as a kid, I never understood the privilege in which I'd been raised, the amount of money my devout father had hoarded to himself instead of using it to help other people in need. What would Jesus think of the way he'd managed his *godly* life?

Standing proud beneath the glow of a bright, full moon, the house was a three story masterpiece, complete with a stone exterior, carved wood detailing, travertine tile on the front porch, diamond paned leaded glass windows and turret style risings from the roof. It looked like a small castle nestled in the center of a small quiet suburb, as large and pompous as my father had been.

I climbed out of my truck, slamming the door shut as I peered out at a house that had been abandoned for years. My mother died before my father and when I'd learned of my parents' fate, I'd inwardly enjoyed knowing that his last few years were spent alone. However, that joy washed out of me now, diluted until empty by the rush of anger and heartbreak pouring through my veins.

So many memories lingered inside that house like ghosts that would never go away. They followed me into sleep from time to time, begging for me to return and set them free. Those ghosts were the reason the walk to the portico took that much longer to make.

Pulling out a plain manila envelope from my pocket, I broke the sealed flap and extracted the bronze colored key given to me by the managers of my father's estate. He'd been surprised to see me arrive in his office unannounced, had told me he assumed neither my brother nor I would return to claim our inheritance. Ignoring the way he'd rambled on, I'd asked him for the key and ignored all the other information he'd given me.

Not caring about trusts, not wanting a penny of the wealth that had been left to me, all I wanted at that moment was to turn around, climb in my truck and get the hell out of town.

Yet, here I was, staring at an empty house, knowing I had no other choice but to walk in. Every step felt like a heavy stone was tied to my foot, each inch I crawled closer chasing a shadow across my bones stuffed full with the reminder of the pain I'd suffered growing up.

Jericho and I had been treated similarly by my father, but it was my antics mostly that were noticed. Many times when people reported some stunt we'd pulled or supposed 'sinful' act, I received most of my father's wrath. I was the darker twin in his opinion, the one closely tied to the devil in his attempts to influence us both.

After a while, I'd grown so accustomed to the constant crawling and vicious lashings that when Jericho had messed up alone and gotten caught by a teacher or a nosy neighbor, I'd lied and claimed it was me. He was always weaker in that regard, unable to bear the painful punishments and unhinged scorn on the part of my father.

Jericho, despite what he'd grown to become, had at one time been soft.

Dad had been right, I was the darker twin, the one more prone to questioning authority and seeking

75

excitement and entertainment in areas and subjects thought perverse or shameful by the members of a conservative Catholic community. But I couldn't help my fascinations, especially when they were waved in my face every day as a possibility that was always just out of reach due to a religion I wasn't quite sure I believed.

So like any rebellious child, I'd explored and tasted the sinful things. I stole gum at ten, other higher priced items as I grew older. I lied to my teachers and parents. I slept with women once their beauty caught my eye. Slowly, but surely, I crept through the places my father always told me to avoid, acting in ways that went against everything he demanded of me, and found that my tastes only grew darker the older I became. Vanilla sex, hearts and flowers type love, innocence and finer things all fell into a state of perpetual boredom until I discovered the true ways to liven up the endless days I spent sheltered in privilege I didn't deserve.

Jericho was a different story. From the minute we were expelled from the womb, he had always shone brighter. The quietest baby, the respectful toddler, the child that found early on how much he loved to sing in the church choir, Jericho was a shining light that only became dim when he went along with something I wanted to do. He was made of the same glimmering gold as the treasures housed in the grand beauty of our parish, and I was the air that tarnished him.

He was also the twin who screamed the loudest during my father's punishments, the one who cried and genuinely repented for his sins.

I guess times have changed since then.

Now I'm the one left licking my wounds while he sits on the throne of evil he'd created in the cult he called his family.

Father Timothy told me the answers regarding my brother's issues might be found in this house, if only I could find where to look. Regardless of what Father Timothy may have known or even suspected, by sending me here, he wasn't only sending me home...he was sending me straight to hell.

13

EVE

When I woke up, I had to blink my eyes a time or two to focus on the familiar surroundings. My stomach hurt so bad that I was curled over myself, cradling my abdomen beneath trembling arms, my hip and shoulder sore from having slept on a hard platform instead of a bed.

The cabin.

I hadn't been near this place since the week I spent with Elijah after we married, hadn't seen it this clearly since the morning I woke up, tired and in pain, foggy and unbalanced. Elijah had promised me the evil had been cleansed, that after the ceremony, I wouldn't get *sick* any longer. The memory of that conversation was broken and disjointed, but I remembered the promise nonetheless.

Why had I run? Why had I opened myself up to the evil he'd worked so hard to chase off? It only left me confused again, sick and in pain.

Like now, with this feeling in my gut that something was shredding me from the inside out.

It was late in the day from what I could tell, the crimson pinpricks of dying sunlight piercing the small natural holes in the wooden walls to stain the room in reds and golds. It wasn't much light to illuminate the room, but much wasn't needed with the plethora of candles lit and swaying on some soft breeze. Dust motes danced in the barely there movement of air.

I would have preferred to push myself into a seated position, but the pain in my abdomen was too intense. Instead, I lay there helplessly, my teeth clenched so hard I was sure I'd crack the enamel. Left with only a partial view of the cabin due to the position in which I lay, I wasn't sure I was alone. Groaning, I gave every indication I was awake. Elijah's voice didn't boom or even whisper in response.

Finally losing the patience to see if he would speak first, I called out his name. Nothing.

Leaving me unattended wasn't like Elijah, especially considering I woke up unbound and free to move around. Unfortunately, the pain inside me prevented it. And despite the oddity of the moment, being alone didn't last long. Within minutes the old door opened and the devil himself walked in.

"I brought you more tea," he said, his lips pulling into a practiced grin.

Devil. It hadn't occurred to me until he spoke that it was the word that came to me when I first saw him. The sickness must have been speaking inside my head. The sickness these demons caused each time they attacked me.

"Thank you," I barely managed to whisper, "but I think I need plain water, too."

I wasn't sure if his expression was sympathy or satisfaction. His lips ran a twisted line, his blue eyes glistened in the candlelight, his eyebrows pulled up just enough to cause small ripples in his forehead. His was always so beautiful, even when you couldn't tell what he was thinking.

"Your throat sounds like someone scrubbed it raw with copper wool. I'll give you some water first."

Setting the teacup on a small table littered with religious figurines and candles, he moved behind me. I heard the water pouring into a glass before he rounded my head to hand it to me. "You'll need to sit up so you don't choke."

"I can't. My stomach, Elijah, it hurts so bad."

Elijah reached out to wrap his strong arms around me. Lifting me from where I lay curled, he watched intently as I tried to straighten my body, each movement even more painful than the last.

"That's the sickness, my love, the evil that is infecting you. It wants out. Wants control. But I won't let it take you from me." His voice was whisper soft, a feather of sound against my senses that was only a tease of what it could be when he allowed it to boom across a room. Always hypnotic, he had a voice that captivated his audience, regardless of whether it was stern or soft. I could spend all day listening to him and never grow bored.

"The tea I brought you should help. I had to heat the water over a small fire outside."

My eyes flicked to the unused fireplace by the platform. "Why didn't you just heat it in here?"

"You were sweating in your sleep. I didn't want to make the room warmer."

His palm caressed my face, the soft touch jarring and unexpected. Since moving back to the parish with him, he hadn't treated me with kindness – only pain, only humiliation.

I couldn't make sense of all the puzzles within this man who called himself my husband, couldn't understand the subtle idiosyncrasies, the changes I'd witnessed in him firsthand. Perhaps it was the illness that made it impossible for me to think clearly, or maybe the demons had become more vicious in their game. I wasn't sure of the cause of my constant confusion, but I had to believe it would end once Elijah had finally conquered the darkness inside me.

Why me? I've always wondered if my fate hadn't been decided the moment Elijah had chosen me for a wife. He was so good – so pure – that perhaps I had become his weakest link, the only method the demons had to hurt him.

"Do you remember the time we spent here in this cabin, Eve? The days and nights that I fought so hard to free your beautiful soul?"

Shaking my head, I winced at the movement, my headache pounding even harder until I swore some hammer was chiseling away at the inside of my skull. "Yes and no," I answered, finally taking a sip of the water he'd given me, the relief instantaneous as it slipped down and soothed my sore throat. "It's a blur. I remember you fighting whatever it is inside me. I remember feeling ill all the time. But that week, those nights and days have blended together until only pieces are available to me. How did it return? Why am I infected again?"

He tsked his tongue against the top of his mouth before planting a soft kiss on my cheek. Standing up, he rounded the platform to retrieve the tea he'd brought in. Steam rose and swirled above the white cup, thinning out as a trail behind him as he moved to stand next to me.

Taking the water glass from my hand, he replaced it with the small cup of tea. "Drink up," he instructed, his eyes studying me as I brought the rim to my lips.

The flavor reminded me of the time I'd spent in this cabin before, sweet, but also rancid. "What's in this?"

"Some herbs I've found in the forest and dried. Did you know my mother taught me all about natural medicine? When I was a boy, we spent a lot of time studying the methods God has provided us for remedy of all that afflicts the body and soul. If you know where to look, you can cure almost any ailment without need of pills or other such medicines."

I didn't know that about him, didn't know much about the man who I'd spent most of my life following. Taking another sip, I ignored the way it burned my tongue. It was good enough for me when it numbed my throat, when it chased away some of the pain in my stomach. "Did she also teach you how to fight against evil?"

His laughter wasn't humorous, it was far darker than that.

"No. My father would have been the one to teach me that. He had to fight it in me when I was young. I can't count how many times I was almost as infected as you. It seems evil knows exactly who to look for in this world, those people so good and pure that it wants to stop them from becoming what they will eventually be. My father told me I had a mission in this world and the Devil himself wanted to stop me."

Caressing my cheek again, he placed his finger beneath the teacup and tilted it to my lips to encourage me to finish it all. "You have a mission, too. By my side, as you well know. It may be my fault you continue to become plagued by the evil forces keeping you ill."

Once the last drop of tea had slipped down my throat, the pain in my throat and stomach subsided. However, the beat of my heart began to quicken in pace until it was a hard pulse against my ribs. Lightheaded, I reached to give Elijah the cup, almost dropping it in the process. He grinned as he took it from me, his blue eyes searching mine.

"Do you feel better?"

Why did it sound like he was speaking from inside a tunnel?

"Do you feel better?" he repeated.

Blinking my eyes, I felt them come into sharp focus. My heart rate continued to increase, my fingertips and toes feeling like pins and needles. Where the pain had once held court, anxiety now reigned, the rush of blood in my head like softly rolling thunder. "The pain is gone," I answered honestly, unsure why I felt out of breath and spoke with clipped words.

A familiar buzzing beneath my skin came to life, a need to move, to rage, to dance and sin. "What's happening to me?" I whispered, unsure how I'd gone from one extreme to the other. Confusion settled in, made more certain by the fact that the fuzziness inside my head had subsided, replaced with a desperation for something more.

"It's the tea," Elijah explained. "I prepared a blend that would alleviate the pain you suffer, but it comes with a kick."

A smile pulled at my lips. "It's quite the kick. I feel like I could climb a mountain, or run a marathon."

His hand brushed down my arm and I shivered at the sensation. The buzzing inside me was a pulse now,

84

every sense I had coming into such keen focus that I felt like I could accomplish anything, if I tried. Was that pride I felt, or something else? My heart beat with the warning that pride was just another deadly sin.

"I'll chase the demons from you, my love. And you will feel many things as I do so. Some you'll remember, others not. But through it all, you can rest assured that I'm with you."

Gripping his fingers over my bicep, he drew me close to wrap me in the warmth of his embrace. I sucked in as much air as I could, my eyes rolling back as the lids closed. I wanted to move against him. I wanted to eat him alive. I wanted so much, so suddenly, that I couldn't understand what was happening to me. Trust. Such a funny thing. But it was the only option I had when it came to him.

He chuckled when my fingers traced up his sides, when my body inched closer to him hungry for the pleasure I knew he could give me. Catching my hand in his own, he squeezed it. Even that small contact sent a shiver through my bones.

"Not yet, Eve. Not like this. Not until I can speak to the family and deliver my sermon."

A sense of pure *need* rushed through me, so violent it pulled the breath from my lungs.

Taking me by the shoulders, Elijah stepped back to watch me, his brows pulling together as air hissed over my lips and I trembled beneath the strain of whatever was happening to me. True fear was a blanket over my heart, the candlelight in the room becoming too much to bear.

"Elijah," I cried out, not able to control the jerkiness of my movements, the fisting of my fingers over my palms. I wanted to move. Needed to move. Was so desperate I fought against Elijah's hold just to expel the energy exploding inside me. "What's happening," I asked again, my entire body shaking now.

"Open your eyes, Eve. Tell me what you see."

His voice was a subtle whisper beneath the noise inside my head, the pounding beat of my heart that pulsed beneath my skin. Forcing my eyes open, I cried out to see that his face no longer looked human. What had been a beautiful man now looked alien, red eyes in place of blue, sallow skin in place of the sun kissed color I remembered. His features morphed and shifted, his mouth curling until a demon stared back at me.

Beyond him the candlelight roared like an inferno, smoke billowing to become shapes, evil dancing behind him until more demons stared back at me, all gnashing their sharp teeth in hopes of being the one who would devour me whole.

I screamed, the sound cutting through the air as I fought against the man holding me.

Speaking to me in quick bursts of urgent words, Elijah held me in place, refusing to budge even an inch from the platform where he kept me seated. His hands were like clamps over my arms, his strength too much for me to rage against. I had to get out, had to run from the nightmare my world had become, and just as I pushed forward to attempt to budge him, movement caught my eye, a door opening to allow in the last of the sun's dying light, three people inching forward that were as frightening as the man holding me in place.

14

ELIJAH

The sun was setting to the west, what little light it fought to beam across the horizon sneaking in as Richard dragged in the damned.

Exactly as I'd asked, he brought me a man dressed in a expensive looking business suit, and a young woman with long brown hair that reached her hips. I hadn't been specific about what I needed in the woman because she didn't matter much for my display, but she looked like an angel, and from what I could tell by the way the man struggled, she meant something to him.

She was younger by far, most likely in her teens based on the pressed white shirt and pleated skirt. I knew well by the emblem stitched on her shirt pocket that whatever school she attended was religious.

Oh, goody.

The girl's eyes darted to Eve, the fear on her face deepening to see another woman in a state of panic. I would have timed it better if I'd realized Eve would react so quickly to the drug, but with the lack of food in her system, the special recipe I'd given her would have soaked into the bloodstream a lot quicker. It was my mistake to not think about the possible effects, but oh well. A show is a show.

"Welcome," I called out, my hands gripping Eve with such strength I was leaving bruises. Shoving her back on the platform, I tugged her wrist to a restraint and locked it in place. She was going nowhere for the moment.

While Eve struggled against the cuff, I turned fully to eye the new friends Richard had brought me. The young woman was frightened to the point of silence, the man held by Richard's other hand not paying me much attention because he was too focused on the woman.

Jutting my chin to a far corner, I said, "Lock the man up, but leave the girl unrestrained. We wouldn't want to be rude to our guest."

I winked at her, and the older man roared out his complaint. Aware that the girl posed no threat, Richard focused his attention on the man, easily overpowering him to drag him and chain him in a corner of the room that gave him full view of every inch of my hidden space in the woods.

From behind me, Eve continued to struggle, the cuff rattling softly as she attempted to free herself. I wasn't sure what she saw in the room as she'd never found the time to answer my question, but whatever it was must have been terrifying. A high pitched keening sound crawled up her throat, only torn apart by the hissing of air over her lips and the rattle of the cuff.

Ignoring her, I stepped toward the young woman eyeing me with fear and trepidation. Prey caught in a trap, she was motionless, an instinctual behavior most victims employed as if the lack of movement would hide them from a predator's eye. "How old are you?" I asked, my voice gentle and soft.

She trembled just slightly but still managed to tilt her chin up in an effort to appear unafraid. What bravery there was to be found in the young. Perhaps it was a natural facet of her personality, or something learned. The older gentleman, whatever his relation was to her, wasn't afraid either - at least as far as I could tell with the way he kept bellowing despite Richard's methods of quieting him.

"S-seventeen," she stuttered, her eyes widening only a fraction as I drew closer.

"Seventeen," I repeated, my lips pulling into a smile that would soothe rather than threaten. My eyes darted to her shirt pocket before meeting her gaze once again. "I see you're in school."

"Y-yes." The poor thing was fighting her tears, still attempting to be brave in the face of danger.

"How is that going for you? Do you like your school?"

Nodding, she swallowed before saying, "I love it. I have a scholarship to attend college because of it."

My brows lifted. "Really? That's quite the accomplishment. I recently met another girl like you. Such a bright thing, she'd earned a full ride." I paused, holding back soft laughter at the thought of Annabelle. "What is your name?"

The man screamed again behind me, his voice cut short by some brute method of Richard's. It must have frightened the girl to see it because the tears welling in her eyes finally fell.

Her hair was a sheet of chocolate silk flowing down her back, her eyes almost as clear blue as mine. With a pale complexion that emphasized the light dusting of freckles over her nose, the girl was as sweet as honey, her features unmarked by the passage of time or a life lived with worry.

"My name," she struggled to answer, "is Colleen. Colleen Quinn."

My smile widened. "Hello, Colleen. Do you believe in God?"

Eyes widening more, she cried harder, her shoulders shaking with each small sob. "Yes," she squeaked out, the answer not sounding as sure as it should have been. People always reacted to questions about God differently and I couldn't tell if this girl was scared her lack of true faith would be apparent to the man struggling with Richard, or if she was scared about *why* I'd asked the question.

Playing along, I led her down a path from which there wasn't an easy return. "Good. Then you'll be happy to discover that God has a plan for you, child, a very important one. You were born for a specific reason and today, you'll find out what that is. But first, I need to take my wife outside to send her on her way. Can you be patient for me, Colleen, and wait for me to return like the respectful young woman I'm sure you are?"

Nodding again, she chanced a peek at the commotion between Richard and the man. Taking the opportunity to lean in and hover my mouth a hair's breadth from her ear, I whispered, "Who is the man that was brought with you?"

She jumped, stepping back quickly when she noticed how close I'd come to her. More sobs broke through her response, but I'd heard enough to know the man was her father.

I couldn't help the soft laughter then. Even better than a husband protecting his wife is that of a father protecting his daughter. It was exactly what I needed. Richard would be rewarded well.

"Stay here, Colleen. I'd hate for Richard to have to force the issue, wouldn't you?"

Another nod of her head, words completely lost to her now that the thin veil of bravery she'd once worn was shredded by the harsh truth of her reality.

"I'm glad we can agree."

Leaving the young woman to cower near a wall, I returned to Eve. Flipping up the fur blanket covering the platform I grabbed a long chain, a steel collar and a simple lock. Eve was now fully engrossed in her delusions, her body trembling with a need so thorough that she was practically purring in response to my simple touch. Ripe and ready, she called to me. I had to be strong not to take what was so easily offered. Nothing could tempt me more than the woman I'd created from dust, the angel stripped of everything but her love of me.

If I had anything in this life to be proud of, it was her. And I'd never let her go, never let her escape the destiny I'd chosen for her. Through everything I had planned, my Eve would survive.

After removing her wrist from the cuff, I picked her up, cradling her close to my chest while still managing to hold on to the tools I'd taken from beneath the platform. Colleen had already stepped deeper inside the cabin. She was smart to keep her distance from the immediate threat. It was unfortunate that despite her best efforts she would be used.

Shoving the door opened, I stepped out into a shadowed forest, the last beams of the setting sun nothing by a glow on the distant horizon. The moon and stars were already visible in the sky, the crisp bite of evening wind nipping at my cheeks. Eve shivered for only a second beneath her simple dress, but was soon heated again by another rush of need and heat, the drug coursing through her veins doing its best to force her into overdrive. She wriggled against my arms, her eyes rolling back and fluttering closed, her lips pulling into a smile before pulling even tighter into a stern line.

"Where are you taking me?" she managed to ask, her words scattered and hoarse with a hiss of air over her tight lips. Teeth chattering in response to the mix I'd given her, she relaxed for only a second before her muscles were clenched again.

I set her on the ground, chuckling as she crawled toward me rather than away. Her back arched so that her hips and shoulders were held up and proud, she resembled a cat in heat just begging for some tom to come relieve her.

"You're not going anywhere," I answered, "not yet anyway." After pulling a length of chain around the thick trunk of a tree, I secured it in place with a padlock. The steel collar locked onto another link and I dropped it to the ground to turn and watch my beautiful girl seduce me.

She was on me in seconds, her hands rubbing up my body as her lips found my neck. I needed to return to the cabin, but I didn't have the willpower to push her off. I adored Eve when she was like this and wished I could find a way to make her so thoroughly useful without the need for intoxication. Yes, my love was always willing to submit whether high or stone cold sober, but she was never so *free* while sober as she was now. She practically growled when my hand found the apex between her thighs from over her dress.

"They're everywhere, Elijah. I need you. I need you to chase them off."

Pulling her closer to me, I smelled her hair. There was a distinct scent to Eve's fear. In ways, it was the same as her need, a calling card letting me know she doesn't trust what's being done to her but will submit regardless. So perfect, she was made for me. And I had been the one to make her.

"Chase who off?"

"The demons. They're reaching for us. Don't you see?"

Twisting around, I saw the thin branches of the trees that hung down, the starlight in the sky twinkling like a million small eyes through the branches. In her state, it would be easy enough to confuse those shapes and shadows for something more nefarious than nature.

Turning, I pressed my mouth to her ear. "Do you trust me?"

"Always," she promised, pressing her body closer to mine as if she would have preferred to crawl inside me.

"Then you must endure them, Eve. For only a few minutes. I have business to finish in the cabin."

"No!" Clinging onto me like I was her only protection against the world, she begged, "Please don't leave me, Elijah. Please!"

My hand found where I'd dropped the collar to the ground and I brought it up to snap in place around her throat. It wasn't enough to choke her, just to hold her in place until I could get back outside to retrieve her and take her to the compound.

93

"Trust me, Eve. I've protected you. The demons won't come near."

She trembled at my words, but her fear was lost to another rush of need, the musky scent of her arousal teasing my nose until my body was growing hard. No woman could affect me like Eve. No other woman was designed specifically for me.

Slowly peeling her off me, I fought my own battle against what I wanted to do, and led her to sit at the base of the tree. She fought at first, but finally succumbed when I kissed her forehead and said, "Hide your eyes, Eve, so that you don't see them. Be brave. God is watching over you."

Nodding her consent, she bent her knees and pulled her legs against her body. Tucking her face down over her knees, she hid from the threat that was all around her. I only had a few minutes before another rush of energy and need caught her in its crushing blow, so I left her where she sat to enter the cabin.

Colleen was now crumpled on the floor crying and I looked past her to see her father's arm twisted behind his back with Richard's foot planted over his spine. One hard yank and her father's arm would snap like a twig, his spine crushed inward if Richard used all his weight.

"Don't break him," I demanded, my voice forceful yet mocking. In truth, I didn't give a damn about what was done to the man. I had one objective only, which I was running out of time to complete.

Richard eased off some of the pressure, but applied it again when the man screamed, "Get the hell off my daughter!"

I'd only wrapped my hand around her bicep to help her to her feet, but I stopped before accomplishing it. Turning to stare at the man who was flat to the floor, the corner of my lips kicked up. "Or you'll...what?"

He struggled for only a second before his face twisted in pain. With skin as red as a tomato, he watched helplessly while I guided his daughter to her feet. Still staring down at him, I had to laugh. "You may want to pay attention, Dad. I think your little girl is about to be all grown up."

A loud snap echoed through the room, the man's mouth wide open as a loud cry of pain tore from his lips. He must have struggled again and Richard had grown tired of it. I grinned. "Did you want to try for the other arm as well? Richard, here, loves breaking his toys."

I dragged Colleen to the platform, inwardly lamenting the fact that I wouldn't have time to stay for the show. Every character had to be in place for what I needed Gentry to see, and my place was behind the pulpit. We only had an hour left to have everything in place. The adrenaline pumping through my body forced a bead of sweat to trickle along my temple.

Colleen cried as I forced her down onto the platform, her body kicking and fighting as I not-so-gently buckled her in place. Under normal circumstances, I would have taken my time with her, would have eased her into the idea of lying down just to eventually strip the veil and show her what I'd talked her into doing. But there was no time left for coddling.

Tucked in the drawer of a small table that held religious figurines and a few scattered candles was a pair of scissors I kept for moments such as this.

Colleen's father screamed and roared, begged and threatened as I made quick work of her clothes. Her sobs were a quiet beat beneath the way he bellowed. Leaving her lying in just her panties, I'd stripped her down to the skin, her clothing a pile of useless rags littering the floor.

Standing over her, I glanced between her naked body and her father's scathing stare. My eyes must have twinkled when I crooned, "My my, what lovely breasts your daughter has. The better to tease me with, I think."

I placed a gentle kiss on her right nipple and her father bellowed out his objection. Another snapped arm was Richard's response, but I needed the destruction to stop. The man had a purpose and breaking him too much would ruin all the fun.

"That's enough, Richard. I need him in one piece."

Colleen continued to cry and I walked away not as interested in what she had to offer as what I wanted from her father. Opening a small cabinet nearest where he was held, I rifled through some small glass jars until I found what I was looking for.

Holding the jar up to the candlelight, I admired the crystalline crumbles, the beauty of a drug that made raging zombies out of men. Over the past year or so, this particular substance had taken hold in some larger communities and people had been caught cannibalizing their friends. As soon as I learned about it, I set out in search, fully knowing that one day it would come in handy.

That day just happened to be today.

Kneeling down by the struggling man, I gripped him by the cheeks and said, "Here's how this is going to go. I need you to stay sill while I inject this substance in your veins. I won't be able to do so with you moving

96

around as much as you have been. And I am not in the mood for a struggle. So, I'll give you the choice..."

Pausing, I turned to look at his daughter, the direction of my gaze obvious before I turned back to lock my eyes with his.

"I think it's obvious what's about to happen to your precious baby, but while you can't stop that, you can save her life by giving up your own. I promise you I won't touch her or kill her, if you do as I say."

He fought, weakly this time, tears welling in his eyes that he wasn't able to hide any longer. "You'll let her live?" he asked through clenched teeth. I imagined the pain he was feeling was the reason why his words sounded rough and clipped.

"I won't kill her," I promised, a genuine smile stretching my lips.

More tears dripped from his eyes that were the same color as his daughter's. "Fine."

Pleased that he would make my job a touch easier, I climbed to my feet and began the process of liquefying the drug and pulling it into a syringe. Once it was ready, I kneeled down again, tied a rag I had handy around the man's arm as tightly as possible before looking him in the eye. "This might pinch a little."

I was sure it wasn't the needle that made him cry out in pain, more like my having moved his arm enough that the snapped bone poked up into his skin.

Once the liquid was safely pumping through his blood, I was back on my feet, my eyes locking with Richard's. "He's going to become quite aggravated here in a few, and I need you to ensure what he witnesses is enough to turn him into a monster. Do you think you can handle that?"

A slimy smile stretched Richard's lips, his eyes focused on the sweet morsel strapped down to the platform. "Yeah. I can handle it."

"Excellent. Afterwards, I need you to have him caged in our special room in the compound. I need him screaming, Richard, but not able to talk, do you understand what I'm telling you?"

His gaze slid to mine. "You want him gagged?"

"No," I answered, my heart rate kicking up in speed. "I need him physically unable to talk, and I need it to look self inflicted. If you go through the drawer in that table over there, you'll find a pair of tongs. Grab his tongue by the tip and drag it out of his mouth. If he doesn't bite down on it himself in response to what I just gave him, help him out by slamming his jaw shut until the pesky muscle comes loose."

Richard grinned. "No problem."

"Be sure to bring the tongue with you and leave it in his cage. Props are important after all. I need Gentry to truly believe what we're about to show him. Understood?"

"You got it, boss."

Patting him on the shoulder, I stalked toward the door before the father screamed out. "I thought you said you wouldn't touch her."

Turning I saw that Richard had already left the man to approach his lovely daughter. A single brow arched over my eye before I returned my gaze to the man. "I'm not touching her, but I never said anything about Richard."

Slamming the door shut, I returned to Eve, finding her exactly as I'd left her. I only had time to free her of her chains and turn in the direction of the compound before two voices could be heard screaming from inside the cabin: the high pitched scream of a very frightened girl, and the low baritone bellow of her raging father.

Eve, lost in her delusional state, didn't appear to notice. I'd be lying to say I didn't regret having to leave.

However, responsibility called and I had a parishioner to meet. I would arrive with just enough time to greet him before delivering my sermon.

15

JACOB

Whatever it was I expected from pushing the old door open, it wasn't what I found. The stark difference between what I imagined and what reality set before me pulled the breath from my lungs on a big rush of air that neither disturbed nor altered the interior of a house I hadn't stepped in for years.

The hinges didn't groan for the door to swing inwards, a gust of musty air didn't billow out until I was caught within its embrace. The smell of mold or mildew didn't attack my senses, and dust didn't dance beneath the overhead lights when my hand found the switch just inside the door.

Nothing had changed and yet everything was different, simply because I was the only breathing body walking into the foyer.

"Dammit, boy, can't you move faster? These groceries aren't light!"

"Be quiet, Jacob, and listen to your father. He knows what's best for you."

"Why is he always so mad at us, Jacob? We didn't do anything wrong."

Three distinct voices, one loud and low, one high and soft, one so small and scared that it frightened me when he whispered. They'd always followed me inside these walls, but now, they were silent.

Nothing had changed and yet everything was different.

The overhead lighting still shone off the polished brass handles of the stately stained oak tables within the large foyer. The black tile with metallic silver striations still gleamed as if hand cleaned by Jericho and me following punishment. On hands and knees, we'd scrubbed until our faces could be easily seen within the stone, our reflections showing us each light bruise forming from where our father had inflicted his reprimand.

The silk flower arrangements my mother had constructed as a means to escape the sounds of crying children were still set neatly within their intricate glass vases, no dust marring the petals or leaves to show they hadn't been handled since her death.

Across the foyer, the staircase rose in a lazy curve to the second floor, the balustrade oiled to a gleaming shine. There were no scuff marks or indentations, no holes in the walls or peeling paint. There was nothing to tell the tale of what madness existed inside this house when I was just a child.

A lie, this house and all its glory was just one giant fabrication, and the twin boys trapped inside had been the only souls to realize it.

Turning to my left as I stepped inside, I saw the formal sitting room my mother had forbidden us to use. The white carpets were pristine, the white couches with nailhead details appeared brand new. The wood tables were unmarked with scratches or water rings, and the crystal coasters sat perfectly stacked in the small brass racks that held them. Never did I step foot inside that room, not even on the day I left home at eighteen. It was my mother's space, her lie hiding the truth that the perfect home she'd put together was nothing more than a farce.

To my right, a doorway opened into the custom kitchen with gleaming chrome and solid oak cabinets. The countertops and appliances were dated from the passage of time, but still you could see the expense in the design. I could smell the savory roasts my mother would cook for Sunday dinner, the same scent that wafted beneath my nose as my father marched me down the basement steps to inflict another punishment.

Another few steps had me inside the hallways leading to the back family room. On my left hung a large, ornate wooden cross, the dark stain contrasting sharply against the brass detail running the edges and gemstones embedded at all four points. In the center was the crucified Christ, his eternal suffering only made worse by our sins.

"Each time you act out, boy, it's another whiplash on Jesus."

My father's belt would come down on me then, giving me strike for strike of what my Savior had suffered as a result of me. I was never one to enjoy the lashings, but I'm convinced my father did. I used to stare at the crucifix and see myself, used to imagine my father dressed in Roman clothes laughing as he beat me

103

thoroughly. Where Christ was made to bear the weight of his cross as he walked to where he'd be erected, I'd crawled along beside him bearing the weight myself, not physically but emotionally.

It took me years to understand that my actions weren't what killed the Savior, that my failures weren't the spear piercing His side. If anything, it had been my father's willful abuse, and my mother's quiet compliance, that drove a man who had never sinned to His eternal cross.

Was I the evil one for childish antics? For disobeying? For having fun during the years where fun was nothing but innocent exploration? Or had my parents been the evil ones, abusing two boys who couldn't fight back, while they draped themselves in holy robes and promised it was better for us to be hurt by them rather than suffer damnation?

The pain returned with phantom fingers tracing each welt, each cut, each bruise to both my body and ego. Pushing forward wasn't easy, but I forced one foot in front of the other, the sound of the soles of my shoes against the tiled floors counting down my penance for having ever been a young man.

While walking me to the front doors of the large parish, Father Timothy had spoken carefully. His choice of words, his tone while speaking them, his patience in delivering a cryptic message, still haunted me as I entered the family room that had surrounded four people who were never a true family.

"You were a priest, Jacob. You understand how we're bound to remain silent regarding a person's confession to God. But what I can tell you is that God wasn't the only

104

person to whom your father confessed his sins. You just have to dig deep enough to find it."

I still couldn't wrap my head around what he'd been trying to say, couldn't think past the deafening white noise that reverberated in my brain as I drove the lonely miles to my childhood home. Even now, that noise threatened to crush me, especially in the moments where it became clear enough for me to hear the whispers.

"What if he finds out, Jacob?"
"He won't find out."
"But, what if..."

My eyes darted to a corner of the room, to the place where Jericho and I used to play with the toys deemed appropriate by my parents. Our father was a doctor and had many books on human anatomy. Jericho and I had found one in particular quite curious. Sneaking the book out of my father's office hadn't been easy. Hiding it in plain sight in our toy corner had been dumb. But somehow my mother never stumbled upon it while dragging a vacuum over the carpets, had never noticed the corner peeking out beneath a pile of Lincoln Logs piled haphazardly on the floor beside their bucket.

"But, what if..."

We were nothing but small boys who wondered about the usual things. How can a bird fly and defeat gravity? How is it possible for a fish to breathe underwater? Why was our mother's body different

105

than our father's, and why did she always keep herself so fully covered?

That book taught us in graphic detail how women differed from men. I remember feeling nothing when I first looked at the pages, my tiny fingers running down the paper over areas much different than what I had seen when standing naked in front of a mirror. It was an idle curiosity, nothing more, but my father didn't agree.

"That's Satan speaking inside you, boy! Drop your pants, let me show you what the good lord created your body for."

It was the first time I fought back. I wasn't able to sit again for a week. He beat me until blood seeped from the wounds his belt had left on my ass. Those images were cemented in my head by his violence...my need to strike out at the very thing that caused me so much pain.

I still liked to inflict that pain, loved hearing them moan and beg for more.

Fuck, how he'd made me crawl. Over carpets, and tile, over wood flooring and the small, hidden, unfinished room he kept inside the basement. The dirt from the floor of that room would always jam itself beneath my fingernails. It would leach inside my open wounds, would kick up into dusty clouds that tickled my nose while I wept. I'd been locked away so many times, that room had become my haven.

Perhaps that's why the darkness crawled inside me. Perhaps I spent so much time locked in shadow, it pulled the dark parts out. The last time I remembered being shoved inside, the light diminishing as he closed the door, was when I was fourteen. I'd broken the door down with angry fists, marched up the stairs to find mom cooking at the stove, and I'd eyed my father where he sat reading his Bible to tell him, "Never again."

The beatings stopped for me that day, but they continued for Jericho.

Turning right, I passed the overstuffed couch where my family often sat to watch television. Never movies or sitcoms, cartoons, or educational shows, the only flickering pictures we got to watch were religious sermons. My father's faith was so resolute that he swore the good Lord resided inside him.

"Do you know how many lives I've saved? How God himself works through me to give my patients life? How dare you question me, boy? I can give life and I can take it away."

There was a time I believed my father saw himself as God, and it wasn't until I walked inside his office that I realized where Jericho might have gotten it.

"So, God sent Christ down to help man, but Christ chose the Kingdom of Heaven as his home. He abandoned mankind when he died. He left us in the Devil's dominion."
"Keep going."
"So, God sent another Christ. And that Christ will eradicate sin and teach us to fight it. To destroy it if we believe in him."
"I told you that?"

Eve had nodded yes to the question.

"And who is the new Christ?"

"You."

Jericho thought he was God, too. At least, according to what Eve had told me that morning in the parish kitchen while I cooked her breakfast.

No. Not Jericho.

Elijah thought he was God.

The light flared on when my hand hit the switch, anger coursing through me like a tidal wave, crushing me and dragging me until I was hopelessly lost in the undertow, drowning beneath an angry, churning sea.

My father's desk still stood proud in the center of the room. His bookshelf still filled with the books he used in his practice. Sitting on the right side of the third row from the top was a book that I'd taken a beating for, its title printed in bold black letters on the spine: *Female Reproductive Anatomy.*

If he didn't want us to find that particular book, why did he shelve it so low that it would be within our line of sight?

If my father had hidden a second confession in this house, it had to be within this office. Creeping forward, I pull the toggle of a lamp on the desk as I passed by. A warm green glow emitted from the stained glass lampshade, a color that reminded me of him.

My knees popped as I bent down, my forearms resting on my thighs. I squatted there for several minutes before reaching to grab the book. Running my fingers down the front cover, I endured the memories for a few quiet seconds. It surprised me when I found myself throwing up a silent prayer.

The book fell open in my hands. I flipped the pages and found nothing.

Slamming it closed, I let it drop to the floor and closed my eyes against the memories. Rage crept inside at the stream of images: the basement door, the way Jericho would look back at me from over his shoulder, the way my mother would guide me away from the kitchen the moment my twin started screaming.

I hated the man who worked in this office, and because of him I'd hated God.

My arm flung out, my fist knocking over the neatly arranged books until they'd spilled from the shelf, their covers opening like the flapping wings of dying birds. They landed in a pile to the left of the shelf and I turned my gaze to the rest of the room.

There was no hesitation to my actions, no time to control the rage. Before long I'd broken every lamp in the room, every anatomical model, every framed photo and degree. I'd dumped every drawer, punched holes in the plaster walls, tipped over bookshelves until every piece of my father's legacy was in a messy pile on the floor. There was nothing in this room but his memory, no written confession, no hastily recorded tape. Out of breath, throat sore from screaming, I ended up on top of that pile, a piece of his legacy just the same.

My chest beat hard with labored breath, my teeth clenched as my shoulders shook, and for the first time since the day Eve showed up on the lawn of my parish, I cried until my tears ran dry. Scrubbing my palms over wet cheeks, I rubbed at my red stained eyes. Every horrible memory continued its battering assault, every voice, every mistake, every stupid fucking decision that led me to this day. To this moment. To this point in my cursed life.

My father pushed me away from God and Cassandra shoved me back. And after twelve years in that sleepy town, I thought I could drop my guard.

Why? Fucking *why* was this shit happening to me? Why couldn't the universe just leave me alone? How fucking fair was it to grant me a life where I'd been forced to climb out from beneath an abusive hand just to discover I wasn't better off alone?

The memories. The whispers. The grating images of what my father had done. Each memory worse than the other, driving me to my feet, forcing another bellowed cry from my lungs until I was marching in a direction I promised myself I wouldn't go.

Within a single minute - sixty short seconds that were nothing remarkable in the span of all time - I found myself staring at the basement door where it stood in the kitchen, my hands clenched into painful fists, my fingernails digging into my palms, and my head pounding with every dark thought that mocked me until I opened the door.

Like any typical basement, a staircase led down. There was nothing especially troubling about the space, at least not in plain view. Yet, as my eyes took in the rows of storage shelves, as I scanned the shadows for memories I knew all too well, I couldn't help the sense that something was watching me as intently as a predator would its lunch.

Charging down the steps, I ignored the way my stomach twisted over itself, the stabbing pains in my gut that threatened to drop me to my knees. Inside my head, all I could hear was my brother scream as he begged our father to stop.

110

I hated the sight of his bruises, couldn't stand the high pitched cries, and for every step I took down into the bowels of my personal hell, those pain-filled shrieks only grew louder.

Three steps led me to a doorway, to what should have been a storage closet if it had been finished, but I knew the room for something else, knew what horrifying secrets it harbored inside.

This room, this cage, this small out of the way prison had been where Jericho and I were left for hours at a time when my father's beatings had ended.

My palm slammed down on the worn metal handle, the door creaking open to welcome me inside. There was no light in the room, not a single bulb to illuminate the dirt-ridden floor my father never bothered to have finished.

As if by God's hand, the chaos of memories was wiped from my head, the smoke clearing and parting until only a few words spoke clearly.

Those words weren't from my distant past, weren't from another day, another time, or another age.

They were Father Timothy's words spoken as he escorted me out, the words I somehow knew he'd chosen carefully.

With a clarity that forced the breath from my lungs, I finally understood what he meant.

"What I can tell you is that God wasn't the only person to whom your father confessed his sins. You just have to dig deep enough to find it."

Dig.

I have to dig.

111

I stared down at the dirt floor before walking away to grab a shovel.

16

ELIJAH

The family had filled the bench seats of the room I called our sanctuary. With the windows sealed shut and blackened by paint, the only illumination inside was the warm glow of overhead bulbs, the yellow cast light that brightened the interior just enough to chase away the shadows. Standing near the door, I waited for my special guest, unconcerned about how the night would play out. Eve was tucked away in her special box and before long she'd have a friend to keep her company.

I knew Richard well enough to know he wouldn't fail in the task I'd given, and I'd be a liar to say I wasn't excited to see the results of our actions against the man we'd brought to the compound.

Just as that thought was flitting through my head, the honored guest of the evening stepped inside. I caught his gaze immediately and used a practiced smile to set him quickly at ease.

"Mr. Holmes," I crooned lazily as I extended a hand in greeting.

Gripping my hand, he smiled hesitantly. "Gentry, please. There's no need to be formal."

"Of course not," I answered, giving him time to scan his eyes around the sanctuary, to take in the altar and religious symbols, the two large crosses at the back that appeared safe and assuring unless one knew what they were for. "I know the drive out here is a long one. Can I get you something to drink before the service begins? Tea, perhaps? Or water?"

Darting his gaze to mine, he nodded. "If you have a bottle of water, that would be appreciated."

"Stay here. I'll be back in a second."

I'd made it five steps before he called out to me. "Don't you need to prepare for the service? Why are you the one fetching water?"

Slowly spinning on my heel to face him, I grinned. "It's like you said, Gentry. There's no need for formality in this place. We are a family sheltered in God's light. This isn't like the Catholic service you're used to. You'll see what I mean soon."

Inclining his head, he returned to studying the room while I snuck into a side room. Pulling a bottle of water from a cooler, I slipped the cap off, added a powder that would help Gentry along on his journey. Not enough for him to notice the effects, but just enough to make him susceptible to suggestion. In truth, it wasn't really needed when considering what I had planned to show him, but it wouldn't hurt. I tightened the cap back on the bottle before stepping back out where he could see me. Once his eyes were locked to mine, I made it appear as if that moment was the first time I'd ever opened the bottle. Handing it to him, I waited patiently as he pulled down a long, deep swallow.

Pulling the rim from his lips, he wiped at his mouth with the back of his hand and said, "That's much better. Thank you. I didn't realize how long the drive would take until I'd actually made it."

"That's understandable. Most people don't even know this place exists, so once they learn of it, they are still somewhat unaware of how far back it was built."

Purposely setting him at ease, I turned my gaze to the family as they took their seats and settled in for my sermon. Most now attended the parish during Sunday Mass, but preferred the sermons I gave here only because I was free to be myself - I was free to speak of the army for God we were steadily building.

"What is this place, anyhow?" Gentry's voice drew my attention back to him.

Rolling back on my heels, I clasped my hands behind my back. It was the posture of a man at ease, a man with no secrets and nothing to hide - a man completely in opposition to me. "It's an old tuberculosis hospital." Seeing the concern in his eyes, I quickly added, "It hasn't been used for that purpose in decades. They were planning on tearing it down thirteen or so years ago, and I couldn't bear the thought of it. You'll have to come out during the day sometime soon and see what I've made of it. The gardens alone are impressive."

The mention of gardens drew his undivided attention. "What kind of gardens? Food or flowers?"

"Food," I answered casually, knowing that he'd want to see the progress of our crops. The weather hadn't been hospitable over the past year, which had led to the failing farmlands. But, I had secrets hidden up my sleeve when it came to maintaining our particular plot of land, secrets I wouldn't be sharing with Gentry. It was better if he believed God has graced this area more so than others. Especially, if I wanted him to believe that we had only deserved that grace based on our steadfast battle against evil.

The family were all seated, quietly conversing amongst themselves while waiting for me to begin. I didn't give Gentry the chance to inquire further into the gardens before lightly touching his shoulder to lead him to a seat. He swallowed down the rest of his water, drawing a smile from my lips.

"I need to begin the service, Gentry, but be sure to wait for me afterwards. I have some interesting *issues* I'd like to show you when we're done."

He cocked a brow, but took his seat regardless. The anxiety of his situation was still riding on his shoulders, and it would only be amplified by what I'd slipped in his drink. Before long, he'd be eating from my hand, begging for assistance as he promised to convince his Sheriff brother to join our cause.

The room grew quiet except for a few hushed whispers. Slowly making my way up the aisle, I didn't raise my eyes to the family until I was in place behind the altar. The room was completely silent by the time I lifted my eyes.

The family stared back, their gazes focused and intent, their ears ready to hear what I had to offer them, their hearts open for the promise of the coming of God's sword. I was only too happy to oblige them.

"It fills my heart with hope to see you all sitting here tonight. It's been too long since we've gathered, since we've taken the opportunity to come together in the name of the Almighty and determine how we can make ourselves fit for His purpose - for His army."

A few low murmurs broke out, my family bowing their heads to humble themselves before their God, others folding their hands together in reverent prayer.

116

Candlelight flickered, creating a myriad of dancing shadows throughout the room, the swirling smoke of incense adding to the effect.

While I'd been a true believer in my youth, while I'd given up every part of my body, heart and soul to a God who sat laughing in his heavenly throne, I'd learned what it took to lead a congregation, what it took to lead a man to the belief that something existed beyond this world.

It wasn't always the meaning of the words spoken, the threats and warnings, the guilt that was heaped upon us until we lay crushed; sometimes it was something as simple as the inflection of the voice, the deep booming tones, the haunting whispers that teased a man's mind with truth.

Music had the same effect for many. It could draw goosebumps from the skin, tears from the eyes, and elation from the heart. And having been one of the Good Lord's small songbirds, having been a part of his choir, I'd crafted my voice through the years to lure the weary into my fold, to make them believe that safety and serenity could be found in the message I delivered to them.

I was using that voice now to soothe them, but soon I would set their hearts aflame, would rouse them until they would commit the greatest of sins in the misguided belief they did it for God's cause.

If my childhood parish had given me anything, it was the knowledge of how to use my voice, as well as the drive for revenge that fueled me.

Forcing those thoughts from my mind, I focused on the message I was giving my family. What I wanted in the end wasn't nearly as important as the path I took to get there.

117

"Our mission has never been more urgent than it is now. In the last month alone, I've run across all sorts of evil. The demons are encroaching. They're invading our lives through our family and friends. Our neighbors and business associates. They're hiding in plain sight, spreading their wickedness through lust and anger, through greed and lies."

Pausing, I gave them a moment to think about my words, to consider where they may have seen examples of what I was describing. My family members wouldn't have had too much experience with the outside community, but Gentry would have, and it was his mind I wanted to bend more than the others.

"I'm sure all of you can give me examples of what you've seen. Just as I'm sure none of you can deny the truth of my words."

They nodded their heads in unison, their hands still folded in prayer. I looked over the faces that had surrounded me for many years, the weary expressions they now had to learn their fears the world was more infected were true. What I said was gospel to all of them, everything illusion until I ripped off the veil to reveal the truth.

I'd just confirmed their greatest fear, and now I was ready to ease them into compliance before pushing them to extremes.

"What can be done about this?" I asked, posing the question and letting the silence fall again to give them time to come to their own conclusions. Never forceful, I liked to dance around the answers, liked to let them think they found the solutions I'd led them to on their own.

"We fight it," one brave family member said, his deep voice resonating against the ceiling and walls of the sanctuary. Silence beat its lonely rhythm before the rest of the family broke it with their agreement. One after the other, their resilient faces heated with the resolve of soldiers.

I knew every one of them as well as they could be known. I'd gathered them from all walks of life and from all four corners of the United States. Some were wanderers, lost vagabonds who sought comfort and inclusion in some place other than the streets. Others were victims of some horrible tragedy, weak and desperate to know that what happened to them hadn't been the result of their decisions or mistakes. Some had been struggling through life barely making ends meet, while a rare few had been successful, but still searching for that hidden piece that would make their personal puzzle whole.

For each one, I'd had an answer to their greatest question, and it had been easy to lure them into my grasp. After years of preaching to them and living with them, I had every single one truly believing I could lead them to the light.

It was too bad there was no light to be found in my darkness, there was no truth to be found in my promises. I was more deceitful than the Devil himself, more convincing than the holy-roller evangelical preachers who'd become wealthy in their wicked games.

Rolling back my shoulders, I stared out of a mass of bodies who would commit evil in my name. Without them I couldn't accomplish what I'd set out to accomplish, and I should have appreciated them for their loyalty, but I couldn't. It was the same bullshit fealty I'd paid to my parish as a kid, the same bullshit faith that led me to a life of torture and pain.

Seeing the heat rolling behind their eyes, the dedication to my cause, I decided now would be a good time to pull Gentry even further into my web. He was a good man, a good Catholic, and it would take blending the two worlds together to bring him around, to convince him what we were doing was sane. Chancing a glance at him, I saw that his eyes had widened, that his pupils filled and darkened what should have been the light color of his eyes. The drug was taking its effect. It was time to lead him closer.

"We should pray," I announced, my voice booming so that it echoed, the tone demanding but not disconcertingly so. I was the point of unity and strength that could bring this group of warriors together. "We should pray for God's holy guidance! That He shines His light on us and shows us the path to our absolution! We should pray that with His power harbored inside our hearts and souls, we do His will in our battle against the evil that plagues us."

I chose not to lead the prayer, keeping my voice silent while the family lifted their voices to the heavens, begging in their undying faith that God would strengthen them against the evil that closed in around their tiny little world. What they didn't understand was that evil had always stared them in the face smiling a friendly grin while luring them down a path that would ultimately destroy them. Casting my gaze about the room, I focused my attention on Gentry Holmes, noticing the way he fell prey to the harmony of voices praying to the Almighty.

Faith, in of itself, can be an uplifting chorus, the music that crawls inside the weary soul to act as a balm soothing its many troubles. Adding to the harmony of voices was the environment: the dim lighting, the flicker of candles, the religious symbols, and the swirling smoke of scented incense that helped elevate the soul to a higher plane, helped make a person falling prey to the vestiges of a long remembered story believe they were communicating with something bigger than their self.

The ease with which religion and faith could warp the mind was a fascination to those who were born into a life of logic. I wasn't the first to take advantage, and I wouldn't be the last. For centuries, religion has warped the feeble minded. Wars have been waged in its name, blood spilled, lives lost, and the victor riding off into the sunset believing that slaughtering men, women and children had somehow earned his place beside God.

Even I had fallen prey at one point, had been beat down and torn apart, made to regret being alive while lifting my voice to a higher power that didn't give a fuck about me.

There were times I remembered being so engrossed in the spirit that my heart would race and my lungs would work harder to draw in air. My mind would float off with the harmonious voices and I believed in God's holy light just because my body had been so affected. Just like Mr. Holmes was now, I assumed, the drug I'd given him heightening his senses, creating the physiological response inside his body that cemented him to the moment, lifted his spirit as high as my family's voices as they sang out in prayer.

From where I stood, I could see that his eyes were glazed over, not because I'd given him too much, but because I'd given him just enough to believe he was connected to this gathering, that he belonged with the group of men and women who were steadfast in their resolve to do God's work.

121

He was right where I needed him: worn down by the state of his life and open to any suggestion I gave him.

It wouldn't be long before I knew his brother would join him in that belief, would turn a blind eye to the odd occurrences and nascent whispers of a town falling quickly under my control.

Unable to help the grin that stretched my face, I joined my voice to that of the family's, leading the prayer into its holy crescendo before bringing it to a close.

The room fell silent and I continued my sermon. By the time I'd suggested the violence to come, and by the time I ended my sermon with feigned sincerity, I knew that Gentry Holmes was mine.

There was only one last thing he needed to see, the jarring evidence of the *demons* that haunted us all.

17

JACOB

The smooth wooden handle of the shovel was gripped against my palm, the heavy metal lodged against the concrete floor as I stared into a small room that I hadn't stepped foot inside in over twenty years. The door was plain and unassuming, the dirt floor torn up and heaped in piles as I peered down into the hole I'd dug.

It hadn't been hard to find where the ground was last disturbed, the dirt smoothed over my whatever tool my father had used to bury the confession I assumed was hidden in the metal box I found. With sweat dripping down my temples and my teeth so tightly clenched they were aching, I couldn't bring myself to reach inside that hole and extract the box my father had buried before he died.

I wasn't sure why Father Timothy's carefully spoken words had echoed in my head the moment I reached this room. Perhaps it had been divine guidance, or some subliminal understanding that I hadn't directly recognized, but I knew as soon as I opened the door that if my father had truly confessed to anything, his words would be contained in this space.

The guilt alone was an insufferable blanket smothering me and stifling my breath, weighing on me with each step I'd taken down into the basement. I hope he died suffocating on that guilt, hope it became a knot in his throat that choked him and stole the last breath from his lungs.

If it had just been about me, I would leave that box in the hole, allow it to rust and rot away without relieving my father of the guilt he carried into death, but my need to understand Jericho had me kneeling down, had me trembling as I reached to extract the confession from its hole.

Knowing what my father had confessed, reading the words and reliving the horror would certainly destroy me, but I was falling down an endless dark tunnel, writhing and scrabbling for some truth - some honest reason - why two boys that were genetically the same, who lived the same lives, the same horrors, had turned out to become opposites.

Nature versus nurture certainly couldn't explain it. We were identical in every way, had lived the same lives, the same traumas, yet in the end, I had walked away only slightly scathed while Jericho had lost his mind.

Why?

It was the same damn question on an endless loop, the one now screaming in my head as I lifted the metal box, brushed the errant dirt from the top and sat back to place it in my lap.

The ice cold temperature of the metal seeped down into my jeans, an icy finger reaching down through my skin to trace the veins of regret and fear, anger and remorse, the memory of lashing and violations that scarred me. Phantom screams erupted inside my head, my brother's young voice only quieted by my own, and as my fingers traced the latch holding the lid of that box closed, one more voice lifted up to remind me that my father's abuse hadn't been the only scorn we'd suffered.

"Maybe if you two didn't break the rules, he wouldn't have to punish you."
"Shush, Jacob. Don't speak of it in public. You'll only destroy the family."
"It helps if you walk away and don't listen. He'll eventually stop and all will be silent again."

I wasn't sure what was worse: my father's abuse or my mother's complacent acceptance. While he beat us down with fists and belts, she kept us silent while painting a picture of the perfect, Catholic family. My father's abuse had been performed in anger, but what was her excuse? Fear? Or was it something else?

My mother, Christy Samantha Hayle, had been a beauty queen when my father met her. According to the stories, at least. She had long brown hair and green eyes that sparkled in the sunlight. I remembered loving her as a child, gravitating to her before the darkness crept in to shadow her gaze. From birth until age five or six, my family had been absolutely normal. Yes, my father had still been a self-proclaimed Saint, a man who believed he wielded the might of God in his hand, but he hadn't been abusive. It wasn't until Jericho and I had been caught with that book that the abuse started.

"Do you look at your mother that way, boy? With lustful eyes? The devil has gotten inside you. He's filling you full of his evil."

125

Thinking back now as the memories flooded me, it was odd he'd dragged my mother into that accusation. We were just small boys, just innocent youth, but he'd immediately assaulted us with disgust. My mother. Why would a young boy ever look at his mother in that way? And why had my father assumed we had? In truth, all I knew about my cock at that time was that it was useful for pissing while standing up. It wasn't until he'd made such a big deal of it that I'd become curious as to its other uses.

Perhaps our curiosity had scared him. Our interest in the female body leading him to believe we'd been touched by some sinful thing. Whatever it was had shattered the happy illusions of a close-knit family, had crushed the belief that his undying faith could protect his sons from real life.

I never saw my father hit my mother, never saw him threaten her or make her fear for her life. But I clearly remember the wineglass in her hand that, through the years, transitioned into a tumbler, a pint glass, a bottle. I'd grown to hate her more than my father's angry fists just because she sat back and silently allowed it. Every time my brother cried out in pain, it wasn't my father I'd wanted to punish...it was her.

As it turned out, it wasn't necessary for me to strike out at her, she'd taken care of that all on her own with the amount of alcohol she drank. It sapped the life out of her as the years churned on, destroying her on the outside as well as within.

My mother wasn't a beauty queen any longer by the time I left home. She was a shadow of the woman she'd once been, a victim of my father's torment even if he'd never laid a hand on her.

Staring down at the box, I flipped the latch and opened the top.

What I thought would be a simple handwritten confession turned out to be so much more.

18

ELIJAH

The family slowly shuffled out of the sanctuary, single woman going through one door toward the women's dorm, single males through another. Married couples were allowed to go back to their rooms together, because it wasn't a sin for them to sleep together.

I didn't have to direct them where to go, they knew the routine, so I took the opportunity to train my gaze on the solitary person still sitting in his seat struggling to understand why I'd brought him here in the first place.

Slowly meandering down the aisle, I inclined my head toward those people who complimented the sermon, smiled when appropriate and carried myself in such a way that nobody would notice my level of excitement. Reaching Gentry's chair, I hovered for a bit before finally training my gaze on him.

"Did you like the sermon tonight? I'll admit it was somewhat tame compared to the normal family meetings." My smile didn't reach my eyes, but it didn't much matter. There was no telling what my features looked like to a man whose pupils were twice their normal size and whose pulse was visible beneath his skin. I watched that flutter of blood flow on his throat and knew he was feeling just fine.

His fingers drummed over his thigh, his expression somewhat strained yet contemplative. "I heard the same thing at the parish, I'm not sure how any of this will help me in my situation. You promised results, Father Hayle. How will you get them by just talking?"

I hadn't promised anything during our conversation earlier that day, but I didn't feel the need to correct him.

"I haven't finished showing you what I have here. A lot of it you'll need to see during the day. You are still interested in the gardens, correct?"

Nodding his head, he was doing his best for it not to appear uncoordinated and jerky. Another hour or so would help his body ease back into a normal state, just in time for him to drive, but until then, I planned to take full advantage of his altered mentality.

"That's good," I replied, "so we'll save that for when we have the sun to light our way. Tonight, however, won't be a complete loss. My family found something very interesting in town and decided to bring it back to show me."

His dilated gaze pinned me in place. "Interesting, how?"

Feigning ignorance, I shrugged my shoulders. "I'm not quite sure, they only told me before I gave my sermon. Would you like to come with me to find out?"

Gentry stood from his chair, perfectly steady on his feet, but his reddened skin still gave away the high blood pressure making him shaky. Waving my hand at my side, I sauntered off without hurry, "Follow me this way."

The excitement thrumming through me was almost too much to bear because I knew what Gentry would now see could only cement him to my cause. Pretending like it was new to me as well as him was an important factor in this game, as it would create the illusion that I was just as shocked as him.

Turning a corner, I led him down a narrow hall, a low sound growing louder as we approached another door. Turning, I raised a brow to Gentry, my mouth cocked and unsure about the *peculiar* noise. "Does that sound like a man screaming to you?"

He nodded, his concerned eyes darting toward the door.

I made a point to look between him and the closed door several times, before suggesting, "I think you should stay here while I find out what's going on."

Adding urgency to my words, I pivoted on my heel and stepped forward as if to leave him behind, but his hand slapped over my arm, his grip preventing me from moving forward. "I want to see whatever it is."

Looking between the door and his face, I shook my head, still playing up the refusal. I needed him to truly *want* to see this, to feel as if he'd forced the issue rather than having been led to see something I planned to show him all along.

"I'm sorry, Gentry, but I don't know what's occurring. It could be dangerous..."

"How so? I'm a strong man. I can defend myself."

The screaming became a primal roar. Stifling my laughter, I made a mental note to give Richard a very special reward for whatever he'd done to force a sound like that out of the businessman's mouth. It was pure, undiluted rage bellowing out from the cage.

Without dropping the role of a concerned priest, I turned to place a hand on Gentry's shoulder. "It's not just your physical wellbeing I'm concerned about. In situations such as this, the potential for something I'm sure you've never seen, I'm more worried about your spiritual wellbeing."

"I'm a devout man. God is with me."

"Is he?" I pondered aloud, my lips turning down into a frown when all I wanted to do was grin like a madman. "Your crops are failing. Your home is about to be taken from you by the bank..."

His eyes widened, the dilated pupils like two black mirrors reflecting my face back to me. "That's not my fault. The evil in this world is attacking me. Like you said. But it has nothing to do with lack of faith on my end."

There wasn't an ounce of doubt in his words. Pleased to see he was fully on my side now, that I'd handed him the Kool-aid and he'd swallowed it down greedily, I relaxed my posture and looked at him as if considering whether I would allow him to follow or not. The passage of those several seconds while I stood presumably in concern as to whether to let him walk with me only cemented his devotion to the cause.

Lowering my voice as another roar bellowed from behind the door, I forced so much fear and concern into my voice that Gentry would have had to been deaf and dumb to miss it.

"Fine. I'll let you come with me, but I need you to protect yourself. You need to pray, Mr. Holmes. You need to surround yourself in the Holy Spirit, and if your faith so much as wobbles while you're in there, I need you to walk out immediately, to go far away as fast as your feet can possibly carry you."

His eyes rounded even more, his pupils dilating with fear and uncertainty. Until all color in his iris was gone. "What is going on back there, Father Hayle?"

Breathing out a heavy sigh, I glanced between him and the door, my shoulders shaking with soft laughter that I passed off as fear. "Do you remember what I showed you last night? The woman infected with lust?"

He nodded, his Adam's apple dipping low as he swallowed hard.

"I suspect what we're about to see is far worse than that woman." Pausing, I let that thought sink in before saying, "I hope I'm wrong-"

Another roar sounded. I closed my eyes and opened them again.

"But it sounds like the situation - the evil - is much worse than I realized."

"Dear God," he muttered, understanding sinking in as he turned his gaze to the closed door.

I stepped toward the door, stopping again before touching the handle. "Keep praying, Mr. Holmes. And if you feel yourself sliding into doubt, you need to leave."

He nodded his head and rolled his shoulders back with the resolve to stare evil in the eyes. My fingers wrapped over the handle, shoving down to open the door. The businessman's voice bellowed even louder now that there was no barrier to muffle it.

Stepping through the doorway slowly, I kept Gentry at my back as if cautiously surveying the scene before allowing him to enter. I made a point to lock eyes with Richard where he stood next to the large cage that held the man. He approached immediately, feigning urgency and consternation.

Good, I thought, *he set the stage perfectly.*

"Father Hayle," he called out, adding such speed to his words that no person would doubt he was afraid. "You have to see this. Thank God you came when you did. The man, he-"

"Let me through, Father." Gentry's voice was resolute in his demand that I step further inside so he could follow. My shoulders and head were still blocking his view.

Richard paused in his rush toward me when I held up a hand. Keeping my face trained on the scene he'd staged, I risked a smile while Gentry couldn't see my expression. It was lovely, so much more than I'd expected.

Stepping back, I forced Gentry to do the same so I could slam the door closed. I rested a shoulder against the wood, my head bowed as I made the Sign of the Cross over my body. Eyes clenched shut, I fought not to peek at Gentry's face. He needed to believe I was frightened of what I saw.

"What is it, Father Hayle? What did you see?"

"I can't take you in there," I breathed out, fear and apology in my voice. "I'm sorry, Mr. Holmes, but I've never seen anything like that."

Chancing a peek at his face, I smiled inwardly to see determined rage written across his expression. By now his interest must have been at its highest, mere curiosity transitioning into a driving need to know he can face evil and walk away unscathed. Hesitant interest had now become full blown belief. Sometimes playing with a person's mind was far too easy, but then I'd had many years of practice.

134

"Fine. I'll allow you in, but you can't show weakness in the face of what you'll see. You need to stay at my side, Gentry, and if you feel your faith failing, you need to leave. Otherwise-"

"Otherwise, what? Are you accusing me of being weak in my faith in God?"

"No," I answered, shaking my head. "I'm only attempting to prepare you fully."

"I'm prepared," he growled.

Inclining my head, I caved in to his demands. "Then follow me."

Playing into his ego had worked perfectly. He was now prepared to believe exactly what I had to show him. I'd even be willing to bet he'd argue with me if I told him it wasn't a demon infecting the raging man trapped in his cage.

Too easy. The human mind was far too easy to toy with.

Opening the door again, I stepped inside and indicated for Richard to hang back, to remain quiet while Gentry took in the scene. The room was nothing special. Scratched white walls that could use a fresh coat, white tile floors that were also worn down and scuffed, a high ceiling lined by air conditioning ducts and exposed electrical made the space utilitarian in its design. Seated in the middle of the large room that had once been used for storage was a large cage just tall and wide enough for a man to pace back and forth without having to stoop. On a normal day, it wouldn't be a shocking or disturbing sight, but the same couldn't be said for today.

The first feature to draw the eye was the crimson splash of blood on the floors bordering the cage. Dripping slowly from the base, it formed a small pool that spread across the tile, slowly working its way down the grout until small streams went in several directions. A copper scent tinged the air, my eyes dragging up to a drugged man screaming and raging in his cage. Dragging my gaze to another drugged man, I grinned to see his wide eyed reaction.

Too fucking easy.

Richard approached me while Gentry remained frozen in place.

"What is this?" I asked, intentionally speaking loud enough for Gentry to hear. Richard played along perfectly.

"Several of the family members brought him in. He wasn't like this at first, Father, but he got worse almost as soon as he was brought into the compound. We had no choice but to cage him."

It wasn't a complete lie, the man had gotten much worse since being brought in. I had to fight to contain my laughter.

"You should have seen what he did to his own daughter," Richard continued, "I'm surprised the girl is still alive."

She would remain alive, I was sure, at least until Richard grew tired of her.

Gentry was listening as he stepped closer to the cage. His eyes took in the feral man, his head struggling to understand what he was seeing. The drug I'd slipped to the businessman had worked better than I'd anticipated. Turning him into a practical monster, the effect was damn near stunning.

Why any person would intentionally ingest such a substance was beyond me. But they did, those addicts seeking their next high, and they were normally found on the side of the road covered in their own blood or that of a loved one.

His eyes catching sight of some strange lump at the bottom of the cage, Gentry jumped back and covered his mouth with his hand, his skin losing all color as he realized what he'd seen.

I had to jump into character once again to play the shocked and concerned priest. "What? What is it?"

Still covering his mouth with one hand, he pointed at the cage with the other. His voice was muffled as he attempted to speak around his trembling fingers. "H - His tongue. I think he bit off his own tongue!"

Bit off, or had it otherwise removed, I thought. Not that it made a difference. Shit, this was going better than I could have dreamed.

My eyes widened with the proper amount of horror, my hand coming down to rest on Gentry's shoulder. "We all need to leave. We can't stay here and watch this. We need -"

"To put that poor man out of his misery," Gentry finished for me.

My fingers gripped tighter over his shoulder. "We should pray over him. Try to relieve him of whatever evil has infected him."

It was my mistake not to consider the area in which I lived before setting up this particular game. Here in rural Appalachia, there were all sorts of threats to avoid. Wild animals on the search for food, coyotes on the hunt for livestock, venomous snakes coiled and ready to strike when you take a wrong step. Most residents understood these dangers. They took steps to protect themselves, often choosing to carry a weapon that would quickly give them the advantage.

Take an armed man, drug him with an amphetamine and then plant him in the face of danger. It would have been a horrible idea if I didn't love the what occurred next so much. Before I could understand what Gentry was reaching behind his back to do, he'd already pulled the gun from the waistband of his jeans, cocked it and pointed it without giving me a second to get one last word out.

The hammer dropped, and so did Mr. Businessman, the loud blast of the gun nearly deafening me.

Good God, how I fought not to fall apart with laughter. Only the true Almighty could have dreamed up such wonderful results.

My jaw dropped in feigned shock, my hand falling away from Gentry's shoulder as I stared down at the dead man in a cage. "What have you done?" I whispered, my soft voice carrying through the room now that the man was no longer screaming.

The .45 shook in his grip, the realization that he'd killed a man sinking deeper into his mind and thoughts. "I -" Gentry looked at me, his gaze pleading and unsure. "He needed to die, Father. What kind of life is that? Possessed? Without his fucking tongue!"

Turning my attention back to the cage, I studied the dead man, the blood, the bits of skull and brain matter now splattered across the cage floor. A grin tugged at my lips, but I fought it back.

"Is this what you brought me here to see, Father? This...this man possessed by evil?"

"No," I answered after a lengthy pause. "I brought you here to see something else. But, now I'm afraid to show you."

In all honesty, Gentry's decision to shoot the poor bastard was the best gift of all. There had always been a chance he wouldn't believe the show, that he would have gone and reported the compound to his sheriff brother. Having killed the man himself, however, he put him in a position where he had no choice but to convince his brother that all of this was real.

"Show me!" he demanded, the gun now held down at his side. With the grip tightly clutched against his palm, the barrel shook so hard that it tapped against his leg. Even Richard was smart enough to keep his distance while an armed man was in such a fragile state.

My next show was through another door, this one far more tame, yet oh so enticing. I couldn't take him there. Not yet. Not until I knew my beautiful girl would be safe.

"You'll need to leave the gun behind, Mr. Holmes. This is a place of God."

Eyes meeting his, I spoke with a neutral tone. The man was shaking so hard, even the lines in his face were doing the tango.

"You said it yourself, Father. We need to fight. And even you have to admit that man was too far gone to have a chance at redemption. You heard your friend there. They'd caught him doing horrible things to his own daughter!"

"Man can be redeemed, Mr. Holmes, for anything."

"It's Gentry!" His voice was bellowing so loud that I had the urge to either cover my ears or cheer in victory. I hoped he didn't stroke out right there in front of me for how high his blood pressure must have been. Maybe I'd given him too much of the amphetamine. Or maybe I'd given him just enough.

"Fine. Gentry," I whispered, holding my hands up between us like I thought he would rush toward me. "But it is not our place to kill these men -"

"Yes, it damn well is! And if my brother was here, he'd tell you the same." Pointing with his gun, he indicated the cage. "It's things like *that* that are destroying this small town!"

Halle-fucking-lujah. Before long I would have complete participation and control of this once sleepy town. Those crosses in the back of my sanctuary were going to see a lot of use.

"Fine," I said again, "I'll take you to see what I intended to show. But you have to put the gun down. I don't think all those infected with evil have to be killed. I believe a good many can be saved in God's name."

Our argument was important, the mercy I was pretending to show in my responses. At some point in the future, Gentry will remember back to this moment. He would question whether what he did was right. And instead of suspecting my ulterior motive for showing him what I did, he would remember that I was the one who attempted to save lives. That memory would always be in the back of his mind any time he wanted to question my future plans for this town.

The gun was still shaking in his hand, but the mention of the Lord drew his attention. After a few tense seconds, he nodded his head and placed the gun on a counter along the wall. Turning back to me, he demanded, "Take me to see whatever it is.

My head snapped to Richard. "Is Eve still in the adjoining room?"

He nodded, his mouth pulled in a tight line as he fought against his true feelings about the situation.

That big son of a bitch wanted to laugh as much as I did.

I knew he wanted to get back to the girl, and without openly saying it, I gave him my permission. "Why don't you get back to your duties for the evening? I can take it from here."

Flashing a snide grin, he schooled his expression before saying goodbye to Gentry and leaving.

"Eve," Gentry said as I approached, "Is she the woman from last night?"

"She is."

"Is she still-?" His voice trailed off before he could finish the thought.

Crossing the room without answering, I flattened my palm against the cool wood of the door leading to where she was being kept. By now, the poor girl was most likely writhing over the floor. Lack of stimulation, light, sound, touch...in her state, it would have driven her close to the brink of temporary insanity.

Drugs are such a wonderful thing.

Twisting to glance over my shoulder at the man who would unknowingly hand me the small town on a silver platter, I forced a frown over my lips, carefully keeping my voice morose on the subject of Eve.

"It will take time with her. She's not as far gone as the man you-"

I allowed my words to die before completing that thought, my expression to wrinkle with regret and horror. "She's not as bad as him, so you have no need for concern."

The crimson tint to his complexion was draining away, his once wide eyes going back to normal. The effects of what I'd given him were deteriorating now that the spike in adrenaline was calming.

141

"I'm sorry, Father Hayle. I know you didn't want the man killed." His expression dropped, guilt now rolling behind his focused gaze. I would eventually use that guilt to my advantage. But for now, I'd offer sympathy.

"I think you may have been right to do what you did, Gentry. Perhaps I'm the one who needs to realize when a person's life is to dire to save."

He smiled, seemingly appeased by my hesitant agreement.

"We should keep going. It's getting late and you have a long drive ahead of you."

Opening the door, I flipped on the light, the illumination flooding the room and highlighting the small woman seated in a single chair positioned in the center of the small space. Her long brown hair was disheveled, her green eyes piercing when they finally opened and flicked to mine. Like Gentry, the pupils were large, two black pools reflecting my image back to me.

I wasn't sure what it was about her particular features that drew me to her, that reached out and called to me with the pull of something familiar. In many ways I loved her more deeply than I'd loved any other - but that emotion was cut through with hatred and deep-seated anger.

It irritated me when she wouldn't shut up - and I loathed her when she was so quiet that she wouldn't speak out against anything.

Why did her silence affect me more? Why did her quiet acceptance of an abusive hand make me want to strangle the life from her body?

I wanted to possess her and cast her aside, protect her and punish her just the same. My power over her

142

was a power over something buried in my past, something I knew subconsciously, but couldn't bring to the surface.

The only thing I could state with utter certainty was that now that she'd been used for the purpose of chasing off my brother, no man besides me would ever touch her again.

Eve trembled against her seat, her teeth chattering and clacking together, her breath still a hissed whisper over her lips. Glancing down at her hands, I saw them clenched at the sides of her seat, letting go only to rub over the skirt covering her thighs.

Opening her mouth as if to speak, she lost her voice to see Gentry walk in beside me. Fear shot through the green of her eyes, confusion and need dancing in to become a toxic combination.

"She looks normal to me," Gentry commented as he stepped closer.

I didn't bother looking at him, my eyes locked on a woman that stole the breath from my lungs. She was so thoroughly compliant, so perfectly created for a man like me. I guess that was only fitting considering I was the God who designed her.

"Come here, Eve. I'd like to introduce you to a friend of the family."

Pushing to her feet, her gait was uncoordinated and off balance, but she eventually found her way over, stopping within feet of where we stood watching.

Gentry looked over the tiny woman, his gaze focused and attentive, his throat working visibly as he studied her behavior and mannerisms that would appear normal to the naked eye - but odd once closely seen.

"Why is she breathing like that?"

Clasping my hands behind my back, I shook my head. "I'm unsure. It's better than it was when she first came to us. The treatment has been working."

"Like what I witnessed last night? The whipping?"

"It's a part of it, yes. The punishment. But what I'm finding with this particular problem is that no matter what I do, no matter who I introduce to her, she's oversexualized, ready and willing if you know what I mean."

His eyes snapped to her again, and if I weren't mistaken, Gentry was considering what she would be willing to do for him.

"Let's test my theory, shall we?"

He nodded his head, swallowing deep again. His eyes were unblinking, his body tense.

"Take off your clothes, Eve," I instructed.

She didn't hesitate to unbutton the dress she wore, didn't care who stood in the room watching. A grin slid across her full lips promising everything I could want and more.

The dress slid from her shoulders, lower until it was a pool of cloth at her feet.

Stepping forward, I was careful not to touch her skin with my body, careful not to give any indication that she would do this for no other man but me. "Do you feel no shame for being naked in front of a stranger? Doesn't it bother you that a man looks at you with lust in his eyes?"

She trembled at my closeness, her eyes closing as my breath brushed over her cheek. Standing behind her where Gentry couldn't see, I trailed my finger down her spine, stopping when I'd reached the small of her back. She bucked against my touch, greedy for any small sensation.

"Would you allow any man to touch you? Any man at all?"

Tears welled in her eyes, glistening against the green. But still, she played her part well, knew not to question me, talk back, or even use my name. I'd instructed her earlier to be compliant, to allow Gentry to fuck her if that's what he wished to do. It was just one more way to drag him in, to lock him in place under my control. His guilt over his own actions would render him obliged to every future request I made of him.

"Yes."

Flicking my gaze up at the man standing before her, I welcomed him closer. "Would you like to see for yourself how deep her lust has infected her?"

Nodding his head, he stepped closer, his eyes roaming her body with obvious want, his hand reaching out to run a finger over her exposed breast. Eve didn't move away, didn't flinch or act with shame as he palmed the weight of her breast, his lips parting and his body tensing more with the carnal need he was feeling.

Anger erupted inside me. Anger and a overriding need to push him away. It had been my intent all along to allow his lust to take over, to tempt him into acting in a manner a good Catholic husband would never abide, to then blame her *demon* as the cause when his guilt set in. I would have claimed it had infected him due to her proximity, to illustrate how easy it was for the madness to spread through the town, but I found the sight of someone else touching her maddening.

Not just maddening...I wanted to wrench his hand off his damn body, stick it in a blender, and feed it to

145

him as a lesson of what happens when you touch something that's *mine.*

Why hadn't I had the same reaction when the hand touching her body had been Jacob's?

Regardless of the question, I decided against the show, decided that his ease in murdering another person was enough for one night. Snatching at his wrist, I yanked his fingers away from her skin, pulling back so hard, that he had to move with me just to keep his shoulder from being pulled from the socket.

"Careful, Gentry. You are a married man are you not? Her lust is infecting you and you're allowing it without question. This is what I mean when I've said how easily the evil spreads." With an ominous whisper I reminded him just how far he'd stepped out of line. It would have to be enough. If he'd done anything else to her, I would have killed him.

He winced at the remark.

Even that small contact had been enough for him to consider himself a sinner. Even more than pulling a trigger and ending a man's life, he would regret his desire to fuck her. It was a central theme through all religions, I'd long ago realized: that the desire for sex was somehow more of a crime than taking another human's life.

"We should leave," I suggested, struggling to maintain my composure.

After clearing his throat, he agreed with a clipped nod.

Turning to lead him from the room, I only looked back at Eve as he stepped through the doorway. My eyes scanned down her body, coming up to meet her eyes and I wondered about the odd emotions I was feeling.

19

JACOB

Running up the steps of the parish at exactly nine in the morning, I had a metal box tucked beneath my arm and a feral determination to find answers to my questions. Anger coursed through my veins, only deepening with every passing hour, my body tense and energetic despite my lack of sleep. I'd spent the entire night reading over my father's confession, damning the man that raised me and staring at several pictures that sickened me.

Bursting through the door, I found Father Timothy standing at the stoup just inside the doors, his hand moving to bless the water.

"How long have you known?" My voice boomed against the vaulted ceilings and thick walls.

He didn't so much as flinch in response to my anger. Calmly finishing his prayer, he lifted his knowing eyes to pin mine with understanding. "Perhaps we should go somewhere private to have this conversation."

I ignored the calm tone of his voice, refused to let it soothe me. "How long?"

Glancing back to ensure we were alone in the immediate area, he returned his gaze to me. "Since before your father died. But I won't have this conversation out here." Turning he took a few steps before saying, "Follow me."

My jaw ticked with frustration, but I quietly followed nonetheless. It didn't matter where and how he gave me my answers, just that he gave them at all. Barely able to control the fury coursing through my body, I walked with him past the large stained glass windows, gold crosses and statues of Mary, finally breathing out a steady breath when we reached his office down the long hall.

He led me inside, turning to stare back at me once I'd walked fully inside.

"Close the door," he requested. My hand hit the knob at the same time someone called for him from the opposite side of the hall. His annoyed expression matched my own. Stepping past me, he spoke low. "Wait here. I'll see who it is and take care of their issue quickly."

He was gone before I could stop him. I considered rushing after him, demanding his time over whatever issue that other person had in mind, but I knew doing so would only work against me in the end. Father Timothy hadn't done anything to warrant my level of aggression, except for keeping his mouth shut on a secret that could tear his parish apart.

I found myself pacing as one minute bled into another, whispers running through my mind that led to memories that led to pain. The questions were endless, the betrayal suffocating, but allowing the weight of my father's confession to crush me would only weaken me and knock me off course.

150

My jaw ached from clenching my teeth, my hair messy from constantly running my fingers through it. And when I came to a point where I felt like I would start screaming, I turned towards the far wall of Timothy's office and froze in the face of the cross.

Not just a cross, the large wood and metal symbol was an ornate crucifix, the detail stunning right down to the nails that held Jesus in place. My heart felt heavy to realize how evil and painful this symbol had become.

The door opened and closed behind me, soft footsteps approaching before stopping at my back. I didn't turn to Timothy when I finally said, "It's such a morbid symbol, isn't it? The image of a man tortured and killed. Of all the ways Jesus could be remembered, this is the one we hold most dearly. Like we're still celebrating the destruction of a good man."

Seconds passed before he finally answered, "I guess that all depends on how you look at it."

"When I look at this, I see the torture and destruction of purity. The proof that even when faced with God and the power of his hand, humans are still evil enough to turn their backs on it. To use it in order to feed their own selfishness and greed. When I was young, this symbol was the ultimate bearer of my guilt. It became so much more when I was ordained as a priest. Hope, maybe, or a promise. But now...now all I see is another means by which human beings hurt each other on a daily basis."

A moment of silence beat between us. I assumed Timothy was absorbing my words and considering how he could respond to them. Softly, he answered, "What I see is a symbol of ultimate sacrifice. A pure being enduring the worst forms of suffering and torture just to save us all."

Pivoting on my heel, I met his gaze. "Tell me then how everything he stood for so easily fell to shit. How the men who stand as symbols of His goodness and His sacrifice are sometimes the most evil."

He winced at the accusation, at the lack of emotion in my voice, at the truth in the words I'd spoken.

Elijah's words echoed in my head, his insistence that after Jesus had risen from the dead, man was left to fall again. I understood what he was implying, and now that I'd read my father's confession, I felt guilty for not seeing what had clearly driven him mad.

"You've known for several years what happened under the roof of this parish. And yet nothing, not a damn thing, has been done about it."

Shadows crossed over his eyes, guilt and regret lining his brow in deep wrinkles. There was no conviction to his voice when he answered, "You know how it is, Jacob. You've been a priest long enough to understand."

I could feel the beat of my pulse just beneath my skin, could feel my blood pressure rising until it was a steady drum pounding inside my head. "Actually, Father Timothy, I don't know. I've come to you so that you can enlighten me."

It was impossible for him to miss the threat in my tone, the menace, the barely controlled violence that flooded me. His throat worked visibly to swallow down the fear he felt. "We should sit down, I think. Take some time to discuss this in detail."

I smiled, the expression not quite reaching my eyes. Timothy moved quickly to take a seat behind his desk, no doubt praying that the large and heavy oak furniture would act as a barrier between his body and mine.

Stalking closer, I didn't sit down before carefully setting the metal box on the desk, its bottom clicking softly against the wood. Somehow that quiet sound carried more guilt and accusation than anything I'd ever known. Timothy moved as if to reach for it, but I splayed my hand over the top.

"I want to know what he told you, first. Then I'll let you see what's contained inside this box."

My father's confession contained a lot of sins. I wanted to know if Timothy had heard them all.

Pulling at his clerical collar, Timothy settled as much as he could against his seat.

I jutted my chin in his direction. "It strangles you, doesn't it? The small strip of white cloth that has become a symbol of your faith."

A bark of laughter shook his thin shoulders. "It definitely has a way of silencing me. Of making me question things."

I knew what he meant. That collar had made me question my entire existence when I was faced with Eve. Slowly taking my seat, I thought back to her. Saw the complacency in her green eyes staring back at me. Just like another set of green eyes I'd known. Two sets actually, now that I was beginning to understand my obsession.

Leveling my gaze on Timothy, I sat silent, not-so-patiently waiting for his explanation.

He spoke carefully, his words more political than heartfelt. "I'm sorry, Jacob, that nothing has been done. And that nothing had been said. But this is a delicate situation."

Delicate, my ass. He just didn't want to risk losing his job. "I'm not here to talk about what kind of situation we're dealing with. I'm fucking familiar with that. What I want to know is where are the two sons of bitches who thought they had the right to touch my brother?"

Did he know they were dead?

Timothy went completely still as the words left my mouth, the room sinking into silence once the reverberation of my voice died off leaving the question to linger between us. Slowly, he sat forward in his seat, the wood creaking beneath his weight. Crossing one forearm over the other on the surface of his desk, he kept his eyes trained on me, sympathy swirling beneath the deep shadows of guilt. "I don't know."

So, my father hadn't openly confessed everything...

He breathed out heavily after answering me, the fingers of one hand drumming over the skin of his opposite arm. "All I know of that particular situation is what your father told me during his confessions."

Eyebrows shooting up, I asked, "Confessions? As in plural?"

"As in multiple. Five or six, maybe. Your father had tucked away quite the collection of skeletons in his closet. By the time he was finished confessing, I'm sure he went to meet God with a clear conscience."

My teeth slammed together, my jaw ticking with the effort. "Hopefully God sent his ass into the pits of Hell as soon as he arrived."

Timothy blinked at the censure in my voice, maintaining the appearance that he was calm and collected despite my obvious hatred toward the man who raised me. "Regardless of your father's eternal fate, what I know of the others is that there was a shakeup within the parish while Jericho still lived in town and attended here. From what I know, Jericho had every intention of going to school, earning a degree and attending seminary school much like you did. However, he made...accusations...prior to starting school."

My lips tipped up into a snide grin. "Let's stop beating around the bush. It's a waste of both our time. I know what you meant to say is that my brother finally came out and spoke about the two men who had been abusing him his entire life, the two men who sought protection from my father."

"As far as your father knew, they were only disciplining Jericho-"

"With their cocks?"

The older priest's eyes clenched shut at the reminder that the attention given to Jericho hadn't been what most would consider good or pure.

The situation didn't entirely make sense to me. After reading what my father wrote so many times that the words went blurry beneath my strained and tired eyes, I'd spent the late evening and early morning hours attempting to understand how something so evil could have happened. How I could have missed what was being done to my twin brother? It wasn't just when we were young. Perhaps if it had been, there would be some believable excuse. But from what I knew, the abuse lasted late into Jericho's teen years, possibly continuing even after I'd already left home.

Opening his eyes, Timothy reached up to scrub his palm over his face. "The priest assigned to this parish prior to me, as well as the music director who led the children and youth choirs were transferred shortly after

155

your brother came forward. The situation was handled quietly in order to spare the parish."

A fire had been lit inside me, rolling and growing until the heat threatened to strangle my lungs. Dragging in a breath was difficult. Keeping from screaming even more so. "So, what you're telling me is that two grown men abused a boy for over ten fucking years, and the only punishment they received was to be transferred?"

"This type of situation-"

"Is delicate. Yes, you've told me that already. But didn't the Church consider that my brother had been delicate as well? Every day, every week, month and year that those two bastards raped him, he had been just as delicate as the *situation*."

Pinning me with his gaze, he managed to keep a straight face. I would have gone across the desk at him if I didn't notice the anger rolling behind his eyes - an anger that matched my own. "I never claimed it was right, Jacob. There's a reason I hinted to you where you could find your father's buried secrets. But, as a former priest, you have to understand the Church's reasoning for keeping this quiet."

"To save money?" I posited, "or to save face."

Timothy cringed. "To save the faith, Jacob. If something like this were to come out, you know as well as I that believers and non-believers both would blame the Catholic Faith. They would question their own belief systems based on the actions of a few evil men who had taken advantage-"

"So, instead of punishing them and jailing them as they should have been, the Church made the decision to transfer them? Are they free to continue molesting small children?"

156

I knew the answer, but did he?

"I assume they're both so old now that even if they wanted to-"

My fist slammed down on the desk, the metal box rattling over its surface. Timothy flinched, but gave no other indication that he would back down. I took several steadying breaths before asking a question that eluded me over the course of the night that I racked my brain for answers. "Why Jericho and not me? We were the same age. We lived under the same abusive hand."

Sitting back in his seat, Timothy's eyes darted to the wall behind me, to the crucifix that hung there, the image of a dying Christ staring over at him. "How does evil choose any victim?" he finally asked. "Ease of access, maybe. The strength of the person? None of it makes sense to me."

Biting back a response that wouldn't have been fair to the man sitting in front of me, I refocused my anger on the two men who were guilty of Jericho's abuse. Not just two, but three. While my father hadn't been sexual in his abuse towards my brother or me, he had remained silent on what he knew happened to Jericho. "What, exactly, did my father tell you?"

The wooden chair creaked again as Timothy adjusted his weight. He wasn't fidgeting, just slightly uncomfortable. I understood his hesitancy to talk. Confessions, especially those made on the deathbed of a believer, were sacred. They were a conversation with God made through the holy men on this Earth who acted as a vessel of sorts. As priests, we are sworn to remain silent even when we know the information should be exposed, but our duty to remain silent is steadfast and irrefutable. The faithful need to know that they can confess their sins without fear of secular reprisal. They must be given a safe place to talk to God, a haven of sorts to unload all the sin and evil they may have committed. Their desire to appease their creator must be maintained by the protections provided by the Church. To allow our lips to fall loose, to allow our tongues to speak the secrets that were spoken through us to God, was to admit that secular law was more powerful than the Faith to which those believers subscribed.

Even now, with my father long gone and buried beneath the ground, Timothy stumbled over his vow to guard those secrets, and his own morality to make known the evils that had been committed beneath the roof of this parish and my childhood home.

Fortunately for me, his morality won that battle.

"Your father was a devout man, Jacob, as I'm sure you know. Everything he did in life he did for the Almighty. He gave God the use of his hands as a doctor to heal people and save lives. And, in his belief, at least until the day came where he knew he was facing death, he'd given over those same hands to God for the purpose of raising his sons. He truly believed that the punishment you and your brother suffered was for your own good, that he was fighting against the forces of the Devil to ensure that both your souls could be saved." He paused, breathing out heavily before darting his gaze back to the crucifix hanging behind me. "He didn't know what was happening to your brother when it first started. And from what he told me, he didn't find out until years later when Jericho and you were close to fourteen. He swore to me that if he'd known, he wouldn't have condoned the sexual abuse of his son."

158

"However," he said, straightening his shoulders against the high back of his chair, "when he did discover what had occurred, when Jericho admitted it to him during one of the punishments your father was giving him, he, at first, believed your brother was lying."

I knew Timothy was being honest about this part. It matched what was written in my father's confession.

"Your father told me that Jericho only admitted the abuse at the parish because, through the years it was ongoing, he'd been made to believe that it was his fault it was happening. Jericho claimed that he believed he was temptation personified, for lack of a better word. That he had been told the priest and music director were innocent of evil because they had fallen prey to his lustful charms. Rather than seeing those words as proof that two men had intentionally warped the mind of a small child, your father initially believed that your brother was guilty of pride. What other person would assume that they were so desirable that two godly men could not resist the temptation to sin?"

My hands fisted over my lap, not because I was surprised to hear what Timothy was telling me, but because Eve had also been made to believe that she was the ultimate temptation. Jericho's warping of her mind hadn't been some original thought created from his evil need - it had been a repeat of the treachery committed by the men who'd first abused him. I'd already gone over the details of that realization in my head while spending the night pacing the floors of my childhood home. I'd already connected the dots that clearly illustrated how Jericho had known exactly how to brainwash Eve before he'd ever had the first chance to meet her.

"I think, at first, your father's refusal to believe the accusations Jericho made was a disassociation of sorts, a dividing line between his Faith and his opinion of his own son. He knew both his children to be *wicked*, as he put it, that like most impetuous youth, you two had a habit of being up to no good. It was difficult for him to see-"

"That the truly *wicked* are the men hiding behind the guise of faith while committing the worst of sin? That they are the men who should be feared above even blatant psychopaths and murderers?"

Inclining his head in agreement with my assessment, he reached out to straighten the cuffs of his sleeves. His voice was soft when he answered, "At least with most psychopaths, you see the evil coming. But with men hidden within and protected by the Church, by men who, in truth, should be the most holy, you never see it coming until it's too late."

"So, my father did nothing."

Nodding his head again, he cleared his throat and answered, "And the abuse continued until Jericho finally came forward after you left home."

Understanding hit me like a runaway train, plowing me over and tearing me apart. I was left as tattered ribbons with one screaming truth crushing my heart. Jericho had a reason for attacking me like he did, at least in his mind, he did. Because, whereas he had been used and hurt in so many ways, it appeared as if I had been the twin to escape unscathed. It made sense, maybe not to an outside person looking in, but in what was left of his fragile mind, I was just as much to blame for what happened to him.

After discovering the truth, I wondered why he'd never told me. Why he'd kept such a horrible secret from his twin. But then, as the evening hours carried on and I rolled all of this through my head, only one reason came to me: I'd never protected Jericho from my father, even after I'd fought back when he'd tried to continue abusing me. Why would I then help him against a form of abuse that was far worse than even my father could deliver?

The sad truth of that realization struck me far harder than anything I'd experienced in life. Flooded with guilt for everything that happened, I couldn't help but feel complicit in the destruction of my twin.

When I'd first come to this city to find answers for my brother's madness, it had been with revenge driving me forward. The same revenge was fueling me now, but rather than it being focused on the bastard that had delivered my Eve, it was towards the men who had originally created the monster, Elijah.

Opening the metal box, I pulled out my father's handwritten confession as well as the photographs he'd left tucked inside. Without bothering to look at them, I tossed them in Timothy's direction. By that point, I didn't need to look at them again. The images were already seared into my brain.

"They were photographing my brother. It wasn't until my brother stole some of the pictures and took them to my father that he believed Jericho's claims." Sad laughter fell over my lips, grief stricken breath beating in and out of my lungs. With flashes of the torment I saw in the grainy, black and white images, I fisted my hands and closed my eyes. "Even after being presented with the evidence, my father did nothing to stop the sexual abuse."

Timothy picked up the photos, his face twisting in revulsion before sliding them under the letter my father

161

had written. Out of sight, out of mind, I guessed, but this particular crime wouldn't go away so easily.

"Why did you bring this to my attention? Did you want me to find out?"

"I thought you should know in case your brother ever contacts you. After the allegations were made, he was quietly asked to walk away from the Church, paid a significant sum to keep his mouth shut and never mention it again." His fingers drummed over the desk just inches from the confession and photos. "Have you see your brother lately?"

I couldn't understand why he cared. "Why does it matter?"

He sighed. "I was hoping you would know where he could be found. I've been quietly looking for him."

My gaze snapped to his. "Why?"

Fingers drumming again, the sound was a quick succession of taps that ended as abruptly as they began. "How much do you know about your father's death?"

My brows pulled together with confusion. "That he died of old age. I don't fucking know. I just heard that he'd died when the executor of his estate contacted me. That was all I cared to know and I never dug any deeper. You told me yourself he was sick, that he gave you these confessions while dying."

His lips pulled into a thin line. "I never told you that your father was sick. I simply said that he'd made the confessions because he knew he was close to death."

Stilled by the implication of his words, the tight fist of my hand released, my palm rubbing over my jeans to dry the clammy sweat. "Are you saying my brother killed my father?"

"I can't tell you what happened, Jacob. All I know is that he knew he was going to die and he was found

162

dead at the base of the stairs in his home. The back of his head had been dented in from blunt force trauma."

It didn't upset me to hear my father had died violently, not in the slightest. But what did worry me was why this priest was so interested in finding my brother. I didn't need the authorities digging too far deeply into my brother's activities. That particular problem was mine alone.

Snatching the confession and photos from the desk, I dropped them in the metal box and slammed the lid. "Can you find the priest and music director? Will the Diocese admit where they were transferred?"

Nodding his head once, his voice was morose when he agreed. "Of course, Jacob. I can do that. But it will take time. Can you come back here in a week to give me time to dig around?"

Frustration was choking me. The last thing I wanted to do was spend a week in this city. "Yeah. I can do that."

It was too important to find out exactly what my father had confessed.

"I'll see you in a week's time, then. But if you feel the need to come to me sooner, the parish's doors are always open."

I highly doubted I would step foot inside this place any sooner than was absolutely necessary. Refusing to say as much, I stood and stormed out of his office.

20

ELIJAH

When I was a young man, I'd learned through personal experience how easy it is to take advantage of a person or situation. Sometimes it was something as simple as stumbling into a place at a time when some other person is doing something they shouldn't. Other times, it took coercion, a simple method of attracting a victim by learning how easily they could be victimized.

Victims aren't so difficult to find. They're everywhere you look while walking down a crowded street. The inferior, the weak minded, the forgotten who stand on the sidelines just hoping that somebody would one day see them as more than just a pathetic stranger struggling to get by. One must be careful though, not all outcasts are looking for companionship. You have the find the ones who are truly lonely, the ones who are outcasts by force rather than choice. Those who are unloved when all they crave is the love they've been refused.

Growing up, I was one of those weak minded. Lack of love wasn't my issue. It was more of too much love, too much attention, too much protection by a strict and uncompromising hand.

Often I'd arrive at my local parish ready and willing to escape the walls of my childhood home, but carrying with me the markers of my unfortunate circumstances. It didn't matter what I said or did, what I believed or how I behaved, the old man always found a reason to worry about my eternal soul. He left his mark on every square inch of my body, small bruises, small splits in the skin, the occasional bump that swelled into a painful reminder of what my punishment had been.

On timid feet, I'd walk the interior of the parish donning the white choir robe all members wore, the length covering my scrawny legs, but the sleeves never quite enough to hide my arms.

The music director would notice the bruises, his eyes darting between the sheet music on his stand and me. When first I'd joined to lift my voice to the highest power, he'd assigned me a spot in the back, eventually moving me forward through the weeks and months until I was the student standing directly in front of him. He'd recognized the victim easily enough, a boy with no support, no champion, no protector to whom he could run.

His attention was innocent at first. A kind word spoken when nobody else could hear, a soft brush of his hand against my back while we filed past him into whatever room into which we were being directed, a well timed compliment on the days when the bruises were new and fresh. It wasn't long until he'd asked the question that didn't require a response. The marks and bruises, cuts and scrapes were the only answer he'd needed.

I was being groomed, my innocent mind being made to believe that someone cared. My mind didn't stay innocent for long.

"You can't speak a word of the sin that I've pulled from your body. What would your father think if he knew?"

The best method of trapping a victim and forcing their silence is to make them believe that they, too, were dirty. The music director had been the first smudge of dirt against my skin or inside my body- the priest following shortly after.

Much like the method used by the men who'd abused me when I'd been too young to understand, that method was how I'd trapped Gentry at my compound, and it's why, a week later, he walked his brother into the parish with an expression of guilt written across his face.

"Gentry," I greeted him, my voice solemn and resigned. Turning my gaze to his brother, I inclined my head, "Sheriff Holmes. It's good to see you."

Whereas Gentry was tightlipped and solemn after sobering up to realize what he'd done, his brother was aggressive, a take charge personality whose only weakness was his kin. "Father Hayle. I hear we have a problem in our town."

A practiced smile stretched my lips. "I assume Gentry told you about the trouble we had the other night. Perhaps we should go into my office to discuss it."

The two men followed me silently down the hall that led to my office. Taking their seats just as quietly, they waited patiently for me to round my desk, sit down and face them with a blank expression. I didn't need to say a word to start the conversation. Sheriff Holmes had enough to say to fill the silence of the room.

"I want to know your take on what happened at the compound you maintain in the neighboring town. What is that place? Why do you have it? And where are you finding these possessed people like Gentry claims?"

My lips stretched into a slight frown, my forehead wrinkling with the dismay I hoped both gentlemen would believe I felt. "I don't own the compound. It's registered to a religious organization and was given to me for my use. You see, I assist the group of devout people who live there in order to escape the reality of the wicked world in which we live. They are people who have true faith in God, but have found it difficult to avoid the poverty and violence implicit in this world. I provide them with my presence, my blessings and my sermons on days I'm not required to perform duties at the parish."

Twelve years ago when I'd taken the money I received as hush money from the parish I attended as a child, I'd purchased the compound and refurbished it to suit the needs of the family I was in the process of growing. However, knowing that I would eventually want to work in the shadows of society and not be known as Jericho Hayle, I'd started a business enterprise in another country, listed the business as a religious organization in the states and then filed all the necessary papers in such a way that the trail would never lead back to me. Knowing little about taxes, and not wanting to deal with any accountants face to face, I ensured that no money was made by the organization and filed the appropriate paperwork yearly. Signing

168

under an assumed name, I'd managed to keep the compound running while preventing a paper trail that would be easily followed back to me. I wasn't concerned with Sheriff Holmes discovering the truth that I owned the facility. I'd dotted every I and crossed every T to prevent such a discovery.

"The family, as they refer to themselves, are humble people, Sheriff. They're meek and afraid of the outside world. The compound is somewhat of a shelter for them. They grow their own food, sew their own clothes, raise and educate their own children, and do so under the oversight of the Almighty. That's how such a place has existed for twelve years without becoming well known. You're welcome to look into all the county paperwork regarding the property, if you're so inclined."

Reaching up, he tugged at his well-groomed beard, the brim of his hat casting a shadow over his eyes. Much like his brother, Gentry, he had a focused and intense gaze, his skin tanned by the sun and wrinkling from age. There wasn't a speck of grey in his hair that peeked out from below his hat, and it was obvious he kept in shape for someone of his age. I assumed chasing down criminals for a living helped maintain his physique.

With a gruff voice, he answered, "I will look into it, but the ownership of the facility is not my concern. I've known of the building since I oversee the county police work, but I never understood how many people lived there."

Shrugging my shoulders, I folded my hands together over the smooth surface of my desk. "It's like I said: they're quiet and they don't cause problems. It's more than can be said for other individuals freely roaming our town and the neighboring towns around us."

"Which leads me to my other questions. Gentry tells me he had to-" His voice trailed off and I assumed it had to be difficult for a sheriff to admit openly that his brother committed cold-blooded murder. "That he had to kill a man who was possessed by the Devil. How often does that happen?"

My seat groaned as I reclined back, my legs crossing at the ankles beneath my desk. "That was the first time I've seen a man as *spiritually tortured* as the man that evening. Like your brother, I was shocked by the condition of him. Members of the family claimed to have found him wandering near the compound. They were concerned and brought him in hoping I could heal him with prayer."

Casting a purposeful glance at Gentry, I added, "Unfortunately, I didn't have the opportunity to try. The man was ... extinguished ... before I could offer the first word."

The two brothers shared a glance at each other, some unspoken thought passing between them before they returned their gazes to me. Gentry was still quiet, effectively trapped in his state of continued shock over what happened just a week prior. Sheriff Holmes, however, had no problem speaking out.

"Is our town under spiritual attack as you claim, Father?"

I smiled, but not so much that they would assume the expression was anything more than a sad, resigned response.

"Between you and me, yes. I believe the entire world is under spiritual attack, but that goes back to the beginning of time. I'm sure you've read your Bible,

Sheriff. Demons, and other such spirits and creatures are warned about. It's spelled out quite eloquently by our ancient ancestors. The only thing that's changed since their time and ours is the method we use to fight against it. It's unfortunate that in today's civilized society, we leave ourselves open to evil. You should know. You deal with the vile and depraved in your line of work. I'm sure you see examples of it on a daily basis. So, knowing what you know, and seeing what you see, you tell me how you'd answer the question you just posed."

Rather than blurting out a response in an effort to argue with my view, Sheriff Holmes took the time to consider my response. He wasn't the typical rural farmer, didn't limit himself to the activities and concerns of the day to day. From what I could see within the myriad of thoughts and expressions that floated through his gaze, this man was critiquing what I'd said with an educated understanding of the crime and terror that flooded the lives of people, the horror that was expanding and deepening day to day. Nobody hated a criminal more than a man of the law. Even those lawmen that were criminals themselves.

"I know what you mean," he finally answered, his voice softer and thoughtful. "Every damn day we're dragging in more people. I once thought it was desperation that led them to the petty crimes they committed, but lately, I've been seeing things that cause my skin to crawl. Just the other day, I visited a farm where some of the livestock had been slaughtered. Not for food or any decent reason, but for fun. It cost the ranch owner not only money, but also peace of mind. He'd lived and worked on that land for thirty years and had never seen something like what we

171

found that day. I didn't write my opinion into the official record, but I believe the slaughter had been satanic. Possibly a cult type influence for people committing their evil on the fringes of society."

My lips kicked up into a grin, but I had to fight the expression. I hadn't heard of this slaughter and I assumed it occurred in a neighboring town – one in which the people didn't regularly visit my small parish. "I'm sorry to hear you had to witness such darkness, Sheriff. I don't think I need to point out that such a display is only proof of my concerns. We're a small town with small town concerns, but it seems the evil that has infected the big cities is now bleeding into our mountains. Not too long ago, I heard there was a murderer who butchered several young girls. It was a state over, so I know you weren't involved, but being law enforcement, I'm sure you must have heard."

His expression darkened, pure hatred now blazing behind his steel colored eyes. "Yes, I'm aware of the incident. From what I know, they caught the man, but worried about additional victims that haven't yet been reported missing. What he did to those girls was disgusting."

Inclining my head, I let the silence fall between us as proof of my point. Evil is all around us in this world. It tiptoes down dark alleyways, spreads through the sewers and contaminates our lives. It trickles down rivers and streams until leaking into our small, peaceful towns. Everybody is affected by the evil that surrounds us. Whether the influence is to infect some with the desire to commit it themselves, the terror of knowing the details of some sicko's crime, the constant influx of horrible events that were daily discussed on the local news, evil had a way of touching our lives, darkening

172

our doorsteps and shaking our hand when we least expected it. And while some people were strong soldiers, able to endure and remain blissful while knowing that evil was just around the corner, others became distraught. They watched their children more closely, lamented the time period when they had been raised and could play in the yard without fear of being snatched and taken away for some nefarious purpose.

What evil had done is cast fear in the hearts of most Americans, and it was exactly that fear that men like me used to poison the mind with thoughts most average people would never think for themselves.

I disguised myself well as a man of God, and as I lurked beneath the mask of a decent man, I was the worst type of demon of all. I couldn't take credit for the idea – the same types of demons had long ago preyed on me.

Tugging at his beard again, the tendons in his hand sticking out against the skin, the veins purple and pulsing, it was obvious how distraught Sheriff Holmes had become in response to our friendly conversation.

"What should we do about this, Father? What can be done?"

I shrugged again and played the resigned priest who saw no other option but the standard: Prayer to God. The useless hope that a man who sat in the Heavens would find it within himself to look out for our lives. "I guess we can keep praying…" My voice lowered before finishing the statement. "Or perhaps we can find another way to fight."

"I say we kill them all," the Sheriff replied. "I say we end this shit now, and hopefully God will find it within himself to return his blessings to us for the war we fight in his name. Gentry isn't the only man facing

173

losing everything he owns. The problem is widespread. The fields have gone barren and the banks are trying to kick us out of our homes. People are desperate and struggling, fearful and withdrawn. Surely you've noticed the despair in your parish? So who are we supposed to turn to? The government?" He barked out a humorless laugh. "They aren't any help. So, perhaps you're right. Perhaps we should be taking this into our own hands."

Nodding my head, I silently agreed. Although my expression and posture were solemn, inside I was dancing. This son of a bitch was leading me down the path I wanted him to go, and I didn't have to do anything but follow.

Quietly clearing my throat, I sat forward and made eye contact with both Gentry and his brother. "I'm at a loss as to what can be done. I'm sure you both understand. My occupation in life ties my hands. I don't see how I can be of assistance other than to offer my sermons and prayers."

"How about giving us use of your compound? How about helping us exorcise these demons so we can send them straight to Hell? You have power in that area, don't you? You are a hand of God, are you not?"

Hesitantly, I answered, "I am, but –"

"But nothing. You are a representative of God's power. You are a holy man and, as such, you can help us in this. The compound is so far out of the way that nobody would know what's going on. And with the woods surrounding it, nobody would figure it out. There's not a single home or farm within several miles."

My eyes narrowed as I continued to play the part of the humble priest. "What, exactly, are you suggesting, Sheriff Holmes?"

He pinned me beneath his intense gaze. "I'm suggesting we exterminate the evil."

I sat back in my chair and steepled my fingers at my chin. Giving the matter some thought, my lips pulled into a tight line as I darted my focus between the two brothers. Where Gentry looked frightened by the conversation, Sheriff Holmes looked resolute. It wasn't difficult to determine which one between the two was the strongest brother.

"Are you saying we should, what? Hunt people down on the streets? Abduct them and take them back to the compound to determine whether or not they've been infected by evil?"

Please be saying that....please!

"No, I'm not suggesting we abduct people..."

Damn...

"I have an idea that's even better. Being the Sheriff, I have access to all the criminals that are leaking their evil into our streets. I say we take them to the compound to find out whether their souls can be saved, or whether they need to be extinguished to keep their evil from spreading."

My brows shot up my forehead and it was difficult as hell to keep a smile from stretching my lips. I'd hoped for taking a few unfortunate people off the streets, but by the sound of it, Sheriff Holmes' idea was even better. I couldn't get too excited. I still needed them to believe I was on the fence with their idea. It wouldn't be too fitting of a priest to be excited about bloodshed and death.

"You'll have to excuse me for my ignorance on this, Sheriff, but how would you remove criminals from jail without their absence being noticed?"

The Sheriff smiled. "If they never make it to the jail in the first place, how would anybody know they're missing?"

My lip twitched, but I forced my expression back into a blank expression. I had to keep up appearances, had to pretend I'd objected to this idea. In truth, I was fighting the desire to jump from my chair, reach across the desk, and pull this big bastard in for a tight hug. Where I'd hoped he would simply turn his head to a few odd occurrences throughout town, he'd gone a step further and offered to deliver the evil I wanted directly to my door.

What more could a sadist ask for?

Schooling my features, I drummed my fingers against the surface of the desk, my eyes casting up toward the crucifix on the wall. The time and silence gave me the appearance of a man who was in doubt with the suggestion being offered, but what they didn't understand was that I'd already accepted the offer, and I was using the time to figure out exactly how I could use it to my benefit.

My gaze returned to the Sheriff. I held his stare for several seconds before asking, "Will I be given the opportunity to talk to these people? Will I be allowed to determine if they can be saved before we decide on more drastic measures in how they should be handled? I don't want to make a mistake and condemn a man who could be led to God's holy light."

The Sheriff exchanged another glance with his brother before returning his attention back to me. "I'm sure that can be arranged, Father. But, some of these

176

individuals are violent men. I want to ensure your safety while we evaluate them. Gentry told me you have a cage in which the criminals could be held."

Yes. Yes I do. I have more than that, but these men didn't need to know it.

Speaking slowly and with feigned reservation, I acquiesced to the terms. "You have to understand that this decision is not easy for me to make. I'm a man of God, a priest, and a Shepherd to my flock of parishioners. I prefer to teach the tenets of peace and love, of salvation and absolution."

The sheriff opened his mouth to talk, but I held up my hand to silence him.

"However," I added, "I'm also not a stupid man who is blind to the fact that evil is infecting this town. I tend to think we can drive it out of people, much like I've been trying to do with the ladies who are trapped within lust's hold. I'm sure Gentry also told you about a woman I've been working with lately who's lust is powerful enough to tempt a married man."

Gentry winced at the reminder of having laid a lustful hand on Eve's body. His brother's expression darkened even more. "Yes," he answered. "I've been informed."

Breathing out, I drummed my fingers again, fidgeted in my seat, and took my time responding. One didn't want to appear too eager.

"Fine. If you think this will help the town, I'm willing to try this approach and see if it helps alleviate the town of its suffering. However, for now, I think we should keep this between us and any other man who thinks he can be of assistance without drawing the attention of the entire town. I think it's also important that children and women be kept away from this ordeal until we know we have a good handle on it. I see no reason to upset them with the details of what we're doing to protect the town's interests. The less people who know, the better, but in time, I think we can make it known that something is being done."

Sheriff Holmes nodded his head and rubbed his palms over his pants. If I wasn't mistaken, I thought I caught the gleam of heady anticipation in his eyes. Perhaps the Sheriff had been looking for an excuse to act against the criminals he encountered on a daily basis, and I was sure the compound was the perfect place for him to carry out his innermost desires without drawing attention.

Once again I was looking into the face of the truly *wicked*: the men and women who hid behind the masks of spiritual leaders, teachers and cops, pretending to be helping us when, in truth, they were preying on us for their perverse pleasure. They were the wolves in sheep's clothing that the world had been warned about. And because they hid in places of authority and goodness, they were the worst evil of all.

"When would you like me to bring the first man to the compound?"

My fingers drummed one more time, my lips downturned when all I really wanted to do was smile wide.

"I have duties in the parish for the rest of today," I answered. "But I have a sermon to give at the compound tonight. Do you think you'll find somebody in time?"

The radio at his side blared with static, a voice coming through to call out for police assistance before rattling off a bunch of letters that meant nothing to any person not employed in law enforcement. I inwardly chuckled to think that the timing of that call had been a Godsend.

Sheriff's Holmes' eyes went wide once the noise stopped. "Yeah," he answered, his voice tight and restrained. "I can have somebody there tonight."

21

JACOB

Staying in the city for a full week had been a bad idea. I understood that Timothy needed time to find the music director and priest who'd abused Jericho, but it left me in a place I didn't want to remember, surrounded by phantom voices from my past.

I'd spent the first night on the couch in my childhood home. Not able to force myself up the stairs to what had been my old bedroom, I'd laughed to myself to make a bed out in the formal living room, to think about how my mother would have screamed to know I'd mussed the room she kept so pristine just so she could pretend everything was perfect in her family and world.

After tossing and turning all night, with only small bursts of panicked sleep, I decided the following morning while I drank coffee at a small café that sleeping in the house would only be hazardous to my health. The next night, I'd rented a hotel room in some glitzy building down the street from the parish. It was the first night I'd slept solid after returning home, but the renewed energy only left me bored and idle – a man in search of something to occupy his time.

While staying with Alan, I'd allowed my desires and darkness to take me over. I'd played with those women, one right after the other, without so much as bothering to learn or remember their names. Much like when I'd been young, I used my looks to draw them in. I'd warned each and every one of them, but like most women, they'd laughed and believed I was only playing. They learned differently once climbing in my bed. I never hurt them enough to make them fear me when they left the next morning, but I gave them enough to make them think twice about climbing in my bed again. Most had been smart enough to stay away, some, however, found that they enjoyed being treated like a toy. Sure, they'd convinced themselves that it was only a game, but I knew in the backs of their heads they'd known that what I'd done to them had been wrong.

I never understood why some women believed they could change a man like me. Although I wasn't as bad as some of the sick fucks out there, I had certain habits that any decent woman would know to avoid. But those women that wanted to *fix* me, the ones who'd convinced themselves that their pussy was magic enough to make me fall to my knees and beg them to be mine, they kept coming back for more regardless of the marks they carried when morning came and I showed them the door.

Some didn't make it to morning. Many times, I couldn't be convinced to share my bed for more than a few hours. Their body heat irritated me when I wanted to sleep. God forbid they wanted to snuggle. I was never in the game for companionship, love, or happy feelings. Women were a means to an end...

At least, until Cassandra.

She had been the first that I wanted to keep by my side. The first who didn't cry or complain when I bruised her skin. The first who wore the marks I gave her as a badge of honor, a reminder of the type of man she was with. She hadn't been ordinary, or the type who was easily disturbed. But in my passion for her – my love – I'd ended her life far too soon, and attempted to hide myself in the Church.

It would have worked. I could have lived the rest of my life hiding behind the misguided belief that a man like me could be saved.

Then Eve happened and my life was once again turned upside down – first with her temptation, and then with her untimely destruction at my hand.

Elijah had asked what kind of monster I am. He hadn't been wrong to ask the question, he'd just phrased it poorly. Because, in truth, it wasn't just me who was the monster – we both had been molded and shaped by the circumstances of our youth.

I could barely hold it against him for the manner in which he'd tormented me, but even knowing what I know about his secrets, I still needed to know precisely *why* I was the target of his rage.

Morning light streamed through my window on the seventeenth floor of the ridiculously glitzy hotel room in which I'd been staying. My eyes cracked open and narrowed against it, my body moving to stretch out the sore muscles from the position I'd held in sleep. Behind me, a woman mumbled in her sleep, my movement enough to rouse her as well.

I'd been too tired the night before to walk her to the door, too tired to hear her arguments or complaints when I told her she'd fulfilled the purpose I had for her. But rather than rolling over and beginning her day with the demand that she get dressed and let herself out, I glanced at the alarm clock on the bedside table and convinced myself that she would be a good distraction to pass the time, a toy to be played with until I had to leave and meet Father Timothy.

Erica...or Erin...I wasn't sure of her name, wrapped her arm over my waist, her body scooting closer against my back as if to steal what heat I could generate. My teeth clenched together at the contact, but my cock was hard. I didn't often let that part of me dictate my decisions, but in this instance, I gave in to the flow of blood that turned a sleeping appendage into turgid and throbbing flesh.

My fingers grasped over her wrist, the strength I used to squeeze the delicate bones a warning of what I wanted to do. A soft gasp filtered over her lips, but she didn't complain, didn't attempt to pull away and run. I felt her large breasts press against my back, felt the well trimmed hairs between her legs tickle the skin of my ass. Her legs brushed against mine as her foot slid down my calf, lower until her foot was pressed against mine.

"Good morning," she said with a sleepy voice, a trace of flirtation edging the words. "Are you up for another round?"

Swallowing down the burst of violence that tore through me, I squeezed her wrist a touch harder, my lips twitching with humor when she gasped again. "Shouldn't I be asking you that question?"

Soft laughter bubbled over her lips. It made me want to kick her out of the bed and shove her out the hotel room door. I refrained from reacting, and struggled not to think about what made me hate certain women so much.

It wasn't until I returned to this town that I had the realization of why my sexual tastes were so violent – wasn't until I'd been forced to face my past and stare into the memories of my youth. However, now that I knew, I couldn't erase that understanding from my thoughts. Even considering it now had my cock deflating.

Erin … or Erica …whatever the hell her name was could fix that.

"You were a bit rough last night," she cooed, "But that's okay. I like a man who knows what he wants and is willing to take it. Any time you need a late night friend, you can certainly give me a call."

I was drunk when I brought her back with me the night before, and because I hadn't yet rolled over to look at her, I couldn't tell you what she looked like. I knew my type, though, and I knew she would have long brown hair and green eyes – just like Cassandra and Eve – just like another woman who wouldn't stick up for herself in life and spent her time cowering in a fucking corner. How sickening is it to discover that the mold for what I would eventually look for in a woman was my mother?

Not that I wanted to sleep with my mom or any sick thing like that, but I couldn't deny I didn't want to punish her for never coming to the defense of me or my brother. Perhaps it was the feeling of finally doing something about what was done to us, or perhaps it was something as simple as getting even for my mother's complacency when we heard Jericho scream.

I didn't know what she did when it was my turn down in that basement, but I assumed her blank expression and drink in her hand were just the same.

No. Fucking women who had the same features wasn't what I was after. Nothing about my mom turned me on. But hurting them, the release that it gave me, had definitely sprung from the desire I'd had to hurt her.

Sitting up, I dropped my feet to the floor and scrubbed my face with my palms. With my bleary eyes only partially opened, I finally responded to what she'd said.

"Why don't you come over here and kneel down in front of me? I have an idea of how you can wake me up."

She purred in response, the mattress shifting beneath me as she inched away and slid her body from the bed. Without one question or word of protest, she rounded the end to walk toward me, making a point to add an obvious sway to her hips thinking that the movement would entice me.

It did nothing for me but irritate me, and I had half a mind to ask her to leave. But when she was standing before me in all her naked glory, when she sunk to her knees and licked her full lips, when she tilted her green eyes up to my face, I closed my eyes and let her do her best to seduce.

Her fingers were warm against my cock and I felt the familiar rush of blood pushing me fuller, longer. Once my erection was at its largest point, she flicked the tip of her tongue over the head, teasing me with the wet torment.

186

My hand slid down my thigh to find her hair and fist it, the muscles in my forearm tense as I struggled not to go too far. Despite how often I tried to convince myself that I wasn't a monster, I couldn't forget the death in both Cassandra and Eve's eyes once I was done.

Letting go to the full scale of my desires was dangerous and I didn't need another body lying in my path. Eventually those crimes would catch up to me, and jail would only stop me from finding and destroying the men who'd made a mess of Jericho's and my life.

The Music Director.

The Priest.

Elijah.

All men who hid behind the disguise of pious men, but like me, hid a monster behind their soft eyes and practiced smiles.

It was too bad I knew certain ones were out of reach.

Lips wrapped around the head of my cock, another teasing flick of the tongue, a soft moan that vibrated against my skin. My hand fisted tighter in her hair as my head fell back. As my body came to life, so did the images.

It wasn't this woman I saw as her lips slid down the length of my shaft, it was Cassandra or Eve, the two women who hadn't been frightened of the man I hid behind the mask. They had known the real me and loved me regardless.

Live green eyes glistening with abandon and need.

Dead eyes accusing me of having gone too far.

Angry eyes judging me as I was accused of being a monster, both in my young life, my college years, and only a few months ago.

The accusations would always follow me. The anger and violence my constant companion. And despite the faith I'd given to a God who didn't know me, I'd hoped that, with time, the monster would die.

He hadn't. He still infected me with the memories of my father's beatings, the fear I saw in women's eyes. He still taunted me with thoughts of how I could use the woman on her knees in front of me and hurt her like I'd hurt so many others.

"Stop," I growled out, the pain and memories too much for me to bear. The woman kept going, soft laughter a vibration against my dick because she believed I was playing.

"Fucking stop!" I roared, my hand jerking her head off me so hard that her teeth scraped against my skin. She fell backwards, her ass impacting the ground with an audible thud, her blue eyes darting up to me in shock and seething anger.

"What the fuck?"

"Get out," I whispered, trying like hell not to scream the demand. It wasn't difficult to figure out that I could only handle sex when I was shit faced and drunk. Too many whispers were filtering in my thoughts, too many memories flashing in my mind. Too much pain, anger and regret were bleeding out of my heart to pretend like anything would be normal again.

"You need to apologize," she answered, her shoulders rounding back so that her tits stuck out from her chest.

My lips tilted in humor. "And you need to get your fucking clothes and get the fuck out before I open that

188

fucking door and drag you there kicking and screaming. If you don't think I'll toss your whore ass out the door completely fucking naked, I dare you to say another word."

She didn't move except to widen her eyes.

I couldn't help the volume of my voice. "GET THE FUCK OUT!"

The anger blazing behind her gaze transitioned into fear. Without another word, she scrambled away from me, gathered her things and quickly pulled on her clothes.

"You know what you are, you son of a bitch? You're a fucking lunatic!"

The door slammed so hard the walls of the room shook when she exited, but I didn't care anymore. Couldn't care when everything I'd thought I knew about my life had been destroyed.

I wanted to pretend that my anger made me powerful, but it was only another symptom of my fear. Fear of my father's fist pounding against me. Fear of the dark, dirt floored room that had been my cage. Fear of the torture I was forced to listen to when my father turned his anger against my brother.

Fear of taking another life just because I couldn't control myself.

I could add it all together into one dark conclusion: I wasn't afraid of all those individual memories and moments of desolation. I was afraid that I'd lost control and become no better than my father and mother.

Jericho had regained his control when he became Elijah, and now I feared him, too.

"Fuck!"

Pushing out of bed, I stormed into the bathroom to jump in the shower. The water scalded me where it rained down from the showerhead, the steam becoming a cloud that threatened to suffocate me in the warm moisture. Breathing in deeply, I pressed my forehead against the cool tiles, my hands fisting and releasing as I fought to get myself under control.

I needed to vent the frustration and anger before it consumed me, needed to find the answers I was desperately seeking so I could at least understand what Jericho had done.

And even though Father Timothy had asked that I meet him at one in the afternoon, I knew that I couldn't sit around and wait any longer.

Slamming my hand down on the knob, I turned off the water, dried off and got dressed. With four hours to go before the time that Timothy told me to meet him, I was out the door and climbing into the elevator knowing that I was headed to the parish despite the early hour.

It only took me thirty minutes to walk there in the busy morning traffic. When I reached those imposing doors, I hesitated for just a second before throwing them open.

Timothy was in the sanctuary, blowing out candles and lighting others. Fortunately for me, there wasn't another soul around to hear me when I walked in.

"You're early," he called out, his eyes cast up to look over at me. With a hand hovering over the candle he'd intended to light, he straightened his posture and turned to face me fully.

"I couldn't wait much longer." My voice didn't give away the anger I was feeling. It sounded more dead than alive. "I need to get out of this city, and the only way I can leave is to know what you have to tell me. Were you able to find the two men?"

His mouth was a tight line, his shoulders slumping with resignation. "We should discuss this in private. I need to finish up some things here in the sanctuary before I can talk with you. Why don't you take a seat on one of the pews while I do so?"

The last place I wanted to be was in a parish pew staring up at God's altar, but I had no choice, it appeared. By the tone of his voice, I knew it would be impossible to push Timothy to tend to his duties any faster.

The room fell into sanctimonious silence as I walked to a nearby pew and sat down on the hard wood. Leaning forward, I buried my face in my palms. I tried to convince myself I was just tired, but I knew myself well enough to know that I was hiding.

Even though I'd once been a priest with the same duties and responsibilities of the man I was waiting on, even though I'd spent countless hours in a sanctuary less dramatic and glamorous than this once, I found it difficult to be surrounded by the religious symbols and relics that were now staring me down. I wasn't a different man just because I'd removed the clerical collar, but with each new memory of my life that surfaced, with each new secret that was unburied, I found myself becoming more jaded and angry at the concept of God.

I couldn't even refer to that heavenly being as if he actually existed, not now and never again after realizing just how horrible he'd allowed my life to become.

There was no telling how much time passed before I felt a hand land on my shoulder, before I heard the soft susurration of cloth against wood as Timothy sat down.

191

"Is it really so hard to look up at the altar? You've been sitting like that for at least an hour now."

Without moving or looking over, I answered, "It's all a lie told to appease the masses, a pretty veil pulled over the truth that we are on our own."

"Can I ask you something, Jacob? Just out of idle curiosity."

Finally ripping my hands away from my face, I looked up, my gaze locking on a large gold cross positioned in the center of God's altar. Beside it was a small, carved box, the jewels embedded in the wood glimmering beneath the soft lighting of the sanctuary. I wasn't sure what religious relic was contained in that ornate box, but what I did know was that it was most likely priceless. The bones of a Saint. A remnant of some perfectly pious man. A lie covered as easily as a shroud that is draped over the face of a tortured Savior. I had been part of that lie when I chose to swallow it down, but now I found it difficult to stare it in the face.

"What do you want to ask?" A knot in my throat made my voice hoarse and deeper. Clearing it several times, I was able to speak again, but still I felt strangled.

Timothy allowed several seconds of silence to float between us before building the courage to ask a question I wished he had left alone.

"What happened in your life to cause you to lose faith in God?"

On any other day, I would have brushed off the question and reacted with contempt. This morning I was weaker, somehow, more willing to lay out the answers to that question only because I couldn't make sense of them myself.

"Are you asking this as a priest would a parishioner? Can we consider this my confession?"

Timothy shifted in his seat to lean forward. With his elbows resting on his knees, he looked toward the altar while speaking to me. "If that's what you need in order to talk. This conversation will never go beyond you or me."

A bark of humorless laughter shook my shoulders. "Did you promise the same thing to my father when he showed you all the skeletons in his closet?"

Silence again before, "I deserve that. But in my defense, I didn't spill his secrets openly. I only hinted to where you could find them. I never understood why he told me about burying the confession in a place where you would know to look for it. I think, secretly, he hoped I'd break my oath and tell you where it could be found." Pausing for a brief moment, he added, "And if I had to be completely honest, I'll admit that I wanted that information out in the open. I've never agreed with the politics in the Church that have allowed for the destruction of so many people."

Glancing at his expression, I saw that he was being truthful. His lips were turned down and his jaw was tight. I wondered if he felt the same chains and trappings of his profession as I'd felt in mine. For me, it was financial, but for him, it had to be more. The larger the parish, the more politics took over, and the easier it was for the wicked to invade and prey on those who believed them divine.

Turning my focus back down to where my hands were clasped together over my lap, I watched my thumb idly rub over my skin, the lines stretching until absent, only to return when my thumb released the tension and allowed the flesh to snap back in place. I watched the blood pool beneath, turning white when I

193

increased the pressure of my hold until the skin was absent of life.

"When I was a kid, our lives were built around the Catholic Faith. I was too young to understand the guilt, the shame of being alive and making stupid mistakes that are inherently human. Up until I was six or seven, I truly believed there was a God who existed to love me, that truth could be found in the happy songs they taught us in Sunday School, that it was truly a miracle every Christmas when we remembered the virgin birth of Jesus in the manger. Life was seemingly magical when I was a kid."

"I assume your father had something to do with that changing," Timothy supposed.

"You assume right," I admitted, my jaw ticking with the tension of clenched teeth. "The punishments started after he discovered Jericho and I looking at a book on female anatomy. We were only curious boys trying to understand the differences between women and men. But my father, in all his glorious wisdom, believed that our curiosity was the worst form of sin." Sad laughter rushed over my lips. "Why is sex worse than murder in this particular religion?"

Timothy's burst of soft laughter joined mine. "It seems that way, doesn't it? Even if the act is so natural that even animals have to accomplish it in order to prevent extinction. I had a priest explain to me once that sex isn't a bad thing if it occurs between a married couple – as long as it was performed in the missionary position and for the sole purpose of creating a child."

"So, we're not allowed to enjoy it. Is that where the sin exists?" Growing quiet, I flicked my thumb against my skin once more, watched the blood push away and

194

come back to color the flesh. "Are we allowed to enjoy anything?"

"We can enjoy our relationship with God," he offered.

Nodding my head, I raised my focus back to the golden cross on the altar. "You mean the God who allowed a grown man to beat on two innocent boys just because they'd grown old enough to know there was a difference between the male and female body?"

His voice was remorseful when he answered, "I'm not sure God can be blamed for that."

"Can He be blamed for anything?" I pondered aloud, more to myself than to Timothy.

"You know as well as I that God gave us free will to make a choice. We can choose good or evil, can act in accord with Grace or devastation. Just because one person chooses to commit mistakes in blatant disregard for the welfare of other people doesn't mean God doesn't care. How often have many of those mistakes led to something good and decent?"

I knew what he was getting at. I'd learned many of the same answers while in seminary school. The only problem was that I had difficulty believing them. Nothing good came from my darkness. At first I'd believed that my mistake with Cassandra led to me saving Eve from my twin brother. But, in the end, it only led to me having the opportunity to destroy Eve as well.

"You haven't finished telling me what happen to lead you to where you are now."

It was funny how his prodding question perfectly fit the thoughts I was rolling over in my head.

"After years of abuse at my father's hand, I found myself questioning his Faith. I often wondered if the

Church wasn't evil for creating men so delusional they felt the need to torture their own children in order to save their eternal soul. I also wondered how the bruises were never noticed by my Sunday School teachers, how something so open and obvious could be missed by the very people who were the hand and mouth of God. I never understood how an entire body of people could remain silent."

Taking a breath, I released it slowly. "So, when I turned eighteen, I decided to abandon Faith for science, for something that could be seen, touched, weighed and measured. I figured if the answers to my questions weren't found in the Bible, surely they could be located in a school of intellectuals."

When my voice trailed off, Timothy filled the silence. "What happened then? Obviously, you returned to the Faith in order to become a priest. Did something happen that showed you God could exist, after all?"

I shook my head. "No. I made a mistake, one that cost a beautiful woman her life."

Timothy turned to look at me and for the first time since we started talking, I turned as well to meet his gaze. "It wasn't murder or anything like that. Just a sexual game that went too far. The medical examiner told me a blood clot had been loosened in her veins, that it had traveled to her brain and caused a stroke. He said it could have happened at any time and I spent the next couple of months wondering if I hadn't sped the process along. I considered myself a monster. I believed that my father may have been right. That my sexual deviance had led to the destruction of a woman who was kind, who was beautiful in every way, who would have never hurt a fly, if it could be helped."

Pain shot through me to think of how gentle Cassandra had been. The woman cared so much about all life that she wouldn't let me kill a bug if it got in our apartment. She always demanded I trap it first and release it unharmed back outside.

I killed someone that gentle.

I destroyed her.

I did that, just like my father had always warned me I would.

"So," I said, clearing my throat and wrestling to untangle myself from the memory, "I decided that maybe my father was right. Maybe the world would be better off if I never had sex, if I never had the opportunity to kill a woman again. It seemed that I'd enjoyed sex a little too much and it led to the worst of crimes. The utter destruction of someone far more beautiful than I deserved to know in my life."

Shifting in his seat again, Timothy must have struggled to find something to say. Eventually he found the words, but they did nothing to appease the painful beat of my heart.

"You could have become celibate without the need of becoming a priest. I think if you dig deeper, you'll find that there was still a small spark of Faith inside you, even when you left home and had convinced yourself it no longer existed."

I didn't answer and he didn't press the topic. Instead, he threw out another question I wasn't sure how to answer.

"What forced you out of the Church a second time? What led you to this particular moment?"

Well, you see, my brother is now a cult leader named Elijah and he brainwashed a woman into being the perfect toy. After dropping her off at my door, he waited long enough

197

for me to fuck her as much as I damn well pleased, and unfortunately, I killed her, too.

No. I wouldn't be giving him that answer. In an effort to be honest without dishing out the dirty details, I responded, "Another woman."

"Ah," he replied, his head nodding in understanding. I only caught the movement out of the corner of my eye. "You broke your vow of celibacy, I assume."

"Yeah, you can say that."

Another silent beat passed between us. "It doesn't mean you have to leave the Faith completely behind. Men weren't all created to be champions for God. There isn't a single one of us who can claim to have lived a life completely devoid of sin. All we can do is remember the beauty of the Faith that God has given us and use it to do our best and set the wrongs back to right."

I was growing frustrated with the conversation, so much so that I ended this moment of confession to talk about what I'd come here to find out.

"Did you find the music director and priest who molested my brother?"

He waited several seconds before answering, "I did. But I'm afraid they are no longer around to answer for their crimes."

So, it was true...

My head snapped up at the answer. Turning to face him, I waited for his gaze to meet mine. "They died?"

Nodding, he confirmed that those two bastards were firmly out of reach. "From what I'm told, both of them died in mysterious accidents. The music director passed very shortly after being transferred, and the priest a few years after that."

198

"How? How exactly did they die?"

He rubbed his lips together and visibly swallowed. "The music director was trapped in a fire in his small apartment, but there was some question as to how he became trapped in the first place. Apparently, he had several broken bones in his legs that prevented him from escaping the inferno." His gaze darted away to something behind me. When he raised his hand to wave at a person who'd walked in, he lowered his voice and suggested, "We should discuss the rest in my office. Parishioners are starting to come in."

I stood as soon as he finished speaking. I was far too impatient to move slowly. Once he was also on his feet, he said, "You know where my office is. Go ahead and wait for me. I'll see to the people who just walked in and make sure they're settled before joining you."

Quietly leaving, I moved through the hallways toward his office, my body tense and shaking, my mind racing over the possibilities of how, exactly, the music director died. The timeline fit for what I knew. Not only was there the means and the opportunity to kill someone so blatantly, there had been motive as well.

Letting myself into Timothy's office, I made a point to turn my head toward the desk in order to prevent staring at the large crucifix on his wall. The last thing I needed was to be reminded of the sacrifice a perfect man had man in order to save a wretch like me.

Wretch.

Hell, I was sure if you looked up the definition, a picture of me would be pasted beside it.

Taking my seat, I bowed my head and continued thinking over the ever deepening belief that I didn't need to take revenge on the men who'd hurt my

199

brother. I would have bet every cent I had that Jericho had been responsible for their demise.

The door creaked open behind me and within a few seconds, Timothy was seated at his desk staring back at me.

"How did the priest die?"

I didn't have time for small talk regarding faith or religion, all I wanted was the details of what I assumed had been done.

"Don't you know?"

When my head snapped up, I found Timothy watching me with intense and probing eyes. "How the hell would I know that?"

Rolling his shoulders back, he settled in his chair before folding his hands together over the desk. "The priest died in an auto accident. It seems his car careened off the side of a cliff into a lake at the base of it. When he was found and his body was extracted, they found drugs in his system and a plastic baggie in his clothes with photographs of other boys he'd molested. Photographs that matched the ones given to your father."

Anger burned me from the inside out, but I played along. "And let me guess...the Church covered up those crimes as well."

Timothy eyed me closely. I didn't know why his demeanor had changed so drastically between the sanctuary and now, but he resembled a man who didn't believe the person sitting across from him.

"There was no prosecution, if that's what you're asking. I assume his death was good enough for the Church. They didn't bother to seek answers to the odd circumstances of his death, either. I believe they agreed that he was a monster who needed to be stopped. Since

200

the photos were never mentioned in the news, the entire situation was written off as handled."

My face must have been blazing crimson for how hot I was. My anger had transitioned to naked fury, a truth I was sure was written all over my face. "How can you continue working for an organization that allows such travesties to take place? How do you reconcile your part in this, knowing how many people have been hurt and swept under the rug by a group of people who are supposed to be helping mankind?"

His expression hardened. "My allegiance isn't to the Church. It's to the Faith. And before you tell me there isn't a difference, I'll insist that there is. However, it's hard to stand on a street corner and lead people to God. So, I've resigned myself to working within the confines of the Church to help the people I can. I don't subscribe to the politics, and I'm never silent on issues that hurt people. I can promise you that nothing like what happened with those two monsters has happened again since I've taken over the parish."

Searching his face for any sign that he was lying, I came away empty. Timothy was a truly good man, the type of priest that I'd never been able to be. If every person who'd worked in the parish when I'd grown up had been like him, I may have never lost my belief in God. He was the type of man who would have noticed the bruises, and I was sure he was the type of man who would have pulled my father aside and explained that the abuse wasn't what God would have condoned. Based on that realization alone, I had to curb my anger because Father Timothy wasn't the type of man who deserved it.

"Why did you think I would know how the priest died?"

Maybe he did know, after all…

The question had been floating in my head since the moment he mentioned I would know anything about the man's death, and the lull in our conversation had given me the perfect opportunity to ask it.

So still that I wondered if he'd heard the question at all, Timothy stared across the expanse of his desk studying me. His eyes searched mine, eventually shifting down to search my face, my neck, the manner in which I held my shoulders. The silence between us was deafening and I could have sworn he was taking his time counting the beats of my breath as my chest pushed in and out in an unsteady rhythm. Finally, after several tense seconds had passed, Timothy opened his mouth to explain.

"While making a few calls and researching online about the location of the music director and priest, I also took a few minutes to look into a smaller parish in the Appalachian Mountains, a parish called Our Lady of Serenity."

My brows pulled together in confusion, my mouth opening and closing again without voicing my question. Why in the hell was this man looking up the parish I'd once led? Why did it matter where I'd come from, where I'd lived before giving up the life of a priest?

"You seem a little stunned by the fact that I'd made the inquiry into *your* former parish. Or should I say your twin brother's current parish…Jericho."

My body flinched at the way he'd spoken my brother's name, thoughts racing so hard that it took me a minute at least to decipher what he'd meant by the name.

But more than that, the realization that I was still named the priest of the parish in that small rural town stunned me so thoroughly that I was frozen in place, caught beneath the weight of the question as to why I hadn't yet been replaced.

Ignoring his pointed accusation that I was pretending to be someone I wasn't, that I was Jericho pretending to be Jacob Hayle, I worried about what his discovery meant for a parish located in the center of a sleepy town in the Appalachians.

"Did you call the Diocese to confirm the name of the priest at my former parish, or did you just look it up on the Internet?"

The corner of his lips tipped up. "I looked it up first and came to the conclusion that perhaps the website hadn't yet been updated. I then called the parish to confirm, but nobody answered. I tried for two days before finally giving up and called the Diocese. It appears there was nothing to update because Father Jacob Hayle had never left the parish as you have claimed. That leaves me with one conclusion: You're not Jacob, like you claim. You are Jericho Hayle, coming here and talking to me under the guise of being your twin brother."

Shock and anger filtered through me, mixing and churning until it was a toxic solution spreading from the center of my chest, up into my head, out into my arms and to the tips of my fingers, down until it soured my stomach and trickled lower into my legs.

"Father Jacob Hayle," I repeated slowly, "is still the priest at Lady of Serenity? You're sure of this?"

He shook his head in disbelief, but rather than his expression denoting anger, it withered into soft sympathy instead. "Of course, I'm sure. I confirmed it with the Diocese, like I said. What I would like to know is why you're here pretending to be somebody you're not? I would have spoken to you regardless, Jericho. Would have given you the same information I gave when you claimed to be Jacob. I'm as angry as you are about what happened to you as a child in this parish, and I'm not concerned with the *accidents* both the music director and priest had later in life. That's between you and God, and I'm in no position to cast judgment." He relaxed against his seat even more, the leather creaking on the armrests as he pulled his arms down to his sides. "Hell," he admitted on a resolute voice, "I probably would have done the same."

I had to get out of there, had to jump online and look for myself to see that he wasn't lying. The only problem was that now Timothy knew something wasn't right in that small parish, that there was a possibility that more attention should be given to the small, rural town. The only way I could knock him off course without killing him and hiding his body was to go along with the assumption that I was someone else.

"I didn't kill anybody," I admitted honestly. Well, not intentionally, at least. Cassandra and Eve both were no longer breathing because of me.

Shifting my position on the cushion of my chair, I slouched like a man who'd been caught in a lie, a man who was giving up the pretenses of being someone he was not.

"Fine, you caught me. And I'll admit that I'm here because I wanted to know what happened to the people who'd abused me for many years of my life. Unlike what you suspect, I didn't kill them. Not my father, not the priest or the music director. I-"

Intentionally letting my voice trail off, I played the part of a shamed man, of a person who was giving up the lie and who wanted nothing more than to abandon it entirely.

"I should go."

Timothy sat up, his movement urgent and sudden. "No. You don't need to leave. I might be able to help you, Jericho."

The sound of my brother's name was a spear piercing my side. If what Timothy was saying was true, than Jericho was impersonating me, acting like the friendly Catholic priest in a town that wouldn't know any better. What the fuck was that sick bastard doing to a town full of people who wouldn't recognize the monster behind the starched white clerical collar?

"I'm sorry I bothered you," I stuttered, "I shouldn't have come here. Please forgive me."

Standing up from my seat, I'd made it three steps toward the door before Timothy was on his feet racing toward me. His hand gripped my bicep and spun me around, his eyes meeting mine with sympathy. "I can help you, Jericho. I can give you the peace of mind you're seeking."

With the amount of anger and concern that was flooding through me for my former parish, I highly doubted he'd give me even a fraction of peace. I knew I needed to leave this city, knew I'd have to face my brother at some point to confront him about the games he played. Learning about what happened to him as a child had softened my heart toward him, but now that I knew he'd stepped into my parish to take my place, I felt only fury and worry for the game he was apparently still playing.

Why would he do such a thing? What did he stand to gain?

Shrugging out of Timothy's hold, I bowed my head in feigned embarrassment. My voice was low and morose when I lied just to have an excuse to leave. "I didn't want you to know I'm Jericho. Didn't want you to look at me and know what was done to me. I need to process the fact that you figured it out and I can come back once I get over my embarrassment and shock. Give me a few days to deal with this. And I hope you can accept my apology for having lied."

Timothy breathed out a heavy breath, but his expression softened again before he inclined his head. "Take all the time you need, Jericho. But it's my hope you return. I'm sure I can help you find peace, that I can help you understand and forgive the evil that was committed against you. It wasn't God who allowed those men to do evil things, and I don't want you wandering lost in this world because you aren't able to see that. Men have free will, they have the ability to prey on people that are weaker than them. But God also has a way of healing the people who have been hurt. Please allow me to help you see that. Not every priest is a bad man."

I knew he was honest in his offer, knew he was one of the good men who truly wanted to help the lost. For that alone, I couldn't give an answer that would hurt him.

"I'll return," I promised despite knowing I'd never come back. The look in his eyes told me he knew I was lying, but that he still hoped I'd change my mind.

Inclining his head again, he reached out a hand to shake mine. When I accepted, he placed his free hand on my shoulder. "Walk with God, Jericho. And when you're ready to come back and let me help, I'll be waiting."

Without thanking him or saying another word, I released his hold and practically ran from his office.

22

†

ELIJAH

After sitting in the parish for several hours listening to the pathetic confessions of townspeople who truly believed their little white lies and common human behaviors were worth the guilt that led them to confession, I made my way home to the compound. Upon arrival, I took the time to talk with a few of the family members, to pretend like I gave much of a damn about their spiritual help. I toured the gardens like I was expected to do, I lavished praise and prayers on the fruits of the family's labors and after playing the role of a man who would lead them all to the gates of Heaven, I slipped away into my private bedroom to look upon a woman I hadn't paid much attention to over the past few days.

Eve hadn't left the compound since the night of my last sermon, and I'd tasked Richard with continuing to give her the special herbal teas I'd prepared. According to his reports, he'd kept her so tangled up and twisted that any inclination she may have had to remember oddities between her time with me and the time she'd spent with Jacob was now buried deep beneath the haze of the chemicals we were feeding her.

As I walked in and found her lying on the bed, unbound because there was no longer a need to restrain her, I hissed out a breath over my lips to see the physical toll our games had taken.

The skin beneath her eyes was bruised a deep purple, and beneath that her cheeks were hollow. So pale that she was pure white beneath the fall of her long, dark hair, Eve looked over to me with death resting just behind her eyes. That blank green stare held no affection or worship, had lost the glimmer of love and devotion I was used to seeing behind it.

My heart pounded slowly beneath my ribs, my hands clenching into fists to see the bones sticking out from beneath her skin, the absence of color that hinted to life inside her body. I never intended this, never wanted to hurt her or risk her life. Yet, as I stood there looking at her for the first time in days, all I saw was an animated corpse.

Crossing the room on three long strides, I took a seat on the bed beside her, ignoring how she winced in pain when the mattress dipped beneath my weight. A sigh filtered over her cracked and chapped lips, but she still managed to attempt a smile.

"Elijah," she breathed out, trying and failing to raise a hand to touch my face. Her arm trembled and she dropped it back down, misery flickering behind her tired gaze for not having been given the chance to touch me. Reaching out, I took her hand in mine to find it cold despite the warmth in the room.

"How are you feeling?"

Several seconds passed before she found enough breath to answer. "Like death is staring me in the face.

The demon is going to win, isn't it? It's going to drag me down until I'm lost." Pausing to catch her breath, once again, she managed to whisper, "I'm sorry, Elijah, for having failed you."

No. I couldn't allow this, couldn't find it within myself not to care for this beautiful girl who I'd created and shaped. I wasn't surprised when my brother failed to resist her temptation because, in truth, Eve was everything the two of us had ever dreamed of. A perfect woman, silent and subservient, an angel on this Earth that didn't know how to say no, and would never complain. Why we both needed someone so fragile was outside my understanding, but I didn't give it much thought. All I knew is there would never be another woman as perfect as the one staring up at me.

"You're wrong," I answered, my voice deep and resolute. "I think the demon is weakening. I think it's time to pull it from your body."

Her green eyes widened as much as they could. They didn't glisten beneath the lights, and the white was stained red, but she tried to appear happy to hear what I'd said. "Now? I'm not sure I'm worthy of your love now. I'm not sure I deserve it."

My fingers squeezed her hand softly. "Not now. You're too weak. I need you to eat something, Eve. If you gain strength, it won't be hard to force that bastard from your body. Once he's gone, evil won't be able to return again. You're my wife. I'll protect you with the might of God's hand."

She simple nodded her head, too weak to respond verbally.

Letting her go, I reached up to brush my knuckles down her cheek. There was nobody home behind those eyes, and I was positive she wouldn't bring up Jacob again. My intention hadn't been to harm her, it had been to weaken her mind and bury the truth that I'd used her to get rid of my brother.

That she called him the *kind* one was comical and I wondered for a moment what had happened to the darkness that had always existed inside my brother.

He was the darker twin. My father had been right about that. But I'd become stronger after letting go of poor little Jericho Hayle and replacing him with Elijah.

"I'm going to get you some food. I want you to stay awake long enough to eat. After that you can rest again and I'll be back later tonight after giving my sermon."

Her lips twitched as she tried to smile. Giving up, she breathed out and back in. "I've missed your sermons," she whispered.

My eyes closed at the breathlessness in her voice. I missed the sound of it against my ear as I buried myself deep inside the heat of her body.

"I'll be back in a few minutes, Eve. Don't fall asleep."

I didn't wait for her to answer before leaving the room. Before going to the kitchen, I set out to find Richard and demand he stop giving Eve the teas I'd set out for her. Her body had grown too weak for them, and had I been at the compound instead of the parish, I would have recognized that weakness before it got to this point.

Joshua was in the storeroom that led to the backyard. So consumed by looking through the shelves for whatever item it was he needed, he didn't notice I'd entered until I spoke.

"Have you seen Richard?"

He jumped in place but quickly regained his balance. His head turned to me and he smiled. "He's

212

out back, I believe. I think he's exploring the woods to see if he can expand the land we have for our garden."

My smile matched Joshua's, but instead of being friendly it was amused. "I'll go look for him out there."

Slipping past the man I'd watched grow from a small boy, I made my way across the backyard and unlocked the chain that kept the fence closed. Only three people had a key to the lock, Richard, myself and Joshua. We were the only people who needed access to the outside as I'd convinced the rest of the family that evil lurked just beyond the border of the wall. The family believed we were brave and strong for managing to travel into the world without being infected by its evil. In truth, we were three secretive bastards who kept the family in the dark as to the world at large.

Slowly making my way down the trail that my prey always followed, I took my time weaving beneath the thick branches of trees, moving into and out of the streams of dying sunlight that managed to break through the leaves. One after another, those rays lit my path until the woods opened up into a small clearing where a small wooden cabin could be found. Smoke rose in slow puffs out of the chimney letting me know that Richard was inside.

Stepping slowly through the twigs and dead leaves, I barely made a sound as I approached and listened closely for any clue as to what he was doing to pass the time. It had been a week since he'd abducted the businessman and his daughter. Surely the girl was dead by now.

My hand wrapped over the handle of the door as soon as I was within reach, my forearm flexing as I turned it and let myself inside.

Turns out the girl wasn't dead after all. The bastard had kept her alive for the entire week. Richard's head spun in my direction as soon as he heard me step in. I looked at the girl with a question in my eye before returning my gaze back to him. He didn't need to hear the question to know what I was asking.

"I want to keep her," he confessed. "I want her instead of my wife."

My lips kicked up into a smile. "And what will you do when she grows older? Kill her and replace your wife again? Isn't that how we found your wife in the first place? You always want to keep them, Richard. I allowed it once, but I won't take that risk again."

His broad shoulders rolled back, his chest puffing out with anger. "She won't say anything. I'll make sure of it. She wants to stay with me."

I highly doubted that, but still I looked over at the young girl who sat naked and shivering on top of the platform, her body wrapped in the same thick blanket I'd used long ago with Eve. Her face was downturned and she didn't bother to look up at me. There was no doubt she'd lied to Richard in order to stay alive, and she'd chosen to endure the rape and torture hoping that someday she'd find a way to escape.

"I'm sorry, Richard. But you'll have to let her go."

The poor girl winced in response to my words. Still staring at her, I noticed her eyes close and a tear slip down her cheek. I had to hand it to her for being a decent enough actress to make Richard believe she really wanted him. Even now I was struggling to see the truth that she was planning her escape.

"When?" he asked, his gritty voice curt and clipped. "When do I have to let her go?"

My eyes snapped to his, a question flickering through my mind that I couldn't help but ask. "You do know what I mean by let her go, right? You haven't forgotten what's to be done with them when we're through playing?"

Darting a glance between the girl and me, Richard stepped in my direction and moved past me to open the front door. I turned to see him silently request for me to follow him outside.

The door closed as we stepped out into the woods and I leaned back against an exterior wall. Folding my arms over my chest I watched in amused silence as Richard struggled to bring himself under control. He was angry that I'd told him the girl couldn't stay, angry that I treated him like the minion he was rather than an equal partner with equal say.

"Why can't I keep her?" he asked, his feet pivoting on their heels, his eyes locking to mine with frustration and rage. "I should have a choice of who I want to fuck on a nightly basis."

He'd taken his current wife, much like he'd stolen the girl in the cabin, and had begged for her much like he was begging now. How many woman would he have to go through to figure out he'd lose interest once they grew older? I wanted to hate him for looking upon practical children with more desire than he did adults, wanted to toss him firmly in the same category as the bastard priest and music director who had laughed at me with the same lust-filled eyes.

"You'll only grow tired of her, Richard. Stop denying it to yourself. She'll grow older just like the other one did and how will we explain to the family that your wives keep mysteriously dying?" Pausing, I allowed my words to sink in. "You can keep this one until we need the cabin for something else. I'm not saying you have to get rid of her immediately. If anybody questions your absence, you can claim that I saw evil approaching the compound and you're outside watching the perimeter. Those brainwashed bastards will believe anything you tell them as long as it points to their bullshit God."

Huffing out a breath, Richard's shoulders relaxed to find out that I wasn't demanding he dispose of the young woman immediately. Shuffling his foot over the dirt in front of him, he swallowed down his hasty rage and took a few seconds to look up at me. "Why are you out here?"

"I need to talk to you about Eve. It seems she's ready to stop consuming the teas I left for you to give her, and I want you to watch her closely when I'm not around. She's close to death, Richard, and I don't want anything happening to my blushing bride."

Nodding his head, he kicked at the dirt again. "I would have told you that, but watching the compound and traveling out to the parish to talk is hard. Nobody answers the damn phone over there."

I was never in the office to answer the phone, my *priestly* duties taking up much of my time. It was a good excuse I could use to explain to the Diocese why I was never available to take their calls.

"Stop giving Eve the tea. Start making sure she's eating and regaining her strength. It was never my intention to kill her. I want her kept safe."

Nodding his head one more time, Richard stuffed his thick hands into the pockets of his pants. "No problem."

"I also came out to tell you that we'll have some special guests tonight. You remember Gentry. He

216

brought his brother by the parish today and the overly excited sheriff decided it would be in our best interests if we remove the demons from the criminals he arrests."

Richard's head snapped up, a slimy smile stretching his face. "Are you saying what I think you're saying?"

Laughter shook my shoulders. "I believe so. It seems the sheriff wants to eradicate the evil that is infecting this town, and based on his brother's account of the possessed man we showed him a week ago, he wants to destroy other demons he believes are in our midst." More laughter fell over my lips. "For fucks sake, it's better than I could have imagined. I was hoping to get the sheriff to turn a blind eye, but instead the son of a bitch wants to lead the condemned bastards to our door."

Richard's laughter joined with mine, the deep reverberation echoing through the woods. A flock of birds scattered from the branches above our heads, the leaves rustling in response to their hasty departure.

Fucking birds. If they're not shitting on your head, they're finding another way to annoy the fuck out of you.

"Well, I'll be damned," Richard spoke around his continued laughter. "This will be more fun that I thought. Once we have this entire town in a state of chaos, we can do whatever the fuck we want."

Inclining my head in agreement, I mentioned, "Yes. I'm sure there will be fun to be had. You can gorge yourself on all the fucking and violence you want. In the meantime, I have a show to put on and will be playing the part of the priest. Do you think you can

217

handle keeping the more sensitive members of the family away from the sanctuary this evening?"

"That won't be a problem," he promised, his smile growing wider until he resembled a cat peering down at its next frightened meal.

"That's good to hear, Richard. Once you have them settled in for the night, you can join us in the sanctuary later. Sheriff Holmes told me he'd be by around ten tonight. That gives us plenty of time to prepare for the festivities."

"You got it, Boss," Richard called out as he moved around me in the direction of the cabin.

Turning as he passed, I shook my head knowing that before he went to tend to the flock, he would let the girl know the good news that he would be keeping her for a while longer.

Before he could shut the door, however, I felt it necessary to warn him. "Oh, and Richard, I'm sure this goes without saying, but don't trust the little bitch you have in there. I want her bound and chained when you're not around to keep an eye on her. She's planning on escaping."

He laughed. "Don't you think I already know that? It's more fun when they think they have a chance."

With that, he opened the door and stepped through, closing it again until I was staring at the scarred wood.

I simply turned around to return to the compound and feed the dying girl in my bed.

23

JACOB

After leaving the parish, I paced the city streets, weaving and winding down the numbered avenues, avoiding the people that walked beside me. While they rushed off to whatever job, doctor appointment, lunch meeting or other obligation they were headed to, I found myself stuck inside my own thoughts, growing angrier with each hour that passed.

I was stuck between a rock and a hard place, wanting on one hand to feel sorry for my brother, while on the other I wanted nothing more than to stop the bastard in his tracks, to expose him and destroy him much like he'd attempted to do to me.

Guilt flooded me for not protecting him more when we'd been children, but I eased the pain of it by reminding myself I hadn't known what the priest and music director had done. Never as faithful as my brother had been, I avoided the choir and the Christmas plays the parish put on. I never had much of an opportunity to know the music director, and I'd hated the priest. He was an old man with slimy eyes, the type that made my skin crawl every time he came near. When I was young, I'd believed it was because I was angry with God, and thus angry with what the priest represented. But now, thinking about it as I continued walking at a clipped pace, I realized that I'd somehow instinctively known that the man was a monster hidden behind his black clothes and crisp white clerical collar.

How I had picked up on that and Jericho hadn't, I wasn't sure. Perhaps darkness calls to darkness, and thus I'd recognized it instantly in the priest. As children, Jericho had wanted to believe good existed in the world. He'd wanted to worship God and be a good boy just so he could earn our abusive father's love. That desperation to please was what trapped him in its iron grip, it's what destroyed him as all the people he'd wanted to love him had let him down, one by one.

I was just another name on that list and perhaps he'd played his games against me to get even. But now that I knew he was now pretending to be me, I understood that his games had a deeper purpose.

What could be gained from pretending to be a priest? The question hadn't bounced around in my head for longer than a second before the answer shot up to slap me in the face.

Was Jericho getting even for the abuse he suffered? Was he preying on the faithful to cope with having been preyed on himself?

The thought terrified me as the faces of my former parishioners flashed in my head. The adults would be fine, I was sure about that, but what would Jericho do to the children?

With that concern in mind, I quickened my pace and didn't understand where I was headed until the bold lettering of the company's name was staring me in the face.

Like all the buildings in the city, the glass doors were freshly scrubbed, the company name positioned with pride. I hated these bastards, and hated having to talk to them, but if I had any hope of stopping Jericho, I needed money.

Slamming my hand down on the metal rail that cut the center of the door, I pushed the glass partition open and stepped inside.

The receptionist was a friendly thing with big brown eyes, blond hair and tits filling out her sweater. Not exactly my type, but I didn't mind the view as I told her who I'd come to meet.

"I'd like to cash out my inheritance held by my father's estate. I need to speak to Eric Cotter. He's managing it."

Her fingernails clicked over the keys of her computer, her hips wiggling over her seat. Even without looking at me with desire behind her eyes, she managed to flirt without saying a thing. Body language is always the most telling, and it was a good thing most people didn't know how to read it. If everybody in the world paid attention to their surroundings and other people as much as I did, there would no longer be any such thing as surprises or secrets.

"Mr. Cotter," the receptionist spoke into the little microphone sticking down from her headpiece. "A gentleman is here to see you regarding cashing out his estate."

Her cheeks tinted with a faint pink in response to what Eric had said, her lips parting on a soft giggle.

"Of course, how stupid of me. Give me one second to find out his name."

She must have been new on the job. Most seasoned receptionists knew that the first thing you did was find out who was standing in front of you.

Peeking up at me with shy eyes, she parted those pretty pink lips to ask, "What is your name, Sir?"

I loved the way the word *Sir* rolled off her lips, but I didn't have time to show her just how much I appreciated it. "Jacob Hayle."

"Thank you," she whispered before repeating my name to Eric Cotter. The receptionist glanced up at me a second later. "He says you can meet him in his office. It's room 203 on the second floor." Pointing to the right, she directed me to the elevators.

Thanking her, I didn't bother telling her I'd been here before and knew exactly where to find the office of the estate managers. It didn't take long for the elevator to climb to their floor and ding as it opened the doors.

The hall was well lit, the lights a bit too harsh and glaring. But once I'd stepped inside the office of Cotter and Baxter, I found the lighting much softer and more to my liking. Another pretty woman sat at a desk, but rather than asking my name, she simply pointed down a hallway I knew led to Eric's office.

He lifted his face when I stepped inside, and as I closed the door behind me, he pushed to his feet. His hair was silver in areas, turning to white in others, which gave away his advanced age. But even older than me by several decades, his sharp brown gaze was focused and attentive, his body several inches shorter than me, and his belly more soft and rotund than mine. Money had the ability to overfeed a man, usually leaving him as soft and round as an overweight baby when he died. It was obvious Eric Cotter had lived a life of luxury and ease in this large city.

"Jacob," he greeted me with a deep, friendly voice that was smooth and cultured. "I'm surprised to see you again. You were adamant the last time we spoke that you wanted nothing to do with the inheritance."

"Circumstances have changed," I explained as I shook his hand. He squeezed my fingers a little too hard, but I ignored the attempt to size me up as a man. Pulling my hand away, I wiped my palm down my pants. It felt slimy and sleazy to be here accepting the blood money my father had left behind in his death.

Motioning toward the chairs positioned in front of his large glass desk, he suggested, "Why don't you take a seat so we can get you what you need? All it will take is for you to give me your bank account information so that I can transfer the money."

My brows shot up in surprise. "It won't take longer? I thought this would take several days."

Shaking his head, he rounded his desk and dropped his weight into the overpriced executive chair. "That's it. A click of a few buttons and the money is yours. Technically, it's been yours since the day the estate was closed, but you never gave me a way to send the money over. Neither you nor your brother seemed interested in it. The only reason I was able to find you through the years was due to your affiliation with the Catholic Church. Your brother, however, has been more difficult to find. It's like he dropped off the face of the planet. You wouldn't know where I could find him, would you?"

"Nope," I lied. "I have no idea at all. I haven't spoken to Jericho in years."

I had to admit it was much easier to lie now that I wasn't strangled by my old clerical collar.

223

Nodding his head until the triple chin beneath his face shook with the movement, Eric slipped me a piece of paper and a pen. "Just give me your routing and account numbers and I'll see that the money is in your account within the next hour."

It took a full thirty minutes for the transfer to go through, and I left without bothering to thank the man for his effort. My head was swimming with all the conflicting emotions I had for my twin.

The last thing I wanted to do was return to that town, but I knew those parishioners were in trouble. With the amount of months that had already passed since I ran from the parish, I wondered how many of the young, faithful women in town had already fallen prey to Jericho's attention.

Gritting my teeth, I ran out of the building and paused as my feet hit the sidewalk. Like a statue standing in the middle of a throng of rushing bodies, I remained motionless as I forced myself to stop and give myself time to think.

Getting to Jericho wouldn't be easy, and entering the compound would be damn near impossible. If he had people watching the parish, I was sure I'd have a gun pointed in my face before I could cross the large lawn.

No. I had to think like Jericho if I wanted to discover what he was doing, and I needed a way to protect myself from his family.

I needed guns, and I needed stealth, and if I hoped to do anything to end Jericho's games, I knew I needed to take my time, rather than rushing in there with guns blazing.

It would take a few days to put a decent plan together, possible a few weeks. But I knew when the time came to travel to that small, rural town, it would take everything I had inside of me to decide whether to let my brother live, or whether to kill him as soon as I saw him.

24

EVE

Elijah stared at me the entire time he fed me, taking his time to spoon the warm soup into my mouth. He never got impatient with me when the liquid dribbled out from between my lips. Much like a parent would do for an infant, he used the spoon to scrape up the spilled food from my chin and guide it back between my lips.

For the past few days that he hadn't bothered to come see me, I'd wished for the demon to end my life. Wasn't that what all evil wanted? The destruction of the good? To rip our souls from our bodies and drag us screaming into Hell?

I'd felt guilty to wish for it to end, felt like my faith in God had failed me. Was wishing for death the same thing as suicide? Was simply giving up considered a comparable sin?

Those questions had circled in my head when I hadn't been sleeping or too agitated to think. Up and down, left and right, over and under, my mind had been scattered in so many places that, at times, I'd forgotten who I was or where I'd been.

But now that Elijah was back beside me, I could think clearer. The pain in my stomach eased with every spoonful of food he fed me, and when the last drop had been scraped from the bowl and fed to me with gentle care, I wanted to ask for another bowl, wanted to beg that he keeping feeding me, just so I could keep him here.

Using a napkin he'd kept tucked in his lap, Elijah wiped the moisture from around my mouth after placing the empty bowl on a bedside table. I was thankful for the way my throat was no longer sore, thankful that I could breathe easier beside him.

"I'd give you more, but I'm afraid it would make you sick. Richard told me you refused to eat since I left for the parish several days ago. Are you angry I didn't take you with me?"

Shaking my head, I resettled myself against the soft pillows of our bed. "No. To be honest, I don't remember much of the past few days. Only that I missed you terribly."

Saying those words had been a lie – at least one made indirectly. It was a lie of omission, the confession of what I'd really been thinking tucked away because I couldn't bring myself to admit that I'd almost given up to the demon inside me, I'd almost believed the whispered thoughts that this life wasn't worth living.

"I'll stay here for as long as you need, Eve. I'll be here tonight, and in the morning, after we eat breakfast and take a walk through the gardens, we'll see if you're well enough to go back to the parish with me. Would you like that?"

Nodding, I admitted, "I don't like being apart from you. I don't like spending so much time by myself."

His eyes softened at the admission, the corners of his lips tilting up into a gentle smile. Brushing his palm down my cheek, he rested his hand on my shoulder. "I've missed you, too. And you'll be happy to know that everything we've worked for is coming to fruition. Soon, we'll have all the demons plaguing our lives running back to where they came from. We'll be free, my beautiful Eve, and we'll live in peace and prosperity. I couldn't have done it without you."

I knew Elijah truly believed he needed me to walk with him toward the light. It didn't make sense to me that he'd accepted me back after I'd run from the ceremony that night.

Leaning forward, he kissed my forehead, the smell of laundry detergent and cologne wafting beneath my nose. I always loved the smell of him, always loved the earthy notes. When I'd first arrived to the parish after running that night, I'd remembered wondering about the lack of his scent when he'd picked me up from the lawn and carried me inside. I was too frightened to give it much thought, too lost and twisted up in the games he was playing.

There was no doubt inside me that I deserved the games he'd played, that he'd been right to push and test me to ensure my faith in him was supreme.

His gentleness with me now reminded me of how gentle he'd been in the parish after I'd first arrived. It was stupid of me to think he was two separate people, to believe that something wasn't right.

He was only two sides of the same person, the man who had to be strong in order to battle evil, and the

229

other gentle one, who loved me like a husband should a wife.

"I love you," I whispered when he pulled his lips from my forehead and planted another soft kiss on my cheek. His fingers tightened over my shoulder, not enough to hurt, but just a firm squeeze.

Pulling away even further, he stared at me for several seconds. "I love you, too."

I couldn't question that he meant what he said. I could question if I really deserved him.

25

ELIJAH

After leaving Eve in the bedroom to get some restful sleep for once, I weaved my way through the compound and scanned the windows to see that night had fallen, the moon having taken its place in the sky surrounded by a myriad of stars that could only be viewed in rural places.

Stepping into the sanctuary, I cast my gaze up at the altar, my body positioned between the two larges crosses from which Sisters Eunice and Joyce had once hanged. At the time, I didn't assume the crosses would be used again, at least for a long time, but it seemed they would find purpose with the criminals that Sheriff Holmes had promised to bring me.

It was five minutes until eight and the men in the family were shuffling into the sanctuary to take their seats. Richard had done well to keep the women and children occupied elsewhere in the building.

My sermon tonight would wake up the bloodthirsty monsters hidden inside the hearts of the faithful. It amused me to think that despite what is written in the Good Lord's Bible, these people still called for war and pain, death and destruction, believing it was the only way to bring peace upon the Earth.

Perhaps in the Old Testament, that sentiment was true, but the New Testament was softer and more forgiving. It's why I didn't read much from the book that discussed Jesus, and I kept going back to read from the passages that made these believers feel justified in a holy war. It was all in how the material was delivered, and that fact wasn't only true for the way in which I led the family. Judgment and hate, fear and condemnation runs rampant in every domination that subscribes to the Christian Christ.

Just look at the way people are judged for their sins. Look at how entire groups of people are shunned and considered not worthy. It's in the churches and Sunday Schools, in politics and religious skirmishes. Even in a day where we should be more cognizant of how different groups should get along, there is still fighting and judging, condemning and shaming – a practice that goes against what their dead Christ had told us.

It's the reason I couldn't practice a faith in a God who was nothing but lies. Religion wasn't a vehicle used to save humanity when entrusted into the hands of man. It was nothing more than a political power play, a balm soothed over the hearts of the masses while the wolves crept in to rip them apart.

I'd trusted the holy when I'd attended my childhood parish. And look what that trust had done to me.

Jacob had asked the question *why* over and over again during the time he was the focus of my games. If he'd searched deep enough, he would have discovered the truth of *why* I was doing any of this.

Revenge is a stone cold monster that settles in the belly rolling endlessly until you were so tired of living with it churning in your gut you finally acted to get rid of it. Some carried the need to get even until it ate at them and poisoned them, following into their early deaths, while other men like myself thought hard about how to attain it.

Twelve years is a long time to put a plan together and play it out to its end. But for something as big as I had planned, I needed to learn to be patient.

The shuffling of feet stopped as every man had taken their seat giving me the cue that it was time to move forward. Reaching the altar, I stood at the makeshift pulpit and delivered a message of death and slaughter.

For each word I spoke, the men's eyes grew wider, their shoulders becoming tense with the need to fight for their God. I opened their mouths and shoved down the hallmarks of violence into their full bellies and greedy minds.

I spoke for an hour, closing the sermon with prayers to the Almighty, and then watched as they sauntered off back to their duties to the compound. I wouldn't need them again, at least not tonight, while I tested whether what the sheriff had promised would actually be accomplished.

At ten on the dot, a family member ran to grab me claiming the sheriff was outside the compound demanding to be let in. I instructed the family member to lead him inside, to deliver him to the sanctuary where I would be waiting.

Waiting patiently as the family member ran off to lead the sheriff in, I leaned against the pulpit and shoved my hands in my pockets. Staring down at my shoes, I only lifted my head again when I heard the sound of footsteps storming in.

I almost laughed to look up and see the sheriff dragging in a man who was both confused and angry for being here.

"What the fuck?" he bellowed from the floor where he was being dragged by the back of his shirt. "You brought me to church?"

"Shut up, you piece of shit," the sheriff roared back before kicking the man in the ribs. He dropped him like a sack of flour and I'd almost expected the man to split at the sides and release his innards all over the carpet.

Unable to smile as I was still playing the part of the solemn priest, I pushed off the pulpit where I'd been leaning and slowly walked toward the sheriff and his captive.

"Sheriff Holmes," I greeted him, extending a hand out. He shook it and settled his weight over his feet. We were about the same height, but his build was more broad and thick than mine.

"Call me James," he said before casting a pointed glance down at the man still lying on the carpet. "I'm not sure you can do much with this one. The son of a bitch was caught raping a girl behind the dumpster of a liquor store. It seems he likes to prey on women that make the mistake of being caught in an empty part of town."

I wasn't sure what liquor store he was referring to, but I assumed it was at the edge of the county. We were living in the center of the Bible Belt and due to our strict adherence to scripture and God's rule, there weren't too many places that sold liquor anywhere close to our town.

Kneeling down, I looked the man in the face and smiled a gentle grin. "Didn't your mother ever tell you to respect women, son? God doesn't like it when you harm people for your own lustful sin."

"Fuck you!" He yelled, his hand grabbing at his side where James had previously kicked him. I angled my head in response and tsked my tongue against the roof of my mouth.

"And here I was wanting to help you."

"Just take me to jail," he roared again, this time getting kicked again for the outburst.

"You won't be seeing jail, you sick son of a bitch. I'm tired of assholes like you in my county."

Standing up, I glanced between the condemned man and the sheriff, careful to keep my expression blank and resigned. Lowering my voice so that only James could hear me, I asked, "And what makes you think this man is infected with evil?"

James looked at me like I was an idiot. "Did you not hear me? He was raping a woman. Thankfully his hand slipped and she screamed loud enough for the store attendant to hear her. If he hadn't been outside on his way to the exterior bathroom, this son of a bitch would have finished the job and been off to rape another innocent woman."

"She asked for it!" The criminal yelled. He shut up when James kicked him in the head.

Rolling his eyes, James stared me right in the eye and said, "They always claim the woman wanted it. Every fucking time. I guess they don't realize that the word no and the tears and fighting mean the woman isn't really into it."

235

My lips tipped down into a frown, my eyes narrowing with feigned disgust. What the sheriff didn't seem to know is that, sometimes, the crying and fighting is half the fun. It wasn't that we didn't know the woman didn't want it. Hell, for most of us, that was the best part.

I wouldn't be the one to tell him that. Being a priest, I assumed raping and killing was frowned upon.

"I tell you what, James: why don't we take this man into the back so I can see if there's a way to save his soul before we do anything more drastic. I'm still not sure I'm a hundred percent on board with all this. I hate to see any life extinguished that can be saved."

James looked at me with disapproval behind his eyes, but eventually conceded to my concern. "You're too soft, Priest, but I guess that's understandable given your profession. Maybe one day I can drive you around with me so you can see the crime scenes and broken lives these bastards leave behind."

Biting my lip to keep from laughing, I answered, "I'm sure that can be arranged, but for now, let's try it my way. At least I'll feel better knowing I did something to save this man from Satan's grip."

"What?" The criminal in question was now sitting up with his head cradled in his hands. Looking up at us, there was pure fear running behind his eyes. "What the fuck are you two talking about? What the fuck is this creepy ass place?"

James grabbed him by the hair and jerked him up off the floor. "I thought I told you to shut your fucking mouth."

A door at our back swung open before we could escort the criminal from the room, and the soft gasp of breath that followed immediately after had me turning around to find Eve standing at the opposite side of the room.

"Eve?"

I moved toward her quickly, hoping like hell Gentry hadn't described the woman possessed by lust to his brother. A quick glance at James told me he didn't recognize her. Reaching her, I laid my hand on her shoulder and lowered my voice to a whisper. "Eve, you shouldn't be in here. Why aren't you sleeping?"

Her eyes were focused over my shoulder when she answered, "I couldn't sleep after you left. I was too restless." She grew quiet for a second, still staring at where James stood with the condemned. Her voice was shaking when she asked, "What is *he* doing here?"

Turning, I glanced back at James and wondered if Eve had ever met him. Not remembering when that could have happened, I returned my focus to her and gripped her chin to direct her face to mine. "He, who?"

Her bottom lip trembled and tears welled in her eyes. "That's him, Elijah. The man from the road. The one who tried to..."

Her voice trailed off and I knew instantly who the bastard was that James had dragged in.

I couldn't thank the universe enough for that small coincidence. Keeping my voice soft, I confirmed it again. "That's the man that made you take your clothes off on the side of the road? The one who tried to touch you?"

Her eyes locked to mine, her brows pulling together in confusion. "Yes. Don't you remember? You were there."

Shit. It never even occurred to me that Jacob had been there that night. Or, as far as Eve knew, I had been there to rescue her.

237

"Of course, I remember, it's why we brought him in. I need you to go back to bed, beautiful girl. You don't need to witness what we're doing."

Her gaze had drifted back to where the two men stood, but at my response, it darted back to me. "Elijah. I don't understand. What are you going to do with him?"

"He raped another woman, Eve. We can't let a demon like him continue roaming the streets and looking for other people to hurt like he hurt you. You know this is God's plan. You know I'm supposed to stop these men. You helped me learn about him the night he found you wandering and now we'll deal with him so he can't hurt again."

Her hair shifted over her shoulder as she nodded her head. Quietly turning to leave the room, she walked back through the door without another word.

When I finally turned back to walk over to James and the condemned, I had a renewed bounce to my step. Knowing who this bastard was would only make my job more entertaining.

"Let me show you back to the cages, James. You can lock him inside where you know he'll be safe and give me some time to see if I can save him."

"And what if you can't?"

"Then we'll decide how to deal with him."

Appeased by that response, James led the man, kicking and screaming, through the large sanctuary, past the crosses, and down a hall that led to the room where Gentry had killed a man right in front of my eyes. I had no intentions for this son of a bitch to live past tonight, but in an effort to appear as Godly as possible – not to mention the fun to be had toying with him – I kept up the appearance of a concerned priest. If

238

it's true that Jacob made a mess of this asshole on the side of the road, I wondered how it was he didn't recognize me.

I'd find out soon enough, but before I could question him, I needed James to lock him safely away. In truth, I could handle the asshole myself, but fighting wasn't exactly the typical behavior of a priest.

It made me laugh to think Jacob had gotten away with it, that he'd hidden his violence in the week it had taken him to go mad.

Opening the door, I held it for James to drag the man through, and remained unmoving until I heard the metal door of the cage snap shut. James passed me again on his way out and made a small motion for me to follow him back into the hall.

The door closed behind us before he breathed the first word. "Do you really think you can save this guy? I'm almost positive today wasn't the first time he hurt a woman."

Positive of the same thing myself, I smiled kindly and touched his shoulder. "At least let me try, Sheriff Holmes. God would want that. You can't let yourself forget that all sin should be forgiven, unless of course the evil has sunk so far in that it can't be stripped from the afflicted."

"And what do we do with him then?"

"Then you take him to jail and let him answer for his crime. If he mentions this place, we'll deny it. Who do you think they'll believe? The Sheriff and the town priest? Or some greasy rapist who thought he could get away with hurting innocent women?"

Nodding his head once in agreement, James shot one more look at the door leading to the cage. "If you need anything, you come and get me. I'll be waiting in

239

the sanctuary and praying that God directs your hand. You are a good man, Priest. A little too good in my opinion, but that's to be expected. I'm not sure how you find the forgiveness inside you for scum like him."

My smile widened, a practiced expression that set my parishioners at ease. "God is a powerful source of love and forgiveness, James. We just have to remember to let him in."

He nodded again and made his way down the hall. Once he was out of view, I turned to walk inside the door, my back leaning against the wood so that I could look at the asshole trapped in his cage.

"Well, well. What do we have here? I'm surprised you don't remember me."

The man squinted his eyes in my direction, his mind obviously scouring itself for what I meant. After several seconds, recognition finally lit his eyes as his eyebrows soared up his forehead.

"I really was beat down by a priest, wasn't I? I can't fucking believe it, I thought I'd dreamt the fucking night up and that I'd gotten jumped by someone else."

This time, the smile did reach my eyes. "You must have been piss drunk, especially if you couldn't remember getting your ass handed to you by a priest."

Once he recognized that I wasn't opposed to becoming violent, his *fuck you* demeanor fell silent. Quickly approaching the bars of his cage, he wrapped his hands around them, desperation flooding his expression.

"Listen, man. Can't we talk this out? I just want to go to jail and serve my time. I don't want to deal with whatever it is you two have in store for me. Please, Father! You're a man of God. Isn't there any mercy inside you?"

Laughter bubbled from my chest. "A man of God? How can you be so sure?"

Eyes scanning me, his brows drew together in confusion. I allowed him to process the confusion, to work through the conundrum that he was staring at a man dressed as a priest, but took too much satisfaction in claiming he wasn't. Leaning against a wall, I faced the poor slouch and crossed my legs at the ankles, relaxing as I scanned him in turn.

Brown greasy hair, red rimmed and bloodshot, beady eyes, a body that at one time may have been strong, but was now withering and potbellied from alcohol and drugs. It wasn't hard to see the signs. I knew men like him. They always came into the family after falling on hard times and eventually took my words to strengthen themselves for God.

An army for the Almighty. Please. I couldn't care less about the silly beliefs that were a balm for the masses, the ridiculous lie that had been told since the Dark Ages that God gave a damn about the unfortunate souls infecting this planet. Meanwhile, the people in power sat on God's throne casting their judgment and filling their bellies as the population starved.

"You're not a priest?" he finally asked, his voice rough from yelling, his eyes narrowed on my clerical collar.

"No, but I play one on television."

His brows drew together tighter, forming one fuzzy patch of hair over his beady, unfocused eyes.

Amusing myself in order to kill time, I smiled back at the man, unconcerned that anything I said to him while we sat alone in this room would leak or be

241

believed, even if he screamed it at the top of his lungs while we dragged him out.

"I'm not a priest," I admitted while holding my hand up to examine my fingernails. "My twin brother was. He's the one who kicked your ass on the side of the road that night after he caught you trying to rape *my* wife."

My eyes dragged up to him. "How easy was she anyway? Did she put up a fight?"

More confusion floated behind his gaze. "Your wife?"

I nodded my head, the corner of my lips pulling up into a lazy grin. "I've heard about what happened on that road late at night, but only from a woman who's too confused to know her own name at times, so why don't you fill in the blanks for me? What happened first when you pulled up and found her walking alone?"

His fingers wrapped over two bars, his lips parted on his breath. "I don't know what you're talking about."

"Sure you do. Eve is a pretty little thing with her innocent eyes and mousy demeanor. You must have recognized her inability to fight the minute you met her."

Smile widening into a snide grin, I watched him shuffle his weight from what foot to the other.

"There's no need to worry about being truthful. I understand men like you, the ones who like to walk on the outskirts of what's considered *normal* and *proper* in modern society. Like you, I've enjoyed a few trysts without asking permission, so I'll play the good Christian and withhold judgment. Lord knows, if a stone were thrown in my glass house, the entire thing would come crashing down to reveal that I, too, am a monster."

"You're lying."

"I'm not," I answered, my eyes pinning him with the sincerity of my words. This man was nothing but a poor rapist, a sick bastard that couldn't keep his dick in his pants but had nobody willing to bounce over it. He preyed on the weak when he had the opportunity to drag them behind abandoned buildings and dirty dumpsters. I'm sure he sweated and grunted as he took his fill, probably giving them the gift of disease that would last a lifetime, or at least until some antibiotic found the means to fight it.

"If I tell you a secret, do you think you can keep it between us?"

Nodding, he reached up to brush the greasy hair out of his face that had slipped from the hair tie he used to keep it all back. I assumed at one point it had been tucked neatly away but had come loose in his struggle with the sheriff. "I won't tell."

A bark of soft laughter burst out. "Sure you won't. I don't believe you, but I'll tell you anyway. I have some time to kill while I pretend to be praying over you while clutching my rosary in hopes I can save your soul."

His knuckles whitened as he squeezed the bars more. "Is that what this is? You trying to convert me?"

"Convert you to what? A lie?" I laughed. "That would be a giant waste of my time. In truth, I'm no better than you. I've enjoyed sneaking behind a woman and taking what should be mine. Men are the stronger gender for a reason, are we not?"

He shuffled his weight again, releasing one of the bars to scratch at an itch on his arm. Watching him

243

closely, I recognized the signs of a man coming down from his high, the itchy need for another hit sneaking up on him that would eventually drive him insane.

"We are," he agreed hesitantly, still not sure he could trust that another kind of predator was staring back at him.

"Who do these women think we are? Pussies that have to ask permission for a fuck? Please. We've been taking it since the beginning of time. Knocking them over the head and dragging them over just so we can get what we want and leave them there to deal with it. Now all these spoiled bitches think they deserve romance, flowers and wine, some type of jewelry that isn't worth the money we spend on it. It's a bunch of bullshit, if you ask me. I tend to think society should return to our roots, ditch the bullshit that makes us civilized and go back to a time where the strongest man survived."

Pushing away from the cage bars, he stepped back and took me in all over again, searching desperately for any sign that I was evil as I told him I was. It was refreshing not having to lie for once, to lay it all out and reveal that I'm not the man everybody thinks I am. I would thank him for being the captive audience to my confession, but I hardly doubted what would soon happen to him was something he'd appreciate or consider as thanks.

"Are you for real? How do I know you're not lying to me right now?"

"You don't, but if you'd rather we sit here and stare at one another, we could do that as well. I just happen to find it boring. Might as well compare notes. I like a good pussy just as much as the next man, especially if the woman is screaming and crying while it happens."

My eyebrow arched and his shoulders relaxed just enough for me to know that he was finally believing I wasn't the friendly neighborhood priest that was *holier than thou.*

His mouth opened and closed a few times, indecision flooding him as he decided whether to admit to his crimes or not. "Well, I mean, yeah. It feels good to take what I want."

I didn't have to look in a mirror to know my eyes glittered with satisfaction. "That'a boy. It's about time you add something to the conversation. So, tell me, with Eve: Do you remember what you did to her on the side of the road? How you convinced her to let her guard down? Nothing against you, it's just that Eve doesn't normally go for men with greasy hair and dirty clothes. I thought I'd trained her better than that."

Rubbing at the back of his neck with his hand, he dropped his arm to his side and answered, "I actually don't remember much of that night. I was out partying, was on my way home and I woke up on the side of the road the next morning, beaten and bloody. My car was popped from behind leaving a big dent. I thought some of the guys I'd pissed off at the bar had followed me. I was drunk. Probably on something."

It made sense, and I didn't doubt he was being honest. Breathing out slowly, I dropped that topic because it was sadly obvious I wouldn't learn more about the night my beautiful girl decided to act like a harlot. I wouldn't hold it against her, and in truth I'd already forgiven the error in her ways.

Glancing at my watch, I saw that only fifteen minutes had passed. Surely, if I were any good at my job as a priest, I'd give this man more time in my attempt to save his soul.

"That's too bad. I was hoping to hear the details. I won't lie and say it doesn't excite me to hear about another man taking his fill. Eve is something to be desired. That woman will do whatever you ask of her and purr when you provide her the slightest bit of pain with the pleasure."

He laughed, the sound sleazy and grainy, but he was started to come under my thumb. If he didn't have to die tonight in order for me to firmly secure the sheriff in my games, I wouldn't have minded taking this man in, cleaning him up, and using him for everything I had planned.

"So, you're really not a priest?"

Shaking my head, I stared back at him, pure honesty shining in my expression. Masks are hard to maintain, they had a way of suffocating you when you were forced to wear them all the damn time. "No. I'm not. I happen to hate everything about the Church and the God to whom all those poor bastards pray. I know a little more about him than I'd like to, and that's why I'm here now, talking to you and waiting for it to appear as though I'd tried to lead you to the light. The sad fact is, there is no light, just power hungry, perverted humans taking a fable and turning it into a way to gain money and control over every stupid fuck that wants to believe it's true."

My friend laughed again, nodding his head as a smile stretched his thin lips. "Yeah, I know what you're saying. I never believed that crap myself. If these fuckers were so holy, why are most of them struggling to get by? Especially in this area where you're either starving, on the verge of starving, or already living in the gutters doing your best to stay alive."

"Exactly," I agreed. "I think it's funny that nobody sees it."

Silence passed between us, but his curiosity had him asking a question before long. "So what's with the getup then? Do you use your job with the Church to have a little fun?"

His eyebrows wiggled up and down, perverted thoughts rolling behind his eyes. "I mean, if I were in your position, I wouldn't be able to stop myself from tasting the good girls that look at men like us and won't even give us the time of day."

That might happen to him, I thought, but only because he was disgusting. The idiot should have thought to clean himself up a touch more, maybe get a haircut and some decent clothes and perhaps the women he fucked would be a little classier than back alley whores.

"I'm not opposed to tasting, if that's what you're asking, but that's not my main motivation. I have much bigger plans in mind." Pausing for a beat, I spent a moment enjoying the fact that I was so close to everything I'd worked for that I could taste it. "I plan on destroying the Church from the inside out. Plan on revealing the truth about the business it's become. You see, the Catholic Church is more powerful than many people believe and they've spent centuries learning how to cover up their crimes. It's too bad for them that they didn't suspect that one person would be strong enough to rip away the veil and reveal them for all that they are. Predators and thieves, the wolves in sheep's clothing we were warned about, the false prophet that Christ himself claimed would appear. Meanwhile, the idiots who look to the Church to read them the Bible don't realize that many passages are left out entirely. The faithful truly have no idea."

"You sound like you have a bone to pick. Either that or you're fucking crazy."

My lip twitched with humor. "Am I?" Shrugging a shoulder, I conceded, "Maybe I am, but only because they brought it out of me." My eyes locked on his, and I felt just a touch of pity for a man who didn't know he was condemned. "Actually, no, I wouldn't say I'm crazy, I would just say that I removed the blinders while everybody else is still sucking down the poisonous lies being spoon fed to them by a Church that's picking their pocket at the same time. It's funny when you think about it. We've been given a book with all these rules, told to follow them blindly and to love our neighbors, yet all you see are a bunch of insolent pricks who judge, who hate, or hold as much money to themselves while not giving a damn about people who are starving. And then those same self-righteous fucks like to turn around and tell people like us how we should live our lives. It's a bullshit game that's been played for too damn long, and I just want to play one myself."

The man was twitching where he stood, scratching at himself some more as he struggled to bring his eyes into focus. Oh well. He probably didn't comprehend a damn word I was saying at this point, and there was no bother wasting my breath.

"I guess I should get back out there and see what the sheriff is doing. It's getting late and I'm sure he wants to get home and go to bed. Do you feel like I've saved your soul in here, son? Do you feel like you can walk out into the world and be a better man for the prayers we've spoken together?"

248

He didn't answer immediately, but took the hint when I winked.

"Ah. I get you now. You're going to help me out by telling the sheriff I'm a saved man." Laughter bubbled from his lips, the movement of his shoulders shaking the hair loose from where he'd tucked it behind his ears. "Thanks, man, that'll really help. I guess you're not lying to me after all. You really are a sick bastard like me."

I winked again. "Actually, I'm not like you, I'm a lot more polished in my games." Pushing off from the wall, I stretched my back and neck before turning to approach the door.

"Hey, buddy. I just wanted to say thanks again. You know, before the sheriff is close enough to hear us."

My hand gripped over the handle to the door and without turning to him, I asked, "Thank me for what?"

"For helping me out."

My shoulders shook with laughter. "I hate to tell you this, friend, but I'm not sure you'll like what my help looks like." Glancing at him, I smiled and said, "Because the truth is you won't live to see tomorrow."

I laughed again and turned back to open the door. Before stepping out I added, "May God have mercy on your soul."

26

EVE

After eating the soup that Elijah had fed me, I felt better than I had in days. I understood the tea was supposed to settle my churning stomach, but it never did, despite the assurances both Richard and Elijah had given me. My head always felt fuzzy and I couldn't sleep when I needed to, couldn't wake up when I was walked outside for exercise. All I wanted to do was lie in bed and wait for my husband to come back to me.

I hated that he spent so much time at the parish without me, but he was back now, and he'd promised to relieve me of the final bit of this demon that plagued my body. I believed him, believed he had the power to deliver me to the divine like he claimed. I know he wanted me to sleep after walking from my room, but the food had warmed me and given me energy. Knowing he would return tonight to our bed, I wanted to be ready for him even when I was so thin I didn't feel beautiful. So, after he left, I jumped in a shower and scrubbed away the dirt and grime I always felt all over me. I'd crawled back in bed and grabbed the Bible hoping the words given to us by the Heavenly Father would soothe me until he returned.

Not much time had passed before the door popped open and a familiar face peeked through. The smile that stretched my lips made my cheeks hurt for how brilliant it was. "Joshua."

I hadn't spent much time with my brother since marrying Elijah, and for the week I spent at the parish after running away, I'd feared he would have been killed for running me off on the night of the ceremony. However, Elijah promised me that no harm would ever come to my family – he loved me too much to let that happen – and he feared the same evil attacking me had gone after my brother. He told me that the men had prayed together night and day, and that my brother hadn't been infected as badly as me as a result. And now, here he was, fresh faced and handsome, visiting me while my husband was away.

"Come in," I said, excited and laughing, the motion of my body from the sound causing a small ache to spread across my bones. It didn't matter. Not with Joshua here, not with my life returning to normal.

It wasn't that I disliked the parish and the time I'd had alone with Elijah, it was simply that I had always felt so unwanted and alone.

"Hey, Eve. How are you feeling?"

He walked across the room on unhurried steps, his broad shoulders and chest covered by the white button up shirt all the men wore. His brown hair had grown out so that it dusted his shoulders. I liked the way the longer hair looked on him. It perfectly framed his face and highlighted his cheekbones and square jaw. With eyes as green as mine, he sat beside me, the light of the room glimmering against those emerald orbs.

"I'm better now that Elijah is back. I missed him so much."

"I know."

I'm sure I looked sickly, that my skin was still pale and my bones protruded so much they pressed against the skin, but I would improve once Elijah was finished pulling the sin from my body and replacing it with his love. He was too powerful, even for Satan himself, and in the coming days I knew he'd make good on his promise to heal me and protect me always.

"I was able to keep down food, for once. I feel like it's been weeks since I last ate."

Joshua's smile didn't reach his eyes, and if I wasn't mistaken, a bare hint of guilt flickered behind his gaze. Reaching out, he took my hand in his, the warmth of his skin sinking into my own. The cold hadn't bothered me until it was obvious in contrast to him.

"I've been thinking," he murmured, his voice soft, but not a whisper. It was gentle, like the way a person would talk during a lazy spring day spent enjoying company beneath the warmth of the afternoon sun. "I'd like to take you on a trip in the next couple of days, just some brother and sister time. We haven't had that in a while and I feel like we're falling too far apart, that if we don't make more time for each other, we'll end up as strangers. Mom and Dad miss you, too, but they've been keeping their distance, giving you time to get to know your new husband."

Heart swelling in my chest, it staggered me to think that I'd missed the company and love of my family, but hadn't thought about how long it had been since I'd spent time with them. Elijah and I had been married for a few months now. I was certain he'd want me going back to the way my life had been before marrying him.

"I'd like that. Where would you like to go? There aren't many places that are safe. Elijah told us that."

A shadow crossed behind his eyes, his expression souring before the shy smile returned. "Maybe just for a walk? I want to talk to you about something, but I –" His voice trailed off, his gaze shooting past my shoulder towards a window. It was night outside and I knew he couldn't see much, but still he stared as if gathering his thoughts.

"I just want some alone time with you. To talk and catch up. I feel like when we're with the family, we never really get to hang out like we used to."

It wasn't that I felt leery about my brother. Except for what happened the night of the ceremony, he'd never led me astray, but something about his poor mood tonight drew my concern. "Is everything okay, Joshua? Did something happen to upset you?"

Shaking his head, he squeezed my hand. His smile stretched wider and the shadow behind his eyes dissipated. "I just miss you. I feel like ever since you've become a married woman, I've lost touch with my sister. I'd like to change that."

My smile matched his. "Okay."

A noise from the hallway outside my door grabbed his attention, his body twisted so that he could glance back to see if someone was coming in. When the door never opened, his shoulders relaxed and he squeezed my hand again.

Eyes locking to mine, he flashed me another smile before he said, "I should probably get going. Elijah wanted me to see to the children tonight and help Richard keep them away from the sanctuary."

That caught my attention. "What's going on in the sanctuary? Is Elijah giving another sermon?"

Reaching up to rub at his neck, he shook his head. "No. Nothing like that. I think he needs to deal with a guest, or whatever. It's nothing for you to be concerned about."

I knew which guest he was talking about after having already been out there to see him. But I didn't want to admit who the man was that Elijah had brought into the compound. I couldn't bring myself to admit the harsh fact that I'd almost given up my purity to a monster. It was far too disturbing. Far too harrowing. Far too...everything...for me to speak the words and make them true. But after tonight, after Elijah vanquished that monster, I knew my life would improve. What was he doing that he demanded the family keep their distance? It worried me and I wanted to know more.

"Okay," I answered, not letting on that I knew more than I was admitting.

The mattress dipped beneath me as Joshua leaned forward to plant a soft kiss on my forehead. He was right in what he said: we had become distant in the past few months, my attention so wrapped up in Elijah and the demons that I'd practically forgotten about the people who loved me. I would fix that as soon as I was well again. I'd show them how much I missed them and work to correct whatever distance had grown between us.

"I'm going to go, Eve. But I'll be around the compound tomorrow. If you get out for some exercise, come look for me in the garden. I want to show you how well the vegetables are doing, I swear the tomatoes are the size of your head."

Laughter bubbled up from my lungs. "I'll do that."

I watched him leave a few seconds later, his boots heavy against the ground as he walked away. The door closed quietly behind him, and while I should have taken the moment alone to try again to sleep, I couldn't help wondering what was happening in the sanctuary. Picking up my Bible, I continued reading passages, but found my mind wandering off so much that I was reading the same sentence over and over again.

Giving up, I dropped the book on the table and sat up to throw my legs off the bed. The floor was cold against my bare feet and it took me some time to find my shoes, but after locating them in the closet beneath a dress that had fallen from the hanger, I set out in search of Elijah.

He would be mad that I ventured out again after he'd warned me off the first time, but I couldn't help my curiosity. How he'd found the man in the first place was a mystery to me, one I'd ask him about when we had time to be alone again.

Pulling the door open, I peeked out to make sure nobody lingered in the halls. I hurried down making a right and a left before coming to the doors that led to the sanctuary. I heard three voices arguing, all low and angry, the words becoming louder and more urgent with each passing second. Fear shot through me to hear someone scream, the sound piercing and unholy.

Pushing the door open as slowly as possible, I hoped the hinges wouldn't squeak and give me away. Not that it mattered much with the way that man was screaming, even the blare of an air-horn wouldn't be heard.

I poked my head out just far enough to have a clear view of the large room, my view obscured by the benches and pews between where I stood and where the men were gathered. I couldn't see the man from the side of the road, but I distinctly saw Elijah standing by the large crosses, as well as the town sheriff and Richard.

"How are we going to hide this once the poor bastard bleeds to death?" Richard asked, the low timber of his voice vibrating across the room. I swear if that man was an animal, he'd be a big ol' grizzly bear given his size and the depth of his booming voice.

"We're not," Elijah answered.

Both the sheriff and Richard turned to look at him, their expressions shocked and questioning. "We can't let the women and children see this. They can't handle it."

Elijah bent down to do something out of my sight, but the scream that tore across the room let me know there was somebody lying on the ground beneath them. Fear shot through my heart, both that I wouldn't be able to handle whatever it was they were doing, and also that I'd get caught watching when I was supposed to be back in the room sleeping.

Despite my brain shouting at me to shut the door and go back to my room before anybody saw me, I couldn't step away. I was too curious to know what they were doing, too damn scared to move and find out later the hard way. If I learned anything in the months I'd spent as Elijah's wife, it was that secrets and surprises would hurt me more than anything else.

I didn't understand why he kept so much from me, as if I were a weak little woman who couldn't handle the truth that, sometimes, he had to destroy the evil infecting this town.

Tired of being alone and stuck in a room waiting for him, I stayed by that door and watching, hoping with everything I had that he wouldn't turn around and notice I could see what he was doing.

27

✝

ELIJAH

"I hate to admit this, Father Hayle, but I had my doubts about what you were telling my brother. Now, seeing this for myself, I don't doubt any longer. I think you may be on to something."

James spoke as I tended to our possessed man, readying him for the moment we would free him of his evil, regardless of the fact it would strip him of life. He screamed and wailed, begging for someone to believe I wasn't actually a priest. Richard laughed it off, and so did the sheriff, one who knew the truth, and the other sinking deeper into the illusion that I was a good man.

Splashing out another few drops of the holy water onto the wounds left behind by the lashings of a whip, the idiot beneath me screamed bloody murder swearing to anybody who would listen that he was just some perverted jerk and not a demon like I claimed.

Sadly, he was being honest, but the sheriff wouldn't believe him. Why would plain water cause so much pain if there wasn't a demon inside?

I'll tell you why that water hurt, and it had nothing to do with the fake blessing. I'd added bleach just to ensure it burned as it soaked into the lacerations and scrapes left by the beating and whipping he took after we had to fight to drag him back out here.

The sheriff was steadfast in his belief that holy water was cleansing the body, meanwhile I was hoping the son of a bitch wouldn't get too close and wonder why the condemned man now smelled like a house that was freshly cleaned.

I hadn't used too much, just enough to make it burn. I doubted it would be a problem.

"So, what do we do next? How to get rid of the demon?"

Richard smiled when I shot a glance at him, shrugging his big, bulky shoulders and waited for me to answer the question.

"We crucify him. Kill him in the same way our Savior was killed by the Romans who were infected with just as much evil as this man. It's God's way of getting even for what was done to the Son."

The sheriff grunted out his approval. "Sounds a hell of a lot easier than that shit you see on television. What's the point of exorcisms if it's easier just to nail their asses to crosses and leave them there to die?"

Face practically purple, Richard fought not to laugh. One would think I'd drugged the sheriff for as easily as he swallowed down the lies I was feeding him. Didn't anybody ever think for themselves anymore? Or was the Faith crammed so far down their throats that it somehow compressed the arteries and cut off the blood flow to their brains?

"Don't believe the lies Hollywood tells you, Sheriff. All of that stuff is put there by the Devil to deceive you. That's why there's so much graphic sex and violence in the big blockbuster movies. The world has slipped in to

260

the depths of Hell and nobody realizes just how bad it's become."

"Not in my town," he growled out. "I won't let this place fall to the Devil. Not now that I know the truth." Glancing up from the man on the floor who was writhing over himself and crying, James locked his eyes with mine. "When do we involve the rest of the townspeople? When do we let them know how much evil surrounds them and what can be done about it? I think the sooner the better. I don't want to see another young woman die like poor Annabelle. I was there when they cleaned up the scene-"

I smiled and placed my hand on his shoulder. "You don't have to tell me, James. I was there, too, remember?"

He nodded his head, the grief of that girl's untimely death still weighing on his shoulders.

Having never intended for Annabelle to die, I didn't feel guilty for being the one that pushed her to it. In fact, if I'd known then what I knew at this moment, I would have shaken her hand and thanked her for the favor. Without her, this town wouldn't have been so stunned as to be deceived. Sure, they may have believed eventually that evil was what affected their fields and had the banks breathing down their necks with the threat of foreclosure, but Annabelle's death only broke them down more, making my job a hell of a lot easier.

"I guess there's nothing to do now than to grab the nails and string this poor bastard up."

James nodded his head in agreement. "How long will it take for him to die? Will it be as quick as Jesus?"

My grin widened. "No. The Son of God died quickly because a soldier pierced his side.

Unfortunately, this poor son of a bitch will have to go out a lot slower."

"What? What the fuck are you talking about? This is insanity! I'm not a fucking demon!" The condemned attempted to sit up, but Richard kicked him in the chest to knock him back down. Even the blow to his ribs didn't stop him from claiming his innocence. "Listen, Sheriff, just take me to jail, okay? I'll confess to the rape today and to several more you don't know about. Hell, I'll even confess for crimes I didn't commit if it means you won't do this! I'll spend the rest of my fucking life rotting in prison, if that's what it takes. How the fuck do you believe this crazy son of a bitch? He's not even a priest!"

James scoffed at the accused and said, "You were right, Father Hayle. All demons do is lie. You've been the parish priest in this town for twelve years and this guy thinks I'd believe him? Let's do what we have to do in order to finish this up. I have more criminals to catch and bring to you. By the time we're through, there won't be any crime anywhere near this town and I'll be hailed a hero."

I laughed at the thought. Of course it would be his over inflated ego that would drive him to nail a man to a piece of wood and leave him there to die slowly.

As for myself, I had far more important reasons for pulling this off, and within a few months, all would come to fruition. I wouldn't call my reasoning evil by any means, just a necessary course of action that would lift the veil of secrecy and expose the true evil in this world.

"Richard," I said, "help me bring one of these crosses down so we can nail this son of a bitch to it. Tomorrow I'll give a sermon explaining to both the family and the townspeople who attend that the war we're fighting for the Almighty has finally started."

28

JACOB

"Four weeks? Is that the best you can do? Isn't there another shop around town that can get the weapons faster?"

The older gentleman behind the counter stared over at me with one big yellow eye, his eyebrow rising so far up his head, I worried it would get lost in his receding hairline. His jowls hung loose and swung as he shook his head in disbelief. Leaning over so that his arms folded over themselves on the counter, he lowered his voice and asked, "Son, I know you passed all the background checks I've done, and you look relatively normal, but is there is a particular reason you want these weapons? I thought you said they were for hunting."

Yeah, I thought, *like I actually need a semi-automatic for hunting deer.* I've never hunted a day in my life and even I knew that line of crap was bullshit. You would think the lie would alert him to the fact that these weapons weren't for what I was claiming, but I went along with it regardless, hoping he didn't pick up on the anxiety I was feeling.

"They are for hunting. It's just that the trip is scheduled to take place in a week and a half and I can't let my friends show me up." Shrugging a shoulder, I flashed him the practiced smile I'd always used as a priest. "You know how it is out there. Men thinking that they're better somehow because their gun is bigger."

His eyebrow pushed higher. Still speaking low, he was half laughing when he answered, "You do know that the size of your gun says nothing about the size of your dick, right?"

I rolled my eyes, but played along. "Yes, I know that. I'm not out there to pull it out and brag that mine is bigger than theirs."

"Yeah, but much like a man's cock, it's not the size that matters but what you do with it. In bed, it's all about rocking a woman's body and making her scream, but when it comes to shooting bullets instead of come, it's all about bringing the animal down as quickly as possible while ensuring it feels as little pain as possible."

We stared at each other for a few silent seconds before he pushed up from the counter and ran a hand through his thinning hair. Breathing out, he looked up at the large clock on the wall and back at me. "I tell you what, it's getting late and I need to close the shop for the night, but I can make some calls and see if I can find what you're looking for at another store in the area. Why don't you come back in a few days and see what I found?"

I didn't like the idea of waiting to confront my brother. With half a mind to just drop it and find another store, I also remembered it would mean another background check, which had the potential to alert some authority somewhere that I was up to something. Sadly, the truth was that if Jericho had controlled the parish for this long, the damage was already done. But still, I wasn't able to just walk away and let him continue whatever game he was playing against the town.

Rushing over there without arming myself would only leave me dead and buried in some shallow grave somewhere, so I had no other option that to do as this man asked and come back to see what he could find for me.

"Do you think the other shops would have what I need?"

Shrugging a shoulder, he moved away from the counter to file away the catalog he'd used to help me select the weapons I would need. "Don't know. With all the bullshit that's going on in this country right now, the particular weapons you're looking for are in hot demand. That's good for us because we suck up the profits, but it just means that people like you have to be patient for the manufacturers to send out more shipments."

He turned back, his eyes darting between the door and me. "I'm sorry I couldn't help you out any faster, but I really do need to be shutting down for the night. You can look around yourself at other stores, but I'm pretty much certain you'll have the same issues everywhere. I have some resources that aren't available to the public. Let me look around for a few days and then you can come back to talk to me. Does that sound good to you?"

Exhaustion withered my shoulders, not to mention the weight of defeat that was crushing me. What the hell was I thinking? That I could rush into a store and walk away with a damn armory in one night? Even in a country as gun crazy as this, it wasn't a possibility. One week wasn't a lot of time to wait. I'd done it for Father Timothy when he needed to get me the information on the music director and priest. I could do it again, in that fucking hotel room, biding my time with the bodies of whatever woman was willing to undergo my fury just to get herself off for the night.

It was too bad I sent Erin...or Erica?... off on such bad terms. Her brand of romance would have been perfect to work out the frustration I was feeling.

Letting out a deep sigh teeming with all the negative thoughts and feelings whirling inside me, I thanked the guy and made my way out of the store to step out onto the sidewalk that had been busy when I stepped in earlier that day.

I didn't know how much damage Jericho had already caused in that small, rural town, and I didn't know how much more he could cause while I waited for the guns I needed. What I did know is that I wasn't stupid enough to believe that I could return to that place with anything less than a full truck of guns and the bullets to go with them.

29

EVE

The four men spoke so quietly that I wasn't able to overhear them. Well, not the four of them, exactly. The one I assumed was lying on the ground screamed and shouted as he begged for his freedom. While I'd been listening he admitted to the crimes he'd committed against innocent women. It confirmed what I knew that night on the side of the road – the man was a demon and had been after me because, at that time, I was the easiest of victims. It was just one more example of how Elijah was saving me from everything evil that filled this world. Just one more example of his power. Just one more example that proved he was so connected to God that he could face down Satan himself and win.

Holding the door open with the tip of my foot, I was careful to keep my head and face out of view. Every time one of the men scanned their eyes over, I pulled back hoping and praying that none of them saw me. Fifteen minutes had passed already and they were none the wiser that I sat in witness of what they were doing. As long as I stayed quiet as a mouse, Elijah would never know I'd been spying.

My plan would have worked if I'd been stronger, if I'd been more able to view violence without flinching. But it all changed from one moment to the next, and I feared I'd be caught for my stupidity.

Poking my head back out, I watched in fascinated wonder as Elijah and Richard brought down one of the large crosses at the back of the church. I would have sworn that thing was too heavy for two men to handle, but then I remembered the story in the Bible of our Savior's death. He'd been made to carry it on his own all the way to the hill even with the injuries from his earlier beating. My eyes closed and a tear leaked out at the thought of how cruel men could be to each other. Even when we had God's son among us, we were too blind to see it. We hurt him and killed him, left him in pain and watched silently while they gave him the wound that ended him. And when all that was said and done, when they'd destroyed someone so beautiful, those people walked back to their normal lives to do their chores, tend to their homes or have dinner. Nothing had changed since we learned the truth of our greatest sin. People were still so horrible and terrifying that I couldn't even go outside without worry that a man like the one being held on the ground won't find me and steal my purity.

For that, I didn't cry to know that they were hurting him and making him suffer, but that still didn't mean I was brave enough to stand and witness how they'd chosen to destroy his evil.

Once the cross was brought down, they dragged the man over and laid him beside it. Richard wrapped one large hand around the man's arm, holding it in place as the sheriff took a hammer and nail and banged it through the flesh and bones to attach his wrist to the cross.

I gasped, unable to handle the sight of the blood, unable to hear the piercing scream that echoed off the ceiling and walls of the sanctuary. I was that one tiny sound that drew Elijah's attention toward the door, that almost gave my position away to the men who hadn't yet seen me.

Holding out a hand, he told Richard to stop for a moment. Still looking over, he shifted his position to get a better look at the door. I backed away but was too afraid to close the door fully. Even that small movement would alert them to the fact that they weren't alone in the large sanctuary.

"Did either of you hear that?"

"Hear what?" Richard answered, his voice gruff and breathless.

Elijah didn't answer immediately, but his approaching footsteps let me know he wasn't going to drop the matter and get back to what they were doing.

"Stay there for a second. I swore I heard something."

Left with no choice, I let the door close, the quiet click of the knob setting into place sounding behind me as I ran down the hallway, turned one corner and then another, pushing myself as fast as I possibly could toward the bedroom. I made it inside, shut the door as quietly as I could and jumped in bed. Kicking my shoes off, I let them fall to the floor, not caring where they landed as I pulled the blanket over my head. I was tucked away, warm and secure by the time that door opened again.

The creak of the hinges squealed slowly, the knob hitting the wall with a soft thump. One footstep and then another slowly beating over the floor, approaching me with caution.

"Eve," Elijah whispered, "Are you awake?"

Clenching my eyes shut, I tightened my fingers into the blanket I held over my head. Still as a statue, I lay on that bed hoping he was just coming to check and hadn't actually seen me.

"Eve?" he whispered again.

I didn't answer. There was no way I would respond, no way I would let him know I'd spied on what they were doing.

The footsteps approached again, soft tapping of the soles of his shoes over the floor. He stopped when he reached the side of the bed and I forced my breath to come out slow and even, prayed with everything that I had that he wouldn't lift the blanket to find that I wasn't actually sleeping.

His palm rubbed over the blanket, the touch soft and tender. My heart must have stopped beating entirely from the fear that he would yank it from my head, would know that I was lying.

A few tense seconds passed before he pulled his hand away, allowing my heart to continue beating, and within a minute from when he'd first walked in, he was leaving again, the door quietly closing, his footsteps beating heavy down the long hall growing silent as he got far enough away.

I let out a long sigh and then spent the next few minutes saying thank you to God for giving me the speed to run fast enough, and the calm to remain still enough for Elijah not to have caught me.

I must have dozed off after he left, the adrenaline rushing from my body so fast that I slipped into dreamless slumber. Waking up having rolled to the edge of the bed, I noticed the mattress dipped beneath me, the warmth of a thigh against my arm, the soft run of fingers through my hair.

"You've been sneaking around, haven't you?"

Elijah's voice, deep and hypnotic. I loved it when he used this tone, could listen for hours as he spoke about anything that filled the deafening silence. Even for as much as I enjoyed him when he spoke this way, I couldn't help the racing of my heart, the sudden shift from sleep to wakefulness that occurred as my mind processed what he'd said.

"I don't know what you're talking about. I've been sleeping."

He was quiet for a moment, contemplative. "When I married you that night in the cabin, I questioned you about many things. Do you remember?"

Thoughts dancing back to a night that terrified me as much as it filled me with hope, I remembered every detail, every sound, sight and smell. I remembered the way he'd chased me through the woods, the freezing rain that soaked me, the warmth of his chest when he picked me up to carry me in the cabin. Even now I could feel his knuckles brushing my chest as he unbuttoned my dress. I could smell the candles and incense, could see the soft dancing light and shadow from the fire. My skin tingled at my shoulder, at the place where I wore his mark, my mind trying but failing to forget how painful it had been when he put it there. I'd been purified by that mark, had found love beneath the glowing heat of metal, had been catapulted

273

from the ordinary life I'd lived to become the woman who walked beside such a powerful man.

"I remember."

Why did it feel like ages ago when it had only been months? Why did I feel so much older now even though I hadn't yet had another birthday? Is this what they mean when they say it's possible to age years for every day?

His fingertips dragged across my scalp, not painfully, but with just enough pressure that it massaged the skin. "Then you'll remember how impressed I was with your inability to lie. Every word that leaked out of you was truth down to the bottom of your soul."

Swallowing hard, I dragged a breath in and released it slowly. "I know."

His fingers fisted my hair, the scalp burning suddenly, threatening to release every follicle from the strength he used to pull. My face jerked up so that I was looking directly at him, I had no choice but to give in to his violence as he brought his nose down to touch mine. "Why, now, do you think you can lie to me and get away with it?"

He'd spoken the words so softly that they were barely a whisper, and I realized that it was in the moments that Elijah was quiet that you had to fear him. When he was loud, his skin was hot and his soul was on fire. But when he was cold, a sheen of ice cracked across the air, splintering and crawling until my body shook beneath its frigid temperature.

Another lie worked its way up my throat to settle on my tongue. Snapping my teeth shut, I fought to keep from voicing it. He would know. He always knows. I had no choice but to swallow the lie back down and endure whatever punishment I deserved for spying.

When I was silent, he released the pressure on my hair, my scalp still pulsing with an ache I knew wouldn't go away for several minutes. "Did you enjoy sneaking around and watching me without my knowledge? Did it make you feel accomplished or strong? Lying to your husband like I didn't deserve better from you?"

Tears welled in my eyes, the lids blinking rapidly to force them out and down my cheeks. "I'm sorry. I was just curious –"

He released me altogether and stood to pace the floor by the bed. "Did you miss him? Is that it? Are your fantasies about him so thorough that you were excited to see him again? That demon from the side of the road. The one who almost stole you from me, who wanted to take every part of you that belongs to me alone?" Stopping suddenly, he pivoted on his heel to glare at me. "Would you like to see him again?"

My head shook before I could utter the word "No."

Elijah's lips twisted into a wicked smile, his eyes blazing with the need to punish, to teach a lesson, to dominate. I've seen that fire behind his stare so many times, and each time only led to a lesson more horrifying than the last. Instinctively, I moved to avoid him when he lunged toward me, but the haze of sleep slowed me down, the weakness in my body from having been sick for what felt like weeks. Wrapping a strong hand over my wrist, he pulled me from the mattress, ignoring the cry of pain that shot from my lips when my hip impacted the floor.

"Get up," he demanded, the frigid temperature of those words freezing me in place.

Shaking my head again, I did so with the knowledge that my refusal would only anger him more. There was no denying Elijah – especially when he was like this. I was going wherever he wanted me to go and seeing whatever he wanted me to see. Refusing only made the journey more painful. But yet, there I was, crying and shaking my head, silently begging him to let me go. Why couldn't I just get up and do as I was told? What remnant still existed of the girl I once had been before he transformed me that night in the cabin? I wanted to find that piece inside me and shake it free. Wanted to become the wife he needed, the one he promised me I could be.

Jerked from the floor, I was planted on my feet, turned toward the door and shoved forward. It didn't take a genius to figure out where he was leading me. Quickly he led me down the same halls and around the same turns toward the sanctuary that I had traveled earlier. Without speaking a word, he stopped me before the large double doors that led inside the room where I'd earlier watched Elijah and two other men punish the man who had attacked me on the side of the road so many months ago. Hadn't the beating he'd endured that night been enough? Why did Elijah feel the need to hunt him down, drag him to the compound and punish him all over again?

Was it because for the original sin the man had committed against me? Or was it because I'd taken what happened that night and held on to it as a sinful fantasy?

I wasn't sure that killing the man would free me of the memory, would vanquish the lustful thoughts I had about another man forcing himself inside me. Even now, I shivered at the memory, both the fear that I'd felt and the heat of his skin pressed against my body.

"Are you ready to face your demon again, beautiful girl? Are you ready to vanquish him from your body entirely? To chase the fantasy until it dissipates into the ether, disappearing into Hell where it belongs?" Elijah's chest pressed to my back, his hand reaching around to splay over my stomach. "Are you excited to know that I'll give you this one final moment with him so that you can finally say goodbye?"

I shook against him, both mortified and anxious, trembling with my own dark needs and anticipation for a release. It had been so long, so lonely with him gone, and despite knowing what horror awaited me in the room beyond those large double doors, I found myself enjoying his closeness, his touch, the whispered threat against my ear. I loved this man, fiercely and without question, and I'd come to understand that if I couldn't have his tenderness in return, I was willing to enjoy the abuse he offered.

It didn't matter to me either way, just as long as it was his hands against my body, his breath brushing my ear, his power pumping between my legs each time he reminded me what it meant to be his wife.

Reaching around me, Elijah's breath was hot against the side of my face, his heart a thumping drum against my back. Slowly he turned the knob and pushed the door open, the sanctuary coming into view with low lighting and the flicker of a thousand candles. Only once had I seen it so beautiful, so mesmerizing that it trapped the breath in my lungs making it impossible for me to breath in the scent of incense that was a haze of swirling smoke through the room.

The stygian silence reached out to embrace me, drawing me into the room as Elijah led me from behind. They worked in tandem, the two threats, the anticipation and fear, the cavernous space and the cold man standing at my back. Before I could look over to where I knew the two crosses stood, Elijah's hand came up to cover my eyes.

"No peeking," he whispered, "I want this to be a surprise."

Walking me farther into the room, he led me around the benches, chairs and pews, guiding me without so much as letting my knee bump against any of the furniture. It was just like Elijah, so angry that he felt compelled to punish me, yet still watching out not to damage me by mistake. Every bruise, every lash, every mark he left on me was with intention, it was an art to a man like him, the type of branding that screamed to any person who saw it that I was owned by a powerful being, that he had left his calling card as a means to keep the demons at bay.

Except for one man, that was, the one I knew he was leading me to see. He hadn't noticed the mark of God left on my skin, he hadn't cared that I was an angel born on this Earth to chase the darkness away and help lead humanity to the light. He'd been blinded by what he thought was my innocent faith without realizing that the power I carried inside me came from the right hand of the Almighty – the new chosen one – the new savior – Elijah.

We stopped finally, Elijah once against pressing his body to mine. Without removing his right hand from my eyes, he used his left to tilt my chin, position my face where I would see the sight he'd created for me, where I would flutter open my eyes to be embraced by the truth of his ultimate power.

His breath a beat against my ear, he didn't speak or make any other type of sound, but I noticed the slight increase in his heartbeat, the way his lungs drew breath harder, letting it out with only a hiss of soft sound. Finally, my head was positioned where he wanted it, the room still silent, the nightmare ready to be revealed.

The heat of his hand pulled away, the cold air in the room coming in to crash against the skin of my face, and when I knew he was ready for me to see what he'd done to a demon who dared to touch what belonged to him, I opened my eyes…and screamed.

30

ELIJAH

I don't think I need to explain the symbolism behind my display of a liar and thief, of a charlatan and criminal, of a man who lured people in to his seductive web with promises of safety and security all while knowing he'd take what was good in them and expose it to the scavengers and predators that exist in this world.

It wasn't necessary for me to spell out the hatred I held inside myself for more years that I wanted to count of a fairy tale told for centuries that, to the good man, would come peace and happiness. Because beneath the robes of those good men existed the demons, beneath the skin of their faces was the mark of the beast waiting for the moment to come out.

Being a child in an abusive household is never easy. Hearing the screams of your brother, the deafening silence of your mother, the terrible, punishing words of a father who swore his allegiance to God and Jesus.

Running out the front door, I would go in search of something that could save me, of a protector, of shelter, of one comforting hand that would promise that it hadn't been me who caused the hatred inside those pristine walls and the small unfinished room with dirt floors. I'd found that promise, and all it cost me was my sanity.

Every day, I was overjoyed to leave my family home in route to a parish I believed was a sanctuary from the horror I lived beneath the roof of my father's house. I would jump out of my mother's car and race to the large wooden doors, fighting against the wind that held them shut so that I could hide inside amongst the golden crosses and jewel boxed relics. I would look up to the doves that were painted into the stained glass windows and bask in the glow of candlelight as I breathed in the incense. I would look up to the music director and the gentle priest with hope in my eyes that one day they'd notice the bruises, that one day they'd approach my father to tell him, "Enough."

Every day I'd appear with that hope in my heart, ignoring the grumbling of my brother who didn't see the parish in the same way. He abhorred the routine, hated the Tradition, had already grown weary of the world to which we'd been born. But not me. I had hope in a story, in a fable, in the imagery I'd conjured of a strong God sitting in the Heavens looking down at me with love in his eyes.

I'd believed in Him harder than I'd believed in anything, and when the time came that the bruises were noticed, the belief I'd held in the Almighty and his messengers had all but destroyed me behind closed doors and secret meetings, on my knees that were burning against pristine carpets, and on my stomach as I leaned over the desk of my parish priest.

For years, YEARS, those men had used me and had relied on my father's wrath to bind my tongue.

"He'll only beat you harder if he finds out."

"Good luck, boy, there is nowhere you can run."

I believed their lies just as much as I'd once believed that God would look out for me and protect me from evil. Once the illusion had been stripped away from my innocent mind, I'd never believed in another thing again.

Not God. Not good. Not evil. Not redemption.

For a boy that was only temptation, there was no absolution.

I was a filthy whore. A petulant child. A mockery of what it meant to be decent and faithful. I was only nine when the sexual abuse started, and by thirteen, those men had shaped me and formed me, beating me down with punishing fists and heavy cocks, until they'd broken me enough to create a monster.

Eight years passed that I endured the abuse while my twin somehow escaped unscathed. And at sixteen, when Jacob and I had tasted our first girl in the basement of that parish, I understood then how good it felt to be the one to punish rather than the one cowering beneath the weight of abusive men.

Their laughter had always echoed in my ear. My father's raised voice always chased me back into their clutches, but I'd come out the stronger man in the end when I'd decided to killed them, one by one.

First the music director, but he'd already been dead by the time I got to him. Then the priest. It was interesting to find out that he too had suffered an unfortunate demise after I'd searched for months to find him. Figuring the Church had done a decent enough job of covering their crimes, I felt robbed of my opportunity for violence, but I couldn't deny I felt a keen sense of happiness after discovering that both men had been shoved into the bowels of whatever Hell devoured them.

My father, well, his death wasn't exactly planned, but after he'd refused to accept his part in the sexual abuse I'd suffered, after he'd failed to acknowledge that if he'd just listened he could have stopped them, he took an unfortunate tumble down the steep, winding stairs. I never intended for that to happen, but then what can be done with a man who will confess his sins to God behind closed doors and in secret while refusing to admit them to his own flesh and blood?

Churning within the mist of all the memories that crowded my head was one symbol that stuck out, one ruse, one lie, one image that was the cause of it all.

Eve's scream tore through the sanctuary ripping at the silence, the volume of her cry like music to my ears as I stared up at that symbol to witness it brought to life.

Oh, yes, those Romans were masters of inflicting the worst of pain.

So absorbed by the sight of a man nailed to a cross, his chest shredded and bruised, his blood still dripping slowly from where he'd been attached to that thick wood, I'd failed to notice how Eve sank to her knees, her body withering at my feet as her forehead was pressed to the floor.

I was mesmerized by the image, my eyes glimmering with the same soft dance of light the candles had given the room. There he hanged in all his brilliance, suffering the same guilt, defeat and humiliation that I'd been forced to suffer for believing his lies in the first place. It didn't matter that the poor bastard hanging wasn't sent by Heaven itself, it meant nothing that nobody had believed him the actual Son of the Almighty, what mattered was that he represented the absolute truth about what the world was about.

Don't believe that lies that good men exist, not in family, in politics or religion. Because, in reality, there is no such thing as a good man or father, just an interloper whispering beautiful lies while dragging you into their Hell.

There was no good in this world, only the wicked, and they were the most beautiful, the most charming, the most deceiving where they sat in their thrones of absolute power.

While staring up at a condemned man who represented everything in this world that I hated, I laughed out loud to realize that it had been me who destroyed him – that it would be me who unveiled the lie and brought His Church to the ground.

My body thrummed with excitement as I stood there staring, my eyes darting between the man slowly dying and the woman kneeling at my feet. Lifting my head so that all I could see was the dying man on his wooden cross, I pursed my lips and whistled so loudly that he could no longer ignore me.

His eyes blinked open, the life in his eyes fading until hazy, but there was still some shred of him left that would enjoy the last experience I had for him.

"Do you remember this woman on the floor in front of me? Do you remember my wife?"

He couldn't answer back, I knew that, but still, it was fun to throw questions out. I wondered if the bastard could even see with the blood dripping down his face, the crown of nails that we manufactured since we didn't have thorns readily available.

Eve was whimpering still, her poor little mind shocked to oblivion by the sight hanging before us. Stripped down to nothing, this man had been positioned over the cross, a white towel draped over his waist as if I gave a damn about modesty. His hair was long and he was missing the beard, but I had to ignore that slight mistake in the image.

Candlelight lit the majority of the sanctuary, but at the base of his particular cross, I'd positioned floodlights pointing up at his body to highlight every bruise, every lash mark, every cut. It was so glorious as to be holy, so implicitly wrong, but I admired my work regardless. He was the symbol of what I'd known about the men pretending to be Godly, the bastards who drag you in to their safe little webs and devour you while shredding you with sharp claws.

I grew hard just at the sight, ready and able to render my beautiful girl pure by removing this bastard's power from her body and filling it with mine.

"Stand up, Eve. Don't cower in the face of evil when you are strong enough to face it. This son of a bitch has no power over you. Only me. Only the one true God."

The man's eyes blinked, his head lulling to the side as he attempted to understand what was happening below him. I was sure he found it difficult to breathe due to the position of his body, that he was consumed by the pain of the nails hammered through his feet, and of his shoulders slowly dislocating. His weight would eventually kill him, his body sagging ever lower with each hour that passed. And here I stood, staring up at a symbol that had once held all the power, to show the world that I was stronger and smarter than their precious God.

Whimpering and sobbing, Eve attempted several times to push to her feet. Once she stood at her full height that was inches shorter than me, she faced the monstrosity I created as the symbol of the Faith she believed I belonged to, like her.

Leaning over, I pressed my mouth to her ear. "Tell me again what this monster has done to you."

Her words tumbled over themselves without making sense. She was in too much shock to complete a simple sentence, the fear coursing through seeping out in a sticky sweat along her temple and jaw. Wrapping my hands over her shoulders I felt the way she trembled when faced with the image of a liar, rapist and thief that I created for her.

"H – He tried – tried to rape me."

Managing to blurt out that pathetic statement, she failed to deliver the details I wanted. Leaning over, my voice was firm when I instructed her, "Tell me from the beginning, Eve, from the moment you met him to the moment I saved you from his sin."

Still shaking like a leaf beneath my hands, she dragged in a deep breath, releasing it slowly as she attempted to look away from the condemned man where he hung from his cross. Gently pushing her face back to where she couldn't look away from the man staring down at us as he was dying, I held it there with my palm against her cheek waiting for her to speak.

"This is wrong, Elijah. He shouldn't be hanging there like the Savior. You shouldn't have done this in God's house."

God's house. My house. Same difference. All I knew by the words she'd spoken was that she didn't appreciate the symbolism, didn't understand that by

287

hanging a criminal on that cross, I was making a statement of what I thought of her Savior.

"What did he do, Eve? Tell me."

Tears ran down her cheeks and over my fingers, her jaw trembling against my palm. Several seconds passed as she gulped in air, her body weakening against mine as she finally found the strength to voice the details of the assault.

"I was walking down the road when he pulled up blasting his music. He pulled over and asked me why I was out on the side of road so late. I told him I was going to the parish to find you and he offered to give me a ride. But he said he wouldn't help me unless I agreed to dance with him. I thought it was innocent. I thought-"

Her voice died off into soft sobs. I gave her a few seconds to gather her strength, to allow her thoughts to travel back to a night that she'd fantasized about despite what was done to her. It would be a lie to say that the image of this man in her beautiful head hadn't bothered me, which was why I decided to end those thoughts tonight. Now, whenever she thought of this man, she'd remember him like this. Bleeding and hanging from the cross I'd erected in *my* house.

"After I danced with him, he told me that he wouldn't drive me to the parish unless I removed my clothes and let him look at my body."

My lips curled at the memory. Whispering against her cheek, I wrapped my arms around her body. "And did you like letting him look at you?"

Body shaking harder, she admitted, "Yes."

My smile stretched wider. "Good. I'd like for you to show him again how beautiful you are."

288

She stilled against me, her breath held in her lungs. Releasing it when she couldn't hold it any longer, she said, "No, Elijah. I can't. That's wrong."

Hands sweeping up her abdomen to rest just beneath her breasts, I hugged her tighter when I said, "You need to purge this man's sins from your system. It's the last bit of sin infecting you. After tonight, after I purge what remains inside and sickens you, you'll be free. You'll be happy. You'll never have to worry again. Trust me, Eve. Trust in your husband."

My fingers were soaked by her tears.

Pulling against my arms, she stepped away when I released her. She wouldn't look up at the man as she reached for the top buttons of her dress, undoing them one by one while he stared down with eyes that were dying. From where I stood, I couldn't see the slow reveal of her body, but he could, and that's all that mattered.

Forcing Eve to bare herself wasn't meant as something against her, but against him. He believed he'd had the right to touch my wife, the right to see her in all her wonderful glory, and I would give him the right again, except this time, he would learn that her purity was never meant for him. She was mine alone.

The navy blue dress slipped from her shoulders, revealing her bare body beneath. The bones of her shoulders protruded more than I remembered, her ribs running in equally spaced lines across her back. Her ass had deflated with the lack of sustenance she'd taken in over the past week, but she would be beautiful again once the last of the *demons* were forced out.

Candlelight flickered softly at my back casting shadows against her skin. Stepping up so that my chest pressed against her, I dragged my hands up her arms, over her shoulders and back down again to palm the weight of her breasts.

"Does it excite you to know he can see you like this again? Does it remind you of what you felt on the side of the road that night?"

Her breath rattled out of her lungs, her words shaky and soft when she answered, "Yes, it does."

"Did he touch you on the road that night?"

Body shaking against mine, she answered, "No. He touched himself."

I wanted to touch myself just for the excitement I felt in that moment, but I decided a better use could be made of my cock. Pressing my hips against her, I asked, "Do you feel my excitement to see you like this?"

Nodding her head, she pressed back against me. "Yes."

Pausing to allow the silence to fall over us, I finally asked, "Will you deny me anything now that I have you here in this place of lust?"

She simply shook her head.

My eyes closed, my heart racing, pumping all that glorious blood down between my legs. "On your hands and knees, Eve. I want to watch this man die while we rid your body of the last of his evil."

Perfectly trained and obedient, my beautiful girl sank to her knees. Forcing her body down farther, she planted her hands against the floor and waited for me to take her.

Glancing up, I saw that the man was still watching. Whether he understood what was happening on the floor at his feet was anybody's guess. It didn't matter, either way, as long as I got what I was after.

I removed my shirt slowly, taking my time to unfasten the buttons and pull it from my chest and shoulders. It puddled on the floor where I dropped it. Unbuttoning my pants, I pulled down the zipper, allowing the material to fall to my ankles as I kicked off my shoes and stepped out of the material. Kicking it all to the side, I grinned up at the condemned, my cock hard in my hands as I stroked it. Nothing about that son of bitch turned me on, but I couldn't say the same for Eve.

Still as a statue, she waited silently while maintaining the position I'd instructed her to take. I sunk to my knees behind her, running my hands up her back to drag my fingernails down leaving red marks against her pale skin in their path. She shivered beneath my touch, her round ass wiggling behind her, because the beautiful thing about Eve was her lack of patience in bed. She wanted it all, the pain, the pleasure, the torment, and she wasn't willing to wait like a good little girl should. No, not this lustful vixen. Rather than playing coy about requesting a release, she used her tempting body to demand it.

I slapped her on the ass for thinking she had the right to demand anything from me, but secretly, I enjoyed it. Never in the years I watched her growing up did I think she'd be so fun in bed, but that just goes to show you never know a person until you've been inside them.

On my knees behind her, I trained my eyes on the condemned man hanging above us as I bent over to take a playful bite of the skin of her ass. She cried out, moisture glistening between her legs as she whimpered and begged, her hips moving slowly as I slipped a finger inside the wet heat of her body to find that she was oh so ready.

Pushing myself back up, I tilted my head to the dying man and smiled. "Don't you wish you'd had the opportunity to taste her before I jumped you on the side of that road? I'll let you watch as your body slowly dies, and along with it the demon of memory that has infected my wife. After tonight, you'll be banished back to the Hell you came from while I continue enjoying her."

He blinked down at me, but it was the only indication he'd understood a damn word I'd said. It was a pity, really, I would have liked to know the thoughts running through his mind while two people fucked on the ground while he was slowly fading.

With one hand gripped to her hip I used the other to position myself at her opening, and with my eyes still gazing at the pathetic bastard nailed to the cross, my grin stretched wider as I pushed inside. Heaven was the only way to describe the tight wet heat that welcomed my cock, gripping at it with greedy muscles as I entered her, inch by glorious inch, until our bodies were pressed together. She moaned out her pleasure, her chin tilting up and her hair falling from her head to tumble over her shoulders. My hips pulled back, pushed back in, my own mouth dropping open.

Sliding a hand up her back, I gripped my hand into the back of her thick hair, using it like reins to tilt her head further, to lift her hands from the floor and force her to look upon the symbol of her savior while I thrust inside her without concern of care. A scream erupted from her lips. Not from fear, but pleasure, and she tightened around me as her body had its first stirring of an orgasm that would rush through her.

"Confess," I whispered, wanting to hear her thoughts, wanting to own every part of her - mind, body and soul.

Yanking harder on her hair, I felt her body tighten around me even more. I bit down on my lip and slowed my pace just to keep from coming at that moment. Her cries were like music to my ears, her need for pain a siren's song that called out to me threatening to wreck my very soul on the jagged rocks of her shoreline. My fingers dug into the sensitive flesh of her hips, my teeth clenching together with the need to sink into the sweet tissues of her body. I couldn't continue like this, I needed all of her.

Pulling out, I ignored her groan in complaint as I wrapped an arm around her wrist and jerked her from the floor to flip her over and throw her on her back. She laughed, her hair splaying around her in crazy waves, the dancing light of candles shimmering across her skin like the fingers of an enamored lover. Nobody would ever be able to deny that my girl was beautiful, the purity of her soul calling out to the parts of me that had once been good.

What would have happened if I'd never been turned into the monster I'd become? What could we have been if I'd been a good man when I met her? I couldn't think of what would never be, couldn't allow the pain of it to dilute the heat of the moment. My cock was pressed to her entrance, my eyes trained down on her face as she stared up at me with true adoration glinting behind her green eyes.

Fuck! What was wrong with me? For a split second I almost felt the skip of my heart, almost believed that it was possible for me to feel love. She wiggled her body against me, begging – always begging – and I pushed myself inside to steal that smile from her lips and force her mouth open on a guttural moan. Her chest arched up toward me, teasing me with the tight nipples of her breasts, and I took the opportunity to do what I'd wanted to do all along. Bending over her while grabbing the backs of her knees to lift her legs and drive myself deeper, I took the tip of her breast into my mouth, biting down until she cried out, and then licked away the pain with the tip of my tongue. Her hips bucked against mine, her legs bending where I held them.

Muscles rippling over my cock, she was swept away by her orgasm, and I struggled to keep from joining her, but lost that fucking battle. Thrusting my cock even deeper, I let go to my need to come, spilling my seed into her sweet body as I watched her fall apart beneath me.

Sweat dripped from my chest to her skin, the drops shimmering beneath the candlelight, and as we both came down from the high, I looked up one more time to smile at a man who endured his slow agony, his eyes still looking back at the fun he wasn't having.

Leaning down to whisper in Eve's ear, I demanded, "Look up at the demon and say goodbye, my love. After tonight, he'll never be able to affect you again. You are pure, freed of the sin and evil that you carried. Wave to him and say goodbye."

A smile spread across her face that only highlighted her beauty. Leaning her head back so that her chest arched up in the position, she smiled at the man hanging from his cross and waved a hand. "Goodbye," she said, the peace she was feeling lacing her words. The man didn't blink in reaction.

Laughter shook my chest just looking at the poor bastard, pride filling my heart to know that this moment was just the beginning of the end.

31

JACOB

Four weeks. I couldn't believe it took four long weeks for the salesclerk at the gun shop to locate everything I wanted. I had my suspicions he was intentionally forcing me to wait it out. Every time I got in touch with him, he questioned me incessantly, making quick comments in an effort to catch me off guard. Although he'd hoped to trick me into revealing the real reason for the weapons, I'd held strong in my ridiculous story that I needed the guns for hunting.

I wasn't an idiot and neither was the clerk. He knew as well as I that the guns weren't for hunting – not unless I was planning on gunning down an entire herd at once. But still, I went through the motions, swearing up and down that I wasn't some psychopath hell bent on destruction. In the end, it came down to one thing for the man: money. From the amount he charged me, he must have made a fortune.

Fortunately, now that I'd cashed out my inheritance, money wasn't an issue. Had I attempted this on my salary as a priest, I wouldn't have been able to afford the handguns, much less the semi-automatics I purchased with them.

The trip between the city where I'd grown up and the sleepy, rural town where I'd lived twelve years of my life as a devout man hadn't been a long one. Three days, with plenty of time taken to sleep at motels, stop to eat when I was hungry, and search the news for any signs coming from that area that indicated something wasn't right. There was never a speck of information to be found. As usual, the small community was quiet, never making waves other than its activities in the county surrounding it.

Driving the long winding roads through the mountains was difficult. The canopy of trees, the rounded peaks of the mountains in the distance, the wild animals scurrying off on the side of the roads reminded me of the first time I'd traveled here after college. At that time, I'd hoped to find peace among the townspeople. I'd hoped to find absolution in a life devoted to God after Cassandra's death. And here I was again, driving into the town with the guilt of another woman's death on my mind, Eve's face flashing in my thoughts as I drove past the businesses that dotted the area and into the heart of the town. I'd never spent much time with her outside of the parish in the week I'd known her, but that didn't matter. She had been a constant thought on my mind as I ran errands and drove about, and, as such, she was on my mind now.

It was Sunday when I arrived, which worked out for me since I knew most of the townspeople would be at the parish. I didn't have to worry about somebody recognizing me before I could park my truck off where it wouldn't be seen and sneak up to check on the

298

activities while remaining out of sight. The walk wasn't long and before I knew it, I was crossing the yard while being careful to watch for anybody who would be watching for me. Jericho wasn't stupid. He had to know I'd return eventually. Unless he was so far gone in his insanity that he truly believed he'd broken me with Eve's death.

In truth, he had. Initially, at least. But as is common with the passage of time, I'd had the opportunity to lick my wounds until they healed and regained my sanity.

Ha. Sanity. The thought of it actually made me laugh as I slowly approached the parish I hadn't seen in months with a gun tucked into the back of my pants and another at my side. There was nothing sane about this situation. Not what I'd learned about the past, and definitely not what I'd learn about Jericho claiming to be me as he continued leading the parish as its priest. We'd long traveled past what it means to be sane and wandered into a fictional world filled with the most wicked men of all.

From what I was beginning to understand, it's the people dressing themselves in the shroud of being good men that can commit the most evil. They are given access to the young. Are trusted with the minds and bodies of the faithful. They lead us in a way of thinking that eventually grooms us to believe that they are infallible and can commit no wrongs. We are constantly directed to look into the light so that our eyes can't adjust to the shadows. And it is within those murky confines that exist behind closed doors and within tight corners that we see the truth. There is nothing good about them at all, we've just been trained to believe the illusions they cast out and told us were reality.

Those are the people to be avoided above all costs. Those are the ones that should be publically shamed and brought out to admit to their horrifying crimes. Because, in the end, it's the deceivers that are the most horrendous of all, and if good men do really exist in this world slowly slipping into Hell, then those men would be better off opening their eyes to the truth that stands before them, because to see it is to fear the wicked.

I don't believe that all men who claim to be good are actually bad. Men like Father Timothy exist, the kind who truly believe they can make a difference. It just sucks that a faith that should have been a beautiful balm to the soul of the devout can be used to disguise pure evil.

It's not like we weren't warned. It's written all over the Bible. But when a society is formed beneath the fantasy that true darkness cannot exist beneath God's light, that society is doomed to fall. We've closed our eyes to the true seat of power. We've covered our ears and refused to believe we were led astray. It's not the fault of the faith that we've sunk so far, it's what's been done with it in the hands of power hungry men.

Money truly is the root of all evil – it's a shame that people have been led astray for so long, they're no longer able to see it.

All was quiet around the parish property except for the faint murmur of noise leaking out past cracked windows to echo across the yard. It was obvious that the pews were filled inside and that Mass was ongoing, which made me wonder even more what Jericho was doing.

A chorus of voices became louder the closer I approached, and I was genuinely surprised that I hadn't yet been spotted or encountered. Perhaps enough time had passed that Jericho was complacent in the misguided belief that I would never return, that I would never think to find out what happened to my former parish.

His complacency was good for me. It made it easier to sneak up and in position. Through a small window I remembered that looked into the sanctuary, I peeked in and damn near froze in shock.

Jericho stood at the altar speaking a blessing that had no roots in the faith. Instead of the relics and religious symbols that used to cover that altar, a woman was laid out over its surface. The entire fucking town was sitting in the pews praying in unison with my twin brother, not a single one of them concerned about the naked woman lying beneath him.

My world spun around me at that moment, reality twisting and bending before finally snapping back into place. What the hell had Jericho done to make everybody believe blasphemy like this was okay?

The prayers ended, the parish growing quiet as the parishioners rose from their knees to resettle their bodies in the pews. Jericho's smile stretched his face as he lifted his head to face them.

"She's possessed with the demon of lust," he called out, his hand resting on the poor girl's shoulder. I craned my neck and narrowed my eyes in effort to recognize his victim.

Molly Harrison was stretched out before him, a fourteen year old girl with the face of an angel. Her blonde hair was swept back so that it fell from the table's edge, her body exposed to the eyes of the parishioners. And rather than appearing afraid or embarrassed for exposing herself to the entire town, she lay there with a peaceful expression.

"But she can be saved. Just like we've saved the others before her. We are powerful as a united front. We've eradicated the other demons. One by one, we are freeing this town of the evil that attempted to consume us. On our own, and individually, we were weak, but together we can face down any of Satan's demons and send them back to the darkness from which they sprung. Who will assist me now in ridding this young girl of the lustful sins that infect her?"

How in the name of all that's holy had Jericho pulled this off?

The answers wouldn't come to me no matter how hard I racked my brain. The only thing I could comprehend at that moment was the force of my building rage. This wasn't what the faith was about. I'd spent twelve years teaching this town about what God intended for his faithful and none of it allowed for something like this. Yet, in a few months, under Jericho's control, the townspeople had become nothing more than the brainwashed members of his cult.

"My son would like to help," Addy Marks called out as she raised a shaky hand into the air. "I know he's young, but I believe it would do him some good to see how much of God's power is inside him."

My eyes rounded into saucers. Addy's son, Jeremiah, was only seven years old.

Jericho grinned like a fox in a henhouse. "Send young Jeremiah up. Don't be shy, young one. We all have the power of God inside us."

The boy pushed from the pew where he'd been sitting beside his mother. His brown hair was cut short to his skull but still managed to look wild. Dressed in a white shirt that was freshly ironed and brown slacks that matched his shoes, it was clearly obvious he was frightened by the changes that had taken place at his parish. His mother, having noticed his hesitancy to approach the altar where Jericho stood, reached out to prod him along by pushing her hand against his back. She whispered something to him that I couldn't hear, but the words had been enough to spur him along. Slowly he walked up the center aisle, his head turning this way and that to see the rest of the parishioners smiling over at him.

I had to fight not to reach for my gun and shoot Jericho before the boy could reach him. But unfortunately he was too far away for the weapon I had. All I would do is alert every person inside the building to my presence.

Once Jeremiah reached the altar, he reached out to accept Jericho's hand. Led around the side, he was positioned to stand where Jericho had previously been, a blade pulled from a jeweled box by my evil twin and placed in the boy's hand.

"Now, young one. What do we know about sin?"

Jeremiah's voice was so tiny that I could barely hear his response. "Sin is bad."

Jericho laughed. "From the mouths of babes. Yes, young man, sin is bad. You are right in that. And how do we get rid of it?"

Shifting his weight from foot to foot, Jeremiah looked less convinced of the answer he was about to give, but still he held on to the handle of the knife and looked over the naked body of the girl laid out on the altar in front of him. It was most likely the first time he'd seen a woman without clothes. "Through pain," he finally answered, shifting his weight once again.

"Yes," Jericho crooned, "That's very good. It shows that you know how to listen. You've watched me release the sin from a woman's body, right? You know what to do with the knife."

One would think that Molly would be struggling against the fate Jericho had assigned her, but instead, she lay on that table smiling up at the man who was convincing a small child to hurt her. I shook my head, far too focused on what was occurring at the altar to notice much else.

Slowly, the boy raised the knife that looked far too large for his small hand, and with a sweeping motion that was clumsy at best, he brought the blade down to run it over Molly's body. It wasn't enough pressure to kill her, just enough to slice the skin, and Molly's mouth opened as that blade ran over her body, the scream tearing from her throat filling the entire parish.

After a few seconds, Jericho took the knife from Jeremiah and whispered something in his ear. The boy smiled up at him before turning back to the parishioners with pride shining behind his eyes. Everybody clapped and began praying again while Jeremiah returned to his seat. Jericho took a cloth to clean the blood from Molly's wound and also to clean the blade.

"This is just the beginning of her purging of the sin in her body. As many of you know, it will take a week at least to rid her of all of it. She's made the first necessary steps by stepping up and confessing the evil thoughts in her head. She's exposed herself to our scrutiny and begged for our forgiveness as a body of the faithful so that she may again be right with the Almighty. After today, I'll take her to the compound to continue her path to the light. But I want to thank you all for your strong faith and the help you are giving me in freeing this town from the evil that has plagued us for far too long."

People applauded his words and began shuffling around to get up from their pews. I watched and identified many of the townspeople, but also recognized the uniforms worn by Jericho's cult family. Knowing I had to leave before anybody walked outside and saw me, I began to turn around when one particular face caught my attention.

It was the face of an angel.

The face of a woman who couldn't possibly be standing among the living.

And as shock burst inside me, weakening my knees as recognition took hold, I understood for the first time the game that had been played against me.

Anger rushed in to replace the shock, my hand reaching for my gun only because the feel of the cold metal against my fingers comforted me.

There, standing among the parishioners and members of Jericho's cult, was a truth that shouldn't have been possible.

My heart constricted to the point where it felt like it wasn't beating, my breath held in my lungs until they burned and forced the air out. My head swam and reality shifted again when my mind finally caught up to what my eyes were seeing and I recognized Eve was still alive.

32

JOSHUA

I was so tired of that arrogant prick who thought what he was doing was God's way. For so many years, he'd led the family to believe that he was holy. I hate to admit that even I'd been fooled by his smooth, proud voice and promises of salvation at Heaven's gates. My parents still believed it, as did the rest of the family, but I wouldn't be fooled any longer.

How he'd convinced us all of his power was simple enough, only because he kept us weak, kept us blind and kept us separate from the world around us. He drove fear into the hearts of every person who lived in that compound and had convinced them all that the only way to God was through him. And even during all the small excursions into town that he'd allowed, he wouldn't allow us to stray far, wouldn't allow us to pick up a book or watch a television claiming that all the knowledge thrown out in the world around us was placed there by the Devil to deceive us.

I'd gone against his rules on the day I swiped a bible from a vendor's table at the market. Elijah had been too focused on Eve to notice what I'd done. After stuffing the book into the bag I carried, I'd smiled and pretended like business was the same as usual. We were there to pick up a few items we couldn't produce on our own and within an hour we were walking back to the compound.

Always with the walking regardless of how exhausted we all were. It seemed like we were starving more than we were fed, but he'd told us to ignore the way our stomachs grumbled.

It's the demons making you believe God hasn't provided, he'd claimed. But if you place your faith in the power of the Almighty, you will see the truth of their deceptions.

Lies, lies and more lies, yet the family sucked them up and truly believed that everything Elijah did was for their own good. I was tired of the lies, tired of being tired and hungry, tired of wearing the same thing day in and day out while I sweated to work the gardens and train the dogs that were intentionally kept starving just like us so that they were bloodthirsty.

I wasn't an avid reader, I'd only been taught how to read until my parents had dragged me to the compound, so it took me a long time to work my way through the pages of the Bible I'd stolen. Elijah would have claimed my desire to read was prideful, and maybe it was. I noticed that he was the only one who knew what the book said, and I figured that's what made him so holy and powerful. I wanted to be as loved by God as him, and I'd wanted some of that power for myself. But after struggling at night when nobody was looking, reading against the glow of candlelight, I realized that many of the lessons Elijah was teaching were just plain *wrong*.

God loved every human equally, we were all his children on this Earth and not one person was placed above the other when it came to his love for us. The savior wasn't the man leading us to his version of the light, it was the one who died on the cross for all our sins, promising that if we would just love each other as much as him, we too could receive God's favor.

So, why was it that Elijah was teaching us to judge every person who wasn't like us? Why was he filling us with so much hate? And why did he think it was right to use the words written in the Good Lord's book to commit evil in God's name?

None of it made sense and I wished it hadn't taken me so long to see it. I could blame that length of time on the fact that I was a slow reader, but it didn't excuse me for my ignorance and what I'd already allowed to happen simply because Elijah told me it was right.

He'd pulled me under his wing after deciding to marry my sister. He'd promised me that she was meant to help him begin the war that would rid all of us of the evil infecting this world. After instructing me to run her off on the night he was supposed to officially marry her, he'd convinced me to stay at the compound and let her run off by herself into the woods. For a full week I didn't know what was being done to Sedra, or Eve as he made us call her. I didn't realize until it was time to collect her from the parish that Elijah had allowed her to sleep with his own brother. It wasn't until we walked to the parish that day that he'd told me the truth of what he'd done, but even then he'd convinced me it was all God's plan, that her sacrifice was as beautiful and holy as God's own Son.

Slowly, the truth had come to me, and during that time I'd watched my sister become weaker and weaker

309

with the teas she'd been drinking. I realized over the week that she was at the compound and Elijah stayed at the parish that if I didn't get her away from him, eventually she would die.

After watching the service today and seeing what he'd convinced a child to do to another child, I was finally to a point where I understood that there was no other choice but to run away. I didn't know where we would go or how we would get there, but I had to believe we'd find our way. So while Elijah was distracted by the townspeople talking to him, I approached Eve where she stood silently waiting.

"Hey, Sis. How are you feeling today?"

She turned to me and the light pouring through the windows sparkled in her green eyes. I noticed her health was returning ever since Elijah claimed to have purified her by crucifying that man at the compound. What most of the family didn't notice was that at the same time he'd *purified* her by killing another, he'd also stopped giving her that tea. I noticed, but kept my mouth shut. I had to keep pretending I was still the ignorant believer in the lies he'd spread since the day I'd met him. Speaking up would only position me directly in his crosshairs and I'd never be able to escape with Eve. I couldn't even tell my parents because they were so far gone in their belief in Elijah, they would run to him in the misguided belief they were saving their daughter from the *evil* that infected me.

"Joshua," she wrapped her arms around me and gave me a strong hug. It made me happy to notice that her bones were no longer as obvious beneath her skin as they had been just a few weeks ago. "I'm so happy to see you."

Laughing, I reached up to rub at the back of my neck, my muscles were tied in knots because I knew this might be my only chance to get her away from Elijah. "Me too. I was wondering if you'd like to take a walk with me? You know, just so we can talk and catch up."

Turning immediately to look at her husband, Eve's mouth twisted with indecision. A few tense seconds passed before she looked back at me and smiled. "Elijah looks like he'll be busy for a little while. And I'd like to go outside and get some fresh air. But we have to stay on the parish grounds. I'm sure he'll be looking for me once he gets done talking to all those people."

Thankfully, the backyard of the parish was large and bordered by the woods. If I could get her far enough away from the building, there was a chance I could quiet her while dragging her off. If there was enough distance between us and the building, nobody would hear her arguing as long as I covered her mouth. I hated the thought that I might accidentally hurt her just to drag her away from the true danger - Elijah.

"That sounds good." Offering her my arm, I waited for her to wrap hers through mine and allow me to lead her from the building. My heart was racing with worry, but I wouldn't let it stop me from at least trying to save my sister.

Stepping outside, the warmth of the sun brushed my cheeks, birds singing from their treetop perches as people shuffled off to their cars or to walk down the sidewalks toward their homes. Fortunately, nobody noticed we'd wandered out and I led Eve around the side of the building and across the yard toward the line of trees at the back. I knew of an old hunting lodge that was hidden deep inside the forest, one that would only

311

be a roof over our head and nothing more, but it would have to be enough until I could figure out where to take Eve to keep her away from Elijah.

My beautiful sister was silent as she walked beside me, completely comfortable beside her older brother that had always looked out for her. She'd never been one for constant conversation and I was thankful for her silence because it gave me the time to think. Was she strong enough to walk the distance to the hunting cabin? Would she complain and fight against me once she found out I didn't intend on letting her return to the compound?

It couldn't matter. If I had to knock her out and drag her, I would.

Approaching the forest, her arm tightened on mine, her head swiveling back to glance at the parish. "Aren't we going a bit far? Elijah will worry if he can't find me."

I patted her hand with mine, a friendly smile pulling at my lips. "Elijah knows you're with me. I told him before I found you inside the sanctuary."

The lie appeased her and she kept pace with me, unconcerned by the distance we traveled away from the safety and security of the building.

While my thoughts were distracted by the questions racing through my mind, I felt Eve break away from my hold suddenly, her eyes rounding and her mouth pulling into a smile as she hurried her steps toward the woods. Confused, I chased after her, my eyes locked on her rather than on what she was running toward.

I should have paid better attention to my surroundings, should have listened to the name that

312

fell from her lips the instant she let go and ran away from me.

If I'd done so, I wouldn't have been taken by surprise when the hard barrel of a gun was pressed to my head and a deep voice growled, "Either you two are coming with me, or I take Eve and leave your dead body for the family to find."

33

ELIJAH

After the night at the compound where Richard and the sheriff of this small town lent their hands in nailing a man to a cross and lifting him above the pews of my sanctuary to let him die slowly, the sheriff and his brother, Gentry, had been instrumental in bringing the town around to my cause, in convincing them that the only way to combat their misfortune was to destroy the evil infecting this area.

In truth, there was no special evil they had to worry about, nothing remotely different than that suffered by the rest of the world, but in the weeks they'd distanced themselves from the news, television shows and other lifelines to the world outside this rural area, the townspeople had sunken deep into my insanity, the seeds planted in their heads over the months I'd played the part of parish priest finally blooming into hysteria that I would use to my ultimate advantage.

While standing by the altar, I shook the hands of the idiots who truly believed I could deliver Heaven to them on Earth, the ones who thanked me endlessly while not realizing that they were being used as a means to my end. The deaths were stacking up, the nightly ceremonies we held while sacrificing the poor condemned souls that hadn't done anything to deserve the methods of their death, and the entire time, I documented the town's activities via the security cameras I'd installed and kept hidden from the family. Not one person knew their faces were recorded for eternity taking part in the cruel and heartless destruction of liars and thieves, rapists and other such violent types.

Eventually, the destruction spread to the parish itself and I made sure to record those scenes as well. Once my plan was finished, once I had all the evidence I needed to show that true evil existed beneath the guise of religion, I would finally have my revenge against a Church that had learned over the centuries how to hide their disgusting crimes.

I wasn't the only man benefiting from the hysteria. Richard, too, enjoyed the fruits of our labors, having his fun and taking his time to help exorcise the lustful demons in the younger girls who believed me when I told them that their impure thoughts would become their destruction. The fact these morons so easily believed me only proved what I'd believed about the faithful all along: It wasn't peace and kind manners that led them inside the parish doors each Sunday to hear the message of God, it was the belief that they gained power and protection by subscribing to a fantasy that someone beyond the Earthly plane gave enough of a damn about them to influence their fate.

Nobody gave a damn, not Christ and not the Father. Because if they had, I wouldn't have been used as a fuck boy for holy men my entire childhood. I wouldn't have been a punching bag for a father who was so far gone in his beliefs that he didn't see the abuse as anything more than an unfortunate necessity to remove the sin from my body.

He'd thought he was saving me from myself without realizing he was weakening me for the true wolves that lived inside the parish, using me for their hidden sins while reminding me there wasn't a soul on this Earth who would believe me if I reported them for what they'd done.

It wasn't an uncommon occurrence. Men such as them had existed since the beginning of the Church in ancient times. And it was for that reason alone that I had to endure the abuse and humiliation in order to become the monster who would be strong enough to destroy them all.

The parishioners saw their way out of the parish, one by one, slowly wandering off to their bleak little lives believing they watched something truly holy this Sunday at the parish. Richard stood beside me wrapping a robe over the newest young woman who believed wanting to kiss her boyfriend was enough of a sin that she needed to turn herself over to the Church for redirection. It was a new type of confession I'd given the parishioners, a public repudiation of their own thoughts, hidden desires and beliefs. They were truly stupid – all of them.

Once we were alone and Richard was practically drooling over the young woman that stood at least a foot shorter than him, I turned to find the woman who had become my obsession.

Eve was growing back into a healthy body, the weight she was regaining forcing her body to round at the hips and breasts, her skin no longer ashen and

317

sallow, but full of life with the rosy glow that always graced her cheeks. She was truly obedient to me now that she believed I'd destroyed the last demon plaguing her and had made her my true and proper wife.

However, when I scanned my eyes through the sanctuary, over the pews, past the walls filled with paintings and other religious symbols, I came to the realization that Eve was nowhere to be found.

My head snapped to Richard. "Have you seen Eve anywhere?"

He dragged his filthy gaze up from the poor girl who had no clue what would happen to her. No, he wouldn't kill her, wouldn't damage her in any way that drew attention, but he would free her of the purity she carried while promising her it was the only way to remove her sin. His eyes searched the room before he shrugged a shoulder. "She was here just a minute ago. Waiting for you like always near the hallway back to the rectory. Maybe she went in your room to wait for you."

Eve knew better than to be out of my sight, but perhaps she assumed the safety of my bedroom was good enough. My legs were moving in the direction of the hallway while I belted out, "Stay here in case she went somewhere else and comes back. I'll go check the rectory."

My feet couldn't carry me fast enough down the narrow corridors leading to the small, boring room Jacob had slept in for twelve fucking years while convincing himself he was a good man. As I turned one corner, walked down another hall to turn another corner, I thought of my wayward brother and laughed to myself at how easy it had been to oust him from his holy throne so that I could take over the town he'd worked so desperately to lead to a light that didn't exist.

In truth, I'd always harbored ill feelings toward my brother. I'd regretted that we were twins, believed that, in the womb, he had somehow reached into me to steal the strength away so that he could harbor it to himself. He had been the one to stop our father's abuse, he had been the one to avoid being used as a human pincushion for those sick fucks who walked around feeding religion to a large parish.

At one time I'd envied my brother, and during the times when we shared women, I'd believed I was the superior brother because I had been the one to take the women first, to steal their purity and watch it drip down my cock as the crimson evidence of my race to their finish line. Jacob never argued who would take them the first time, and I'd believed it was because he understood that I would fight him for that honor, but then as the years passed by and as I watched him transition into the worst kind of monster, I understood that, to him, it had never been about stripping the good little girls of their virginity, it had always been about who would control them in the end.

They may have fucked me with sweet smiles on their bullshit faces, but their eyes had always been locked on my brother, their hearts becoming his as soon as he stepped up to take what remained after I was done with them and transform it into the perfect slave.

It was Jacob who had taught me what to do with Eve, and it was Jacob who I could thank for the perfect woman I'd created from the girl I'd met when she was first brought into the family.

Perhaps I should have thanked him for that one small favor, but I couldn't find it in myself to forgive

319

him. Still, even with the hatred I held for him and the anger that coated my tongue each time I thought about the unfairness in our young lives, I couldn't bring myself to kill him. I still harbored something inside me that needed my brother alive, I still *loved* him despite the way he'd sat with our piece of shit mother and had listened to my cries.

My father would beat me until I couldn't stand any longer and neither my mother nor my twin could find it within themselves to climb down those steps into the basement to free me from the violence of a madman.

Reaching the bedroom door, I slammed my hand down on the knob, twisting it as I shoved the door in. I'd gotten one foot inside by the time I had a full view of the room to realize Eve wasn't here as I'd hoped she'd be. Quickly crossing the small space, I peeked inside the bathroom to find it empty as well.

Rage crawled through me, clinging to my bones with desperate fingers begging to ignite into the intolerable heat of pure, undiluted fury.

I was practically racing on my way back to the sanctuary, my eyes sharp and my muscles tight across my body. Richard was standing in the same place, patiently waiting for me to return with the good little girl standing still in front of him.

"Did she come back here?" I asked, practically screaming.

Richard shook his head, his eyes rounding as he came to the same conclusion as me.

Throwing my hands out, I directed him to the back hallways of the parish, while I ran toward the front. "Find her, Richard. I don't give a shit if you have to tear the walls down until she's found. If we don't find her inside the parish, we'll search outside. Where the fuck could she have gone?"

Richard lumbered off to do as I said while I peeked a head inside the kitchen to find it empty. The offices and bathrooms were empty as well, not a soul to be found in any of the small rooms of the parish.

Within minutes both Richard and I were outside scanning the large yard and the woods beyond, my fury ratcheting higher until all I saw was red.

"What do you want to do? Is it possible she went back to the compound?"

I shook my head, completely irate that she'd wandered off without me. As soon as I found the son of a bitch that led her away, I'd be sure to nail his body to one of my crosses.

"You better hope she's at the fucking compound. If not, I will kill each and every son of a bitch inside this town until I've found my fucking wife!"

34

JACOB

My foot was planted firmly against the gas pedal of the truck, the tires screeching along the asphalt as we peeled off onto roads that wound their way through the Appalachians. Eve was as compliant as ever, her eyes filled with hopeless adoration for the brother she thought I was. Every so often, Elijah's name would roll off her lips like a reverent prayer as she wrapped her arms around mine and tried to pull it from the steering will.

I'd expected the man who was walking with her across the field to put up more of a fight, but instead, he'd taken one look at me and nodded his head, wordlessly following me into the woods without complaining that I'd just stuck a fucking gun to his head. I'd recognized him as he led Eve from the building, knew he was one of the assholes who had stood in the room staring at my naked cock while Elijah carried on about how I'd killed a member of their family. Obviously, that shit wasn't true and I was still in shock for having a woman sitting beside me that for months I'd believed was dead.

As we wound our way along the road, I thought about how convenient this entire abduction (that I'd never actually planned) had been. After Mass had ended and the parishioners filed out of the building, I'd moved quickly to hide in the tree line hoping for the opportunity to have a moment with Elijah alone. But then Eve stumbled out on the arm of this guy and it was like he was leading her right to me. I couldn't help the way I'd stared, couldn't stop the way my heart had clenched in my chest only to pick up its pace as they approached. I felt something for this woman that I couldn't name, and the *something* that eluded me every time I tried to identify it had come to life to see her face, to know that she wasn't just another one of my victims.

"What's your name," I asked the guy sitting quietly by the passenger window, Eve settled in place between us on the bench seat.

She turned to look at me with confusion lining her face, answering for the man before he could get a word out. "What are you talking about, Elijah? You know my brother, Joshua." A nervous laugh filtered over her lips, her green eyes staring up at me like I'd lost my fucking mind.

Breathing out, I clenched my fingers over the steering wheel so tight that the blood drained from the knuckles leaving the skin white. "I'm not Elijah." I wouldn't play the same games with her that I'd played when she first arrived at the parish. The poor girl was sick in the head and I hadn't helped her by playing along. I knew that now, knew that in order to save her from my twin who had lost his fucking mind, I had to burst the bubble that had been built around her. Sheltering her from the truth wasn't the way to free her from the bullshit lies that had created her.

"Not this again," she breathed out. "Have I done something?"

Dragging my eyes from the road for only long enough to stare down her brother, I jutted my chin in his direction and said, "You know who I am. Why don't you do the right thing for your sister for once and tell her the truth?"

I would have sworn the asshole would argue, but instead, he sighed heavily and turned to his sister. "Eve..." his voice trailed off, the flicker of anger obvious behind his eyes. "Sedra, I mean."

"No!" Eve's body stilled at the mention of her real name. "You won't call me that. I haven't been Sedra since the day I married Elijah. Sedra was a stupid girl. A faithless brat that was full of sin. Elijah freed me of that-"

Joshua surprised me when he reached out to take his sister's cheeks between his hands and turned her face toward him. "Sedra," he repeated, his deep voice calm, yet authoritative. "I need you to listen to me without arguing for once. I need you to really listen, okay? There's something you don't know. A lot you don't know, actually, and it's time you found out before it's too late. Please. You have to trust me when I tell you that Elijah has been lying to you for a long time. He's not as holy as he says. He's been hurting you, Sedra-"

"No!" she screamed, her arms flailing and damn near hitting me in the face. "I won't listen to this! Not again! You won't do this to me again!"

The truck swerved as her arm knocked against mine, and as I corrected it to keep up from driving off a fucking mountain, I raised my voice to grab both of their attention. "Get your sister under control now before I kill all three of us by wrecking!"

On one hand, I was still in shock to see Sedra alive. On the other, I was in shock that this son of a bitch seemed to agree with me about his sister and was going along with what I wanted. And if I'd had a third hand on which I could balance some emotion, it would be gratitude to discover that I wasn't alone in the realization that Elijah had become a fucking monster.

Poor Joshua had to practically pull his sister onto his lap to keep her from knocking me out with her flailing hands, but eventually he got her under control and was holding her in place with his arms wrapped around her.

"Listen to me, Sedra. Elijah is not who you think he is. That man over there, the one driving the truck is not Elijah. His name is Jacob Hayle. He was the priest for the parish before Elijah made him believe you were dead and chased him off. Elijah let his own brother fuck you just to get what he wanted, so I'm sorry, sister, but you're not as pure as you think you are. This entire thing has been a game so that Elijah could take over control of the parish without the townspeople knowing."

Sedra's eyes flicked to me, the green orbs rounding with recognition before the brainwashing and lies slipped in to make her scream again. It wouldn't be easy to convince her of the truth, but that couldn't be my problem. I was here for one reason only and that was to stop whatever games my brother was playing from ruining the town and destroying the lives of the parishioners I'd spent years trying to help.

I knew my brother was insane, and after learning about what happened to him when we were young, I understood why. But that didn't mean I could feel pity for him and allow him to destroy other innocent lives. Hating the thought of having to harm him in order to get him the help he needed, I was willing to do whatever it took to ensure more people weren't hurt because of whatever end it was he was trying to achieve. There were better ways to handle what happened. And going on killing people and making them believe in evil wasn't one of them.

"We need to get off the road," Joshua screamed just to be heard over the voice of his sister. "She's not going to stop flailing. We have to get her somewhere we can calm her down so she'll listen."

Well, fuck. I hadn't intended on taking anybody captive, so I hadn't thought of finding a place where I could hide and wouldn't be found. "We can go to the police," I suggested. "We could tell them what we know and send them to that damn compound so they can raid the place."

Joshua shook his head, still struggling to hold on to his sister. "That won't work. The sheriff is working with Elijah now. They've been killing people at the compound because Elijah has them convinced that those people were possessed by demons."

"What the fuck? Are you shitting me?"

Shaking his head again, Joshua looked grim when he answered, "I wish I was, but they've been crucifying people on the large crosses Elijah has at the back of the sanctuary. Two people were up there dying this morning when I left for the parish."

My eyes closed, but I forced them open again. I didn't have time to fall victim to my feelings while driving at high speeds over winding roads. "So where can we take her? We're too far out into the county for me to know where the hell I am."

"I know of a hunting cabin that's been abandoned for years now. I don't think Elijah knows about it or that I know about it. I've been sneaking off over the past few months looking for somewhere I could take my sister to escape. I figured out Elijah was a fraud a few weeks after he chased you off."

"Well, thank God for that," I muttered.

Joshua made me laugh when he answered, "I've been thanking Him for a while. Turn around and when you hit county road five, take a right. It's a distance away, but I'm sure nobody will find us. We can hide the truck in the woods and walk the rest of the way."

Unsure whether I could trust the guy, I turned to look him in the eye. All I found there was determination to get his sister to safety. Nodding my head in agreement, I turned my attention back to the road and followed the directions he barked out at me. Within an hour, we were pulling Sedra out of the truck even though she was still kicking and screaming.

It took both of us to drag her through the woods while trying to avoid roots that were tripping our feet and low lying branches that hadn't been cleared away by hunters or forest animals in their search for food. The sun was beginning to climb into the center of the sky letting me know it was midday. The heat had sweat sliding down my skin, but I wouldn't allow it to slow me down, and eventually, despite the way Sedra had struggled, the cabin came into view. Joshua and I both breathed out a sigh of relief.

The door banged open as we plodded through, the interior nothing but some broken furniture and dust covering every surface. Joshua wrestled his sister down to the floor with minimal effort. Thankfully, the small girl was running out of steam. While he knelt down softly speaking to her, I checked out the broken windows ensuring that I hadn't just been led to a place where Elijah wouldn't come riding up on his imaginary white horse to take back his bride. Nothing moved around the boundary of the cabin, and I relaxed a little to discover we were alone.

"We're going to need supplies," I said. "Food, water, toiletries. I didn't bring anything with me because I was pretty sure it would become a gun battle as soon as my brother saw me."

Joshua laughed softly. "If you'd gone to the compound instead of the parish, it would have. He told the sheriff about you and the order was to kill on sight. He claimed that you were just another evil entity hell bent on destroying the town."

Curiosity filled me. "Why are you helping me out? Aren't you part of the family?"

Peering up at me with eyes the same color as his sister's, he smiled sadly. "I was part of the family. But then Elijah started letting me in on some of his secrets. At the same time, I'd stolen a copy of a Bible from the Farmer's Market and was secretly reading it without him knowing. I realized quickly that all the stuff he says in his sermons isn't what's written in that book."

While we spoke, Sedra sat quietly on the floor, her eyes glistening with tears and her face red and ruddy from having been crying for so long. Her energy was tapped out, however, which was a damn good thing because I couldn't think clearly with all the screaming.

"So, when you took her outside the parish today?"

Joshua darted a glance between his sister and me. Finally turning back, he admitted, "I was planning on

329

walking her all the way here, if need be. I couldn't let Elijah poison her anymore. He would have killed her eventually."

"He wasn't poisoning me," Sedra argued, tears still spilling from her eyes. Joshua turned to look at her with pure remorse written into the expression on his face.

"Yes, sister, he was. Those teas he was giving you weren't to make you better. They were meant to mess up your head. He didn't want you to remember what happened at the parish when you were with Jacob. You were beginning to understand that there were two different men that looked the same and Elijah couldn't have that. I knew about it. I was there when Elijah gave you the herbs to make you appear dead. He did that on purpose so that Jacob would run off and think you weren't alive. I was the one that carried you back to the compound. You have to try and remember."

Shaking her head, she bit her bottom lip, anger spilling across her features as she tilted her head up at me. "Elijah. Please tell me what he's talking about. Why are you letting him lie like this right in front of you?"

I dropped down on one knee so I could look directly in her face. "Joshua's not lying to you, Sedra. My name isn't Elijah. It's Jacob. Hell, even Elijah's name isn't Elijah. When we were young, he went by the name Jericho."

She spit in my direction. "I haven't done anything to deserve this! Why are you lying to me again! I've done everything you asked. You freed me of the last demon. Why are you doing this to me?"

Shaking my head, I knew there was nothing either one of us could say or do to convince her. She had to see it for herself. Had to see that there were two of us.

The only way to accomplish that would be to have her present while I confronted by brother, but I didn't like the thought of taking her along. Perhaps the benefits would outweigh the danger, because until she saw it, Sedra would always believe the lies he'd fed her while creating the perfect submissive.

"I'm sorry, Sedra. I really am. Not only for what my brother has done to you but for what I did to you myself. I took advantage and I lost control by being with you when you believed I was someone else. But I'm not taking advantage of you now. I'm ending this entire thing, once and for all. You'll understand some day. Or, at least I hope you will."

"She will," Joshua responded. "If I have to spend the rest of my life convincing her that she's been lied to, than that's what I'll do. I won't let her continue loving a man who only hurt her and used her."

In truth, he could have been talking about both Elijah and me. It had been wrong of me to have sex with her. It was wrong of me now to still want her despite everything that happened. But I couldn't help it. There was just something about her that called out to the darkness inside me that begged to devour her.

"I'm sorry," I said again before forcing myself to my feet.

Pacing the floor of the cabin, I thought about the stash of guns and ammo I had stored in the truck. It would have been enough for the bastards at the compound, but now that I knew the Sherriff was under Elijah's thumb, how the fuck was I going to compete against that? After they discovered that Sedra was missing, he'd have every deputy out looking for me with the specific instruction to gun me down on sight. I had to take some time to think of a plan that would not only bring an end to my brother's cult, but also keep Sedra and her brother out of harm's way. I couldn't blame the guy for having been fooled by Elijah for such a long time and I was thankful to God and everything holy that he'd seen the truth before I'd arrived.

"We need to figure out what to do," I finally said. "We can't just take off and leave the town to Elijah. After seeing what he did to those children today, I know he'll end up killing them all."

Joshua nodded his head in understanding. "But how? He has everybody believing that they're fighting some holy war against demons. The entire town, Jacob. There's no way the two of us can take that on and hope to win. The compound alone has a small arsenal and every one of the men know how to use those guns. I say we just take off and hope for the best."

My teeth ground together as I thought up a plan of attack. Elijah may have the county sheriff on his side, but that didn't mean he had influence over the state police or the federal authorities. I could call in the fucking Army if that's what it would take to bring the son of bitch down.

On my way into town, I'd bought a cheap cell phone just in case I needed to get in touch with anybody outside of the state. Thankful for having thought to do so, I realized there was one person I could call for help, somebody with enough influence to make people in power realize they had one hell of a problem on their hands.

Stepping toward the door, I turned back to Joshua before running outside. "Do me a favor and keep Sedra inside. I think I know who I can call to help."

Stepping outside, I closed the door behind me and marched to my truck to retrieve the phone. I also grabbed a business card that was given to me before leaving the city.

Nobody would believe me if I went to the cops and told them about a town that had turned into a cult, but I knew that if the right person called with enough influence and money, the state authorities would be sent out to raid the compound.

Dialing the number, I brought the phone to my ear and prayed someone would answer. When it stopped ringing and a familiar voice spoke, I felt some of the tension drain from my body.

"Father Timothy. This is Jacob Hayle. We need to talk."

35

ELIJAH

I arrived at the compound about to explode from the rage that was a seething, rolling inferno inside me. Who the fuck thought they had the right to take Eve away from the parish without me? What son of a bitch was going to die for daring to touch something that was mine? I hoped it was one of the women, hoped like hell it hadn't been some stupid brother that thought Eve could be touched by another male hand, but when I walked inside and questioned the family, they all looked at me with confusion behind their expressions, not one of them knowing where my wife had gone.

Richard had already walked the young girl to the cabin to assist her in the exorcism of the demon, so I was left alone to wander the compound and come to one conclusion. It wasn't just Eve that was missing, I hadn't seen hide nor hair of her brother, Joshua, either.

Winding my way through the empty halls, I was in route to the men's section with thoughts of murder echoing in my head. That stupid little fuck couldn't possibly have made it far with Eve. I knew my wife well enough to know she would fight him the entire way as soon as she realized he wasn't bringing her back. Joshua didn't have a car, didn't even know how to drive one if he did, so the only way he could escape would be on foot. He would have no clue where he was going either. I'd ensured that by keeping the family at the compound rather than allow them to travel freely around the county. I would find that son of a bitch and I would drag him back here by his damn eyelids so that he could answer for daring to act against me.

Reaching his small bedroom, I opened the door and looked around at the bare minimum furnishings. A simple bed, a cross on the wall, a stack of clothes all the same style and color that the entire family wore. There was nothing out of place, nothing surprising, but that didn't stop me from tearing the room apart. After going through everything that was out in the open, I flipped his mattress of the bed and found the Bible that lay beneath.

My eyes locked on the book as every curse word I knew flew from my lips. Snatching it from the hidden place he'd kept it tucked, I flipped through the pages to find small notes written into the margins, notes that revealed that by reading these words, Joshua had figured out that everything I'd taught had been bullshit intended to elicit fear and judgment.

More fury arced through me, the sudden influx painful and barely contained. I wanted to break every fucking thing in this room just to release some of the anger I was feeling. Doing so would only draw the attention of the family, and I couldn't afford for them to see me lose control. Pacing with the Bible in my hands, I took steadying breaths in an attempt to figure out how I would get my wife back and bring Joshua to his knees.

A thought chased through my mind, just the merest whisper, that perhaps Joshua hadn't been alone. And when that little tidbit began speaking louder, I realized quickly that I had to find my wife and end this bullshit before everything I'd worked for was ruined.

Dropping the Bible to the floor, I kicked it so hard that it bounced off the walls, some of the pages fluttering as they tore away from the bindings. Setting off down the hall, I ignored the family members that I shoved out of my way and slammed the door to my office when I was alone inside. I picked up the handset of the phone so quickly that the cradle fell from the desk and crashed to the floor.

The phone on the other side rang only a few times before a gruff voice answered, surprised that I'd called before our nightly meeting.

"Father Hayle," Sheriff Holmes answered, "why are you calling?"

"We have a problem, James. How big of one, I'm not sure, but it needs your immediate attention."

Grunting into the phone, he must have been moving around to get to a quieter place. Behind him I could hear the voices of police officers and secretaries, the typical clitter clatter of an office space as people bustled about their duties on their computers and others machines. A door clicked closed and his end went silent except his deep baritone voice speaking through the receiver.

"What kind of problem?"

"My wife is missing. Eve, the woman I cleansed so that I could marry her. You know who I'm talking about."

337

He didn't answer immediately, but eventually the deep drawl of his voice refilled the line. "Do you know where she might have gone?"

Shaking my head, I realized he couldn't see me. I started pacing the floor of the office, not giving a damn that the cradle of the phone was dragging along on the ground behind me. "I have no clue. I know that her brother, Joshua is also missing. I also suspect they had help. Neither of them could have made it far on foot without being noticed."

More silence fell between us before he asked another question. "What kind of help do you think they had? Are we talking normal shit or something spiritual?"

A bark of laughter burst from my lips but there wasn't anything funny about that sound. "Remember when I told you about my twin brother, Jericho, the evil son of a bitch that tried to pretend like he was me when we were kids? He may have found me, James, and if so, if he has been watching, then he knows that Eve is my wife. I fear for her safety and her purity if that evil asshole got his hands on her. I need every man you have out looking for my wife. And if you find Joshua or even my brother, you need to tell your men to bring them to me alive. I'll stay at the compound so there's no confusion. It's like I told you before, he's not just my brother, he's my identical twin. If he's with them, I'm sure they could walk down the street without anybody blinking an eye or knowing the difference."

James breathed out heavily. "I'll put the men on it that I can afford to lose right now. I can't make it too apparent that I'm working with you at the compound. You know that. I can turn a blind eye, Father Hayle, and I helped convince the town that what you're doing is necessary when faced with the kind of evil we're battling, but I'm not immune to the County's regulations either. The men I bring you aren't recorded as having been arrested and I don't need some curious son of a bitch lifting rocks and figuring out that I've been doing things under their nose. You get me? I have a few men I can trust and they know this county inside and out. If anybody is going to find your wife, it'll be them. Hopefully, they haven't gotten far."

My hand clenched around the phone and I had to bite my tongue to keep from screaming. "Thank you, James," I spat out, "I appreciate the kindness. I don't want any harm coming to my wife, and you and I both know this is the evil striking back at us. We have those fucking demons on the run and now they're out to get both of us. If I were you, I'd worry about the women in your household as well. You may want to tell them to go over to your brother's until you can get home to protect them. Don't forget about what happened to the nuns only a few months ago. We wouldn't want the same fate to fall on your wife or daughters."

James bit out a curse. "Yeah, I hear what you're saying. I'll send the men out now, and I'll tell my family to get over to Gentry's. Thanks for the warning, Father. I'll let you know when my men have located Eve and her brother."

The line went dead and I dropped the handset of the phone to the ground, kicking it against the wall much like I had the Bible in Joshua's room. Those slimy sons of bitches better find my wife before I completely lose it and fly off the fucking handle.

36

JACOB

"No, you can't get the sheriff involved in this, Agent Ross. He's part of the fucking problem!"

Twenty-four hours. That's how long it took for Father Timothy to contact the Diocese, convince them there was a madman who could expose the hidden crimes of the Catholic Church, and have them get in touch with people even higher up the food chain to send a federal agent to the small cabin where I was hiding with Joshua and Sedra. The agent had brought a team ready to storm the gates of Jericho's compound, he was sent to investigate first, but after speaking with Sedra and discovering how brainwashed the poor woman was, he spoke with Joshua and found out exactly what was going on inside the walls of a building that Jericho had managed for over twelve years.

The agent, with his tawny brown hair and shrewd amber eyes, squinted against the sunlight pouring through the thick branches of trees above us. Dressed in simple khakis and a black button up shirt, he didn't draw attention to himself like most agents would. He was familiar with the rural areas in the mountains and had located the roads leading to the hunting cabin rather quickly. He drove a truck that was more beat down than mine, and I was thankful to him for hiding his identity when I knew the sheriff was most likely watching. By now, Jericho knew that Sedra was missing and I was sure he'd set out an entire army to claim her and bring her back to the compound.

Reaching up to rub at the back of his neck, the agent stared at me with disbelief obvious behind his eyes. It wasn't that he didn't believe what he'd learned about Jericho and the happenings inside the small town, it was just that he'd reacted like any person would to find out people were being crucified on crosses like we were back in Biblical times.

"You have to understand my shock in all this, Jacob. That's a lot of crazy shit to digest. As far as I knew, nothing happened around this area except for the occasional theft of somebody's hunting dog, or perhaps an argument over zoning boundaries. It's not too often a person finds out that a cult has been operating directly under their noses for twelve fucking years. And then to hear about what he's doing to people? To learn that the sheriff is helping him? Jesus Fucking Christ! What kind of insanity is this?"

Pacing out a few steps, he turned back to stare at me. "You know, if the Church itself hadn't contacted the Bureau, there would have been no way in hell that we believed it. Sure, we may have made a drive-by, but left it at that. Now we've got the Catholic Church breathing down our necks threatening all sorts of hell if this isn't handled quietly."

Quietly certainly wasn't going to happen. Not with my brother. By the time this was all over and done

342

with, I was sure this particular problem would be labeled another Waco. Bringing down that cult had spurred national attention, thousands of citizens crying out in anger over the deaths of women and innocent children just because some whackjob had decided he wanted to run a cult.

I hoped it wouldn't come to that with Jericho, hoped there was a way we could get all the innocent family members out and also save my brother. I didn't want him killed, only locked away where he couldn't hurt another person. I was sure that deep down inside, he was still the same brother I'd known before those assholes changed him into a monster.

"So, how do we go about doing this?" I asked, hoping like hell this guy could come up with a decent plan because I was running on empty.

Unable to get out and buy food or water, the three of us had stayed in the cabin until the agent was able to bring some with him. I'd snatched a water bottle for myself, but had given the rest to Sedra and Joshua. Who knew how long it had been since either of them had been allowed to eat something nutritious? I remembered the dietary requirements Sedra had told me about during the first nights she'd spent with me at the parish. It didn't matter much to me if they ate every last bite. My stomach was churning so hard with apprehension that I wouldn't have been able to keep the food down regardless.

He sighed before scrubbing his palm over his face. "I think we'll need to get the state police involved. I'll explain that local law enforcement is involved and needs to be kept out of the loop. If they're killing people like you say they are, then we need to get in there tonight in hopes of saving whoever else they have ready to go up on those crosses."

Wincing at the thought of the horrible deaths being delivered to the people dragged into the compound, the agent breathed out heavily and turned his face to the sky. "You know, I'm a faithful man, always have been. It's hard being born and raised in this part of the country and not having Christian values shoved down your throat, but I never imagined an entire town of people could be led so far astray as to believe anything like this is right. These are good people. Hardworking people. Faithful people. But to hear about this? To know they're involved?" He shook his head. "None of it makes sense."

Stepping toward him, I tried to refocus his thoughts on the solution to the problem and not how Jericho had managed to brainwash an entire town. "Can you have a team out there tonight? How long will it take you to bring all of this together so you can get in there and rescue those people?"

He frowned. "Normally an operation like this takes weeks or months to put together. But with the Church breathing down our necks and with the possibility that a damn war could break out if your twin decides he's angry about his wife disappearing, we need to move faster. I'll have some agents come into town. Prepare them for what's to come and I'll have the state police ready to go. There's a chance we can have this ready for tonight." He stopped then, his feet going still over the dead leaves he was crushing with each step. Turning to me, he narrowed his eyes. "Why are you asking that question, anyway?"

Crossing my arms over my chest, I shot a look toward the cabin. "I have no supplies where I am, and

I'm sure my truck will be easily recognized if I drive down the roads. I can survive out here on nothing if I have to, but Sedra and Joshua need food and water. I can't keep them here for long with nothing to eat or drink."

He shrugged, not in an effort to dismiss what I'd said, but more like my issue wasn't much of a problem. "I planned on taking the three of you with me. I can't fit you into the truck I'm driving right now, but I can come back with vehicle that will fit all of us. I wasn't going to let you spend another night out here without some kind of protection. If the sheriff is looking for you, I'm sure he's been instructed to kill you on sight and dump the body. That's not going to happen under my watch."

Kicking at an errant stone on the ground near my foot, I confessed that I had another idea. "I wasn't planning on staying here. As soon as you can get Sedra and Joshua to a safe place, I was planning on heading to the compound."

The agent's eyes rounded into saucers. "Like hell you are. Are you fucking crazy?"

I locked my gaze to his. "Maybe I am, but it's doubtful my brother has told the family about me, and we're identical twins. There's a good chance I can sneak into the compound without Jericho knowing I'm there. Especially if he's out searching for Sedra and Joshua. The members won't know he has a twin. They'll let me in as soon as I approach the gates."

"And what good will that do?"

Smiling, I answered, "That means you'll have someone on the inside who can open the gates for you. If your team can get in without a gunfight just to enter, there's a chance we can keep this quiet." Growing

345

quiet, I chewed on the inside of my lip before admitting, "and if it's at all possible, I'd like the chance to save my brother's life. He's crazy. I know that. But that still doesn't mean he needs to be put down like some kind of animal."

The agent frowned, pacing a few more steps before turning to look at me. "Listen, I think what you're suggesting is fucking insane, but you're a free man and I can't stop you. You don't have to get in my car when I come to pick up those two inside. You hear me? You can go off and do whatever crazy thing you want to do, but it will be without my immediate protection." Pausing he squinted against the sun again before wiping the beads of sweat from his brow. "But, I'm telling you now, Jacob, you'd better not breathe a word of this to your brother. Doing so would only mean that more people inside that compound will die."

My expression softened, my heart beating with the truth of his words. "I know. I won't say a damn thing. I'll just make sure I'm inside and can open the gates when you need me to."

I started to walk off toward the cabin when it was clear our conversation was over. Before I could reach the door, he called out to me.

"Hey, how will we be able to tell the two of you apart? Didn't you say you're identical?"

I'd given that question a lot of thought after leaving the Appalachians and returning back to the city where'd I'd been raised. Fortunately for me, buying the guns had been the perfect answer. I found it funny that I hadn't thought of it long before I'd pressed my fingers against the inkpad on the counter and left the marks on a piece of paper that would tell Jericho and I apart.

"I purchased a shit ton of guns and ammunition before coming back here. I won't lie. I'd intended to deal with my brother myself in this hopes that I could save him and keep him out of trouble. I'll give you the receipt from the gun shop where I bought everything and you'll know where you can find a copy of my fingerprints to use to tell us apart. It'll be the only way. Everything else about us is the same."

The agent's expression twisted with hidden knowledge, an unspoken understanding between two men that even he didn't want to voice into the silence of the forest.

"You try to stay alive in there, you hear me? You seem like a good man with a good head on your shoulders. Dying to save your brother isn't the way a former priest should leave this world."

Inclining my head, I smiled. "I helped create the monster my brother became with my silence about our father. If I deserve anything, it's to die by his side as a way to tell him I'm sorry."

The agent shook his head and cursed under his breath, but he didn't attempt to argue. "Stay here until I get back to pick up your friends. After that, I hope I see you alive again once all of this is said and done."

He stalked off and I watched him disappear through the woods on the way back to where his truck was parked. I wasn't sure what I would do once I entered the compound, but I knew that if it was time for my brother to die, I would be the one to end him.

Jericho was a monster. He did horrible things to other people. But could you really blame a man for losing his mind when everybody he'd ever trusted had used him and hurt him so badly?

If nothing else, I could give my brother a compassionate ending, even if his beginning had been nothing short of a living nightmare.

37

ELIJAH

A full day.

It had been one full day that James or his men couldn't seem to find one small woman and the brother that had taken her from the parish. How incompetent did you have to be to allow two people I'd intentionally kept stupid and unable to care for themselves slip through your damn grasp?

I would have gone out in search of them myself, but I didn't want to cause confusion by my presence. At this point I wasn't sure whether Jacob had anything to do with their disappearance, but I wouldn't put it past him. A smile slithered over my lips as I remembered the pure pain that was written across his face on the day he believed he'd killed Eve. I wondered how long it had been since he returned to find out the woman he'd spent an entire week loving had actually been alive and in my bed.

The realization must have killed him – at least, that was, if he was involved in her abduction. It wasn't like Jacob to sneak around. That was more my style than his. No, my brother was the type to march right up to the compound gates to make his demands known.

Sometimes I had to wonder about the way the universe worked, the odd coincidences that occur leaving many to believe there's a holy figure upstairs - a giant puppet master deciding our fates and pulling our strings.

It hadn't been very long between the time I thought about Jacob and the time Richard walked in, his gut protruding over his large belt buckle and a shit eating grin on his face. "We've got company."

My head snapped up from where it had been angled down to study an errant scratch running over the surface of my desk. "What do you mean? Did the sheriff find Eve and Joshua?"

Shaking his head, Richard barked out a laugh. "No. But your twin brother is at the gates pretending to be you and asking to be let in. Shane came and grabbed me. He was confused because he thought you were inside with the rest of the family."

Lips stretching into a feral grin, I practically growled out my response. "Well, now, it would be rude of us to keep my brother waiting. You run back there and let Shane know to open those gates and let Jacob inside. He wouldn't happen to have my wife with him, would he?"

Shaking his head, Richard frowned. "No. Eve is nowhere in sight. If he has her, he's got her stashed somewhere."

"That's just fine," I drawled, "We'll see what the bastard came here for and then give him no other choice but to give her up. He can't keep her hidden forever. Not with the methods we have to make people talk. Run along, Richard and let him in. I'll be waiting in the sanctuary."

Richard lumbered out, the weighted pounding of his boot steps dying off as he walked farther away. When silence returned to the office, I leaned back in my chair and sighed. I'd never figured my brother to be a stupid man, but in this, he was practically signing his death warrant.

Wondering if he had Eve, I decided that there wasn't any other way to find out than to ask him. And I knew exactly the place I wanted to question him, exactly the sight that would throw him off guard because even he had never been so evil.

Pushing out of my chair, I rounded the desk and was out the door on three long strides. I meandered my way through the halls of the compound, finally bursting through a door to enter the sanctuary, thankful that Jacob hadn't yet been led inside. Taking a position by the altar, I leaned back against the wooden wall of the pulpit and clasped my hands together in front of my body. My eyes had just shifted up to look at the dying man on the cross, his hands practically ripped through for how long he'd been hanging, when I heard a commotion in the front hallway. One of the double doors swung open and Richard walked through dragging a pissed off looking Jacob behind him.

I knew the minute my brother saw the man hanging on the cross. His face lost all its color and he fell to his knees staring up at a symbol that for so many centuries had belonged to the faithful.

"What do you think of my sanctuary, brother? Is it everything you imagined and more? I fashioned it to look like our old parish back home with all the glittering golds and jewel encrusted treasures. Unlike the parish, however, my jewels aren't real. But I have something they didn't. I have the living embodiment of

351

the dying Christ, a thief and a liar looking down on us like he didn't deserve what happened to him.

Dumping Jacob in the center aisle, Richard stood back and looked to me for his next instruction. Knowing that this conversation was intended for brothers, I jut my chin in the direction of the doors and said, "You can go do whatever it is you need to do, Richard. I can handle my brother all by myself. Stay close, though. If I need something, I'll be sure to let you know."

Inclining his head, Richard stalked off. I knew he wouldn't go far and I assumed that was a good thing in case this conversation with my brother didn't go as well as I hoped. Pushing off from the pulpit, I moved around the altar to step down into the center aisle and walk toward my brother.

Unlike when he'd been a priest, he was dressed in a plain pair of jeans and a black t-shirt. I thought it suited him better than the stuffy black clothes and clerical collar that he'd always worn when he lived at the parish.

He didn't get up from where he'd been dumped on the floor and upon closer examination, I could see that Richard roughed him up some while bringing him inside the compound. Kneeling down, I reached out to grip his chin between my fingers and bring his eyes level with mine.

"You mind telling me why you decided to return to town after all I did to warn you off? You're not a dumb person, Jacob. I know you better than that. Were you just feeling like dying, but couldn't bring yourself to commit suicide? Don't tell me after everything that's happened, you're still the devout Catholic boy who believes any of the religious bullshit."

His eyes searched mine and it was like looking into a mirror. Even after all these years, Jacob and I hadn't changed much except in lifestyles, but then again, he hadn't lived through what I'd lived through. He'd only been witness to parts of it.

"I came back after returning home, Jericho. After visiting our former parish and the old family home. I discovered a few things and decided to come and talk to you about what I found out. I know why you hate me now. And I wanted to apologize."

Breathing in, I held the breath for a few seconds before letting it out slowly. It didn't take a genius to figure out what secrets he may have discovered. I just found the timing of his arrival suspect. "This wouldn't have anything to do with Eve, would it? You wouldn't happen to know where she is, would you?"

His brows pulled together with confusion. I didn't buy the expression for a second. Like me, Jacob could play any part he wanted to play just as long as it got him what he wanted.

"I assume she's buried wherever you put her. And no, this has nothing to do with Eve. This has to do with our father's confession and what I found out about the abuse you suffered at the parish."

Leaning back on my heels, I stared down at him. He wasn't lying about what he'd discovered, and I was a little surprised he'd taken the time to go back home. However, hearing there had been a confession from our father was surprising. I hadn't exactly given him time to go running to a priest before I'd shoved him down the stairs.

"A confession? I didn't know dad had it in him. Tell me, what did this confession say?"

353

He reached for his back pocket, and I allowed him the slow movement knowing full well that if he had any weapons on him when entering the compound, Richard would have stripped them away.

Pulling a folded piece of paper from his pocket, he handed it to me and said, "Maybe you should read it for yourself."

Taking the paper, I toyed with the edge of it, noticing that it was old and thin. I had no interest in reading a damn word of what my father had written in order to clear his conscious before death. "Why don't you just give me a summary? As I'm sure you know, I have no happy feelings toward dear old dad."

Jacob frowned, the corners of his lips turning down into a steep shape of disapproval. "You may feel differently if you read the note. It might surprise you to discover what he did in the end."

Laughter tumbled out of my lungs. "I know what he did in the end, Jacob. He screamed while falling down a flight of stairs. His last seconds on this Earth were spent staring up at the son who had shoved him down those stairs and wouldn't move a muscle to help him as he lay there slowly dying."

Blinking at the confession, Jacob didn't seem surprised to hear it. "I was told after returning home that it was possible dad hadn't died from natural causes."

"Well, now you know," I grinned, the expression not quite reaching my eyes. "What does the confession say, Jacob?"

Crumpling the paper in my fist, I made it clear I had no intention of reading it.

Jacob's gaze followed the movement of my hand before returning to my face. It felt like I was staring at a mirror, the image reflecting back one that I wanted to shatter beneath my fist.

Swallowing down whatever lump had clogged his throat, Jacob shifted his weight over the floor until he was fully seated. He swallowed again. "I think you should read it. The impact won't be the same coming from me."

Rolling my eyes, I was tired of the drama and mystery. "Where's my wife?"

His eyes snapped up to mine. "Your what?"

I knelt down, a smile stretching my lips to see him struggling to play the role of a stupid man. "My wife," I said again. "You may remember her. A pretty little brown haired woman named Eve."

There was shock in his eyes at my admission, but I didn't believe it was genuine.

"Eve's alive?" he asked, true confusion in his deep voice. "How is that even possible?"

My eyebrow cocked. "Would you believe I lied?"

He didn't appreciate the humor rolling through my voice. The anger coloring his skin was surprising. And in that surprise, I started to believe he truly didn't know that Eve was still among the living.

The realization only pissed me off more. If it wasn't Jacob who helped Joshua take her from under my nose, then who?

Staring at my twin brother, I paused for a moment before asking, "You really don't know. Do you?"

He shook his head. "No, Jericho. Not until now. My only reason for coming here was to give you that confession."

38

JACOB

Disbelief had shadowed Jericho's expression when I first lied and claimed I didn't know Eve was still alive. However, after a few minutes of me clinging to that lie like it was a lifeboat saving me from the waves of a churning sea, he settled back on his heels and studied me, belief finally settling behind the crystal blue of his insane gaze.

I knew my brother had lost his mind, knew that evil filled him so completely that there was no room left in his heart for compassion or humanity, but I hadn't realized until truly looking at him how deep his insanity was engrained.

Lips moving slowly over words spoken carefully, Jericho asked, "What is it about an old man's confession that you think I need to read for myself? I just told you I killed him. Do you think I give a damn about anything he had to say?"

My eyes darted to where our father's confession lay crumpled on the floor of this sanctuary. Trying not to think of the body hanging above me in some sacrilegious display, I angled my head toward that piece of paper and said, "You should read it, Jericho. Before you lose the opportunity to know the truth."

If you stared hard enough, you could see the gears grinding in his head, the back and forth of indecision. He wanted to know. Of that I was sure, but he was having difficulty admitting it to himself. It doesn't matter how evil a parent has been to a child, there is always a small part of the adult the child becomes that mourns never having the approval of the person that created them.

At least, for me, it was true. Perhaps Jericho's madness had separated him so much from the past that everything had become meaningless.

Finding it difficult to remain calm when I knew there was little time for him to read the confession, I remained perfectly still, perfectly quiet in hopes it would spur his hand to reach for the crumpled paper. No matter what happened once the police arrived, whether Jericho was killed or captured, I wanted him to know that our father's guilt had made his final acts in life a gift to his son rather than the God for which he'd always beaten us.

Jericho finally relented and snatched the paper from the floor. Quickly smoothing it out, his eyes moved as he read the first few lines, his brows pulling together in confusion before shooting up his forehead in shock.

"This can't be true," he muttered. "He would have never done this."

"He did," I answered. "I confirmed it with the priest who currently leads our former parish. Our father killed, Jericho. After you were expelled from the parish and left home, our father went out in search of the music director and priest that hurt you. I didn't believe it myself, so I made the current priest search for them. I thought it must have been madness on his part. I didn't believe he would stain his soul with murder before he died. But, he did. Both of those men died under suspicious circumstances. The priest confirmed it."

Jericho dropped the paper, anger rolling behind his eyes that only led to more madness. Standing up, he paced in front of me, his mouth opening and closing several times before he finally stopped his movement and pivoted to stare down at me.

"Even this is beneath you, Jacob. You can't possibly believe I'd fall for this. Coming in here like you're delivering me some gift. Did you think it would stop me? Did you think it would make me fucking care about what I am doing to your insolent little town? What I'm doing has nothing to do with our father and everything to do with the fucking RELIGION that led to the abuse I suffered!"

Kicking at my leg, he caught my ankle so hard, the bone snapped. My mouth opened as a howling scream tore from my throat, the pain so intense that the room spun around me before once again coming to stop. Bending over, I reached to grab the ankle, but Jericho reached for it faster. Pulling me by it down the aisle, he relied on the pain to keep me from fighting against him. I was dragged over the floor toward the crosses, Jericho's lips pursing as a shrill whistle blew over them. A door behind us opened and closed, the rumble of heavy steps approaching.

How that confession had angered Jericho, I wasn't sure, but to look in his eyes now, I only saw hatred and death.

Dropping me when we reached the crosses, he stomped me in the chest with his boot fracturing several ribs. Again the pain consumed me, my mouth opening wide as I tried to breathe past it.

Turning to the man who approached us, Jericho demanded, "Help me bring down the second cross. It seems like we have another demon that needs to be eradicated."

My eyes widened, my head shaking in disbelief. "Jericho –"

"The name is Elijah, brother! It would be best for you if you learned that. Jericho hasn't existed since the moment he was raped in the parish as a small boy. He hasn't existed since OUR FATHER refused to believe him when he finally confessed what was being done to him. Jericho died in that fucking parish and nothing you say or do will bring him back to life."

His boot slammed against my abdomen, several hard kicks knocking the breath from my lungs. Walking away to bring down the cross that stood above my head, he left me in place struggling to breathe again.

By the time they'd brought down the cross to lay on the floor behind me, I was breathing again, but not without difficulty. Rounding my feet, Jericho knelt down to look me in the eye, his face red in color from his fury.

"Now that I have you here, Jacob, why don't you tell me what you've done with my wife? Do you think I'm so stupid that I don't see the coincidence that you reappear in town and she's suddenly missing? You took me for a stupid son of a bitch when we were children and even as teens. Let me follow you around like a little lost fucking puppy while you enjoyed

360

breaking women and teaching me how to do it. But I'm not that fucking puppy anymore and I don't believe a fucking word that comes out of your mouth, so I'm giving you one chance to fess up and tell me where I can find Eve."

I coughed up blood before trying to speak again. Barely able to move, I stared at the face of my brother, my thoughts racing with what I could say to stop him from doing whatever it was he planned to do. "I don't know what you're talking about," I lied.

His expression twisted with feigned remorse. "That's too bad, Jacob. And here I thought you would have become a smarter man after leaving the Church. But just like the rest of the fucks who called themselves holy, the only thing you know how to do is lie."

Jericho looked up and within seconds I felt the other man grab me by the arms to drag me backwards and over the surface of the cross. I attempted to fight back, tried to roll both directions in hopes that I would evade them. But, the pain locked me in place, and each time I attempted to move, the man's fist came down to slam against my face. For a minute, the room went black before coming into soft focus, my consciousness fading.

My brother slapped at my face. "Careful, brother, I wouldn't want you falling asleep during this process. It wouldn't be as much fun."

The two men held me over the cross, the one positioning my feet together over the rough surface of the wood while Jericho removed my shoes and socks. Once bare to the skin, Jericho placed a large nail above the skin, holding a hammer with his other hand, ready to pound the metal into my feet.

"Last chance, Jacob. Tell me where my wife is."

361

I didn't want to give away the fact that the police now had Eve. To do so would be to warn him that his game was done, the violence and evil he'd spread across this rural town coming to an end. There was nothing I could do to stop him, nothing I could say that would appease him. All I could do was buy time.

"Fine," I answered, "I'll tell you."

His hand clenched tighter over the handle of the hammer, his eyes locking to mine with the promise of pain if I didn't tell him where he could find the woman he'd abused for so long.

"She's at the parish. I took her back there after you came here. She's in the bedroom…waiting."

His lips quirked into a grin. "That was, by far, the worst lie you've ever told."

The hammer came down on the head of the nail, the metal piercing my skin as it was driven through the bone. The scream that tore from my lips was inhuman, pure pain pouring out of me because my body was helpless to contain it. After the first smack of the hammer against the nail head, Jericho held the hammer again over his shoulder, ready and willing to drive the nail further after whatever it was he had to say next.

"Did you want to tell me the truth now, or are you going to continue lying like all the other assholes who call themselves Christian?"

My heart broke for Jericho in that moment. Despite what he was doing to me, despite the blinding pain, I still found it within myself to feel compassion for my brother. Perhaps this had all been my fault for not standing up for him against my father. Perhaps I deserved this for not noticing the pain and torture he'd endured while those sick men used his small body for their own twisted desires.

Perhaps this was my absolution for never giving enough of a damn to look for him after I left college. If I hadn't been so concerned with my own sins, could I have prevented Jericho from slipping into madness?

Spitting out more blood, I stared my brother in the eye. If I was going to die today, I wanted to cleanse the wounds of my soul, wanted to confess to him how I had failed him.

It's true I'd never been a good man – a good brother. I'd surrendered to the darkness more times that I could count, and for that I knew I'd pay eternally. But to carry these secrets to my grave would be a mistake I wasn't willing to make. I'd failed Jericho in our youth. I'd failed him after we'd grown into adulthood. But I wouldn't fail him in this final moment.

"I'm sorry, Jericho. I truly am. I never should have abandoned you."

The hammer swung down, the nail being driven farther into my foot. I screamed again, the room spinning around me as the pain consumed my entire body. Like the savior who had died for us so many centuries ago, I endured that pain while allowing love to fill my heart for the man who was inflicting it.

Barely able to talk around the agony inside me, I forced the words out regardless. "I never should have stood by while he hurt you. I should have made our mother do something – anything – to stop his abuse. I failed, Jericho, and I'm sorry. I love you."

The hammer came down again, the nail now being driven through the bottoms of my feet into the wood. The pain was blinding, the room going in and out of focus, my stomach heaving as my body attempted to expel the force of the torment.

How ironic it was that in this moment I learned my faith was still a part of me.

Closing my eyes, I opened them again, my throat torn apart by the volume of my screaming. I was losing the ability to think, much less speak, so I repeated the only four words that had any meaning.

"I love you, brother."

"Shut up!" he screamed, bringing the hammer down one more time. The nail embedded the wood.

Blood leaked from the side of my mouth where my teeth had cut into my tongue. It dripped down my skin as quickly as the blood dripping from my feet. I was swimming in pure suffering, lost to the cruelty of a man gone mad. Even then, I wouldn't stop trying to make him hear me.

"I love you," I whispered, knowing full well they would be the last words to ever leave my tongue.

The words meant nothing to my twin. He brought the hammer down several more times until the nail was firmly embedded into the wood, my feet splitting apart as the bones were crushed. I couldn't speak anymore, couldn't think past the pain that consumed me. Realizing that I wouldn't tell him where his wife was hidden, Jericho lost his patience.

"His hands," he said, although, to me, the words sounded like they were coming from a deep tunnel. I felt my left wrist grabbed by the man holding me down, felt it pressed to the crossbeam. Jericho positioned the nail where he intended to drive it through, but then light flashed so brightly that it drew their attention away from me.

I existed inside that light for a moment, not understanding what it was, but believing that perhaps it was the beginning of death. My spirit soared as I felt warmth spread over me stealing the pain away and replacing it with comforting numbness. There was peace in the loss of sensation, peace that was lost as soon as I was returned to the present.

Voices shouted around me, a team of bodies moving through the room. So blinded by the pain inside me, I couldn't make out one voice from another, didn't understand that the compound was being raided around me.

"Jericho Hayle," a voice called out, drawing my attention to the right. Blinking my eyes I attempted to bring the men into focus. "Put up your hands and surrender now."

My brother looked at the men with their guns trained on his chest and head before darting his gaze to me. There was nothing left inside him, no soul that gazed out from behind his blue eyes. Even still, I wanted him to surrender, to live despite all the horrible things that had been done to him, and that he had done to others.

But his hatred was too much.

He lunged for me at that second, his mouth opening on a scream as gunshots rang through the air, the bullets striking him in the back as his body fell on top of me. I felt the bullets, too, felt them pierce my arm, my hand, my shoulder.

As my twin brother lay motionless on top of me, I fought to keep the room in focus, fought against the pull of death that dragged me from consciousness. It was too strong, that pull, the light returning with serenity and warmth beckoning for me to release the spirit.

And for the first time in my life, I decided to do what I should have done all along:

Rather than walking away from my brother and failing him, I put my own life aside to join him.

EPILOGUE

SEDRA

"Are you sure you can do this, Sedra? It's only been a few weeks since you left the hospital. You should take some time before –"

Placing a hand over my older brother's mouth, I smiled. Just as when we were kids, he still tried to protect me, still attempted to shelter me from the world that only wanted to devour me whole. But I was done being the helpless victim. Done being the scared little girl who couldn't walk out on her own to find the path that life had always intended for her.

I was a woman now, one who wasn't confused, wasn't scared and wasn't weak like Elijah had made me. I was healed finally, all because of a man who had pulled me from the clutches of evil and delivered me into the arms of safety.

"I'm sure about this, Joshua. It's what mom and dad would have wanted if they weren't killed at the compound. They would have been standing right beside me if they had been given the chance to learn the truth about the man they'd followed blindly. I need to do this. If not for me, than for others like me."

It has been a year since I was taken from the parish by my brother, a year since I was rescued by a man who had failed in his vows as a priest and had fallen for the temptation that Elijah had molded me to become. After being dragged from the small hunting cabin on the final day I saw Jacob Hayle, I was taken to a hospital because I'd refused to believe that I'd been lied to. The first nights had been terrible and reminded me of Elijah's anger. They'd drugged me and strapped me to my bed, restrained me so that I would stop fighting against them. I remember believing that the demons had finally found me again, believing that my brother had forced me from the light into which my husband had led me.

But as the weeks wore on and I was force fed and given other medications so that my body would heal, eventually I succumbed to the treatment and began the therapy I'd so desperately needed to overcome the lies that had been forced inside my head.

Day after day, I fought against the truth that Elijah had lied to me, but now, sitting here after being discharged from the hospital and proclaimed a healthy woman, I found it difficult to look back and believe that I had so easily been misled.

Joshua had been the only one to visit me in the hospital, and it wasn't until he'd heard from the doctors that I was healing that he finally admitted to me what had happened to not only our family, but to the priest that had sacrificed himself in order to save me.

He told me about the fire that destroyed the compound, about the people who were trapped inside. He told me about the arrest of the town sheriff and the townspeople who had taken part in Elijah's cruelty. He explained that in the wake of Elijah's games, the news had spread like fire across the United States, the Church having to answer for all the evil committed by a mad man in its name.

It was hard to hear about what had been done to Elijah when he was a child, that he had turned around and hurt others because he wanted to bring to light the abuses that had been committed against him and covered up. And despite the Church not having anything to do with the injustice that had plagued the small Appalachian town, it still coughed up money to heal the victims that had survived.

I was one of those victims, my image and name spread across the media as a survival story and a warning. It didn't make me happy to become the poster child for what can happen when you are raised as a member of a cult.

Joshua sat back in his seat, but still kept his eyes on me, concern shadowing his gaze as he let out a loud sigh. "I don't think you should do this. I don't think it will be good for you, Sedra. You've worked so hard to leave the past behind you, seeing him will only remind you of what happened. It'll only hurt you in the end."

Smiling again, I reached out to stroke my fingers down my brother's cheek. In truth, I was terrified of what I would think or feel to see him again. But I agreed to take part in this conference if it meant I could prevent this type of thing from happening again. The media had made me a victim in their stories, and now I was ready to take that image and transform it into what it should have been.

I wasn't a victim, I was a survivor of every horrible cruelty that could be imagined.

"It wasn't his fault," I argued, shaking my head when Joshua's expression twisted in disagreement.

Nothing would convince my stubborn brother.

It had been religion that almost destroyed me, and faith that had helped me heal. The hospital to which I'd

369

been taken was run by a non-profit foundation that believed in faith healing as well as medicine. I'd learned that all the lessons Elijah had forced down our throats were twisted and construed in order to keep us afraid and alone. But in the year I'd spent learning the truth of the faith to which I'd always belonged, I'd seen the beauty in its message of love.

We weren't to condemn others so easily.

We weren't to be violent and wish for their death.

We were intended to find hope in the darkest places and to help others who also were lost.

And although the message had been perverted by a man who'd used it for pure evil, we were to forgive the acts committed against us so that, in the end, we could forgive ourselves.

I wanted to forgive, but my brother wasn't so sure. His stubbornness made me smile.

"I'm doing this, and if I don't get up now, I'm going to be late. You're welcome to come with me."

He shook his head. "I can't. I know I shouldn't feel like this, but I can't help worrying about you. Are you sure, Sedra? Are you positive you want to do this?"

"I'm sure," I said one last time before standing from my seat to walk to the doorway leading to the interview room. Casting one backwards glance at my brother, I smiled sweetly. Opening the door, I blinked against the harsh lights that illuminated the grouping of chairs that were arranged to be a small seating area for the interview to be conducted.

On furtive steps, I crossed the distance between the door and the seating area to take my seat. A few minutes later, a man walked through a door on the opposite side of the room, a pen tucked behind his ear and a notepad in hand. Laughing to myself, I thought of how he reminded me of the doctors that had spent countless hours convincing me that all the beliefs inside my head were only illusions put there by a madman.

There had been so many that it took months for me to return to using my own name.

Taking a seat in front of me, the man pulled the pen from behind his ear and scratched out a few lines on the pad in his lap. He smiled at me finally and said, "It'll be just a few minutes. We're waiting on the last of the attendees." He leaned forward and offered his hand. "Thank you for agreeing to this. I think it will be helpful for people to understand what happened to you. How something like that can happen in this day and age."

I nodded, my throat suddenly swollen with fear and indecision. With no choice but to push past it, I leaned back in my seat and waited.

Eventually another woman walked through the door that I didn't recognize. Petite and with pretty blond hair, she took a seat next to me. Turning, she offered me her hand. "I'm not sure if you remember me. My name is Molly Harrison. We only met a few times at the parish."

Shaking her hands, I tried not to stare at the scars crossing her face. Looking down, I noticed those same scars were white lines across the tops of her hands. Although, I didn't remember her from my time spent with Elijah, I did recognize Richard's handiwork. Thankfully, he had been shot dead when the police raided the compound.

My heart hammered in my chest as we waited for the last guest, the minutes dragging on until I felt like I would scream in frustration. I was so scared, but it wasn't something I would admit to Joshua before

371

coming into this room. He would have never allowed me to take part in this interview if I had.

But I needed to face my demons, the true ones and not the ones Elijah had sworn were consuming me. In the end, we all have something inside of us that can be considered evil or tainted, but it's what we decide to do with that part that matters.

Elijah had taught me to hate my own humanity, had convinced me that the dark parts of myself were only a symptom of the evil he believed plagued the world. But I knew now that what I had been taught was just another illusion, one that had led me further into darkness because I couldn't accept it existed.

I accepted it now, knew that to be human was to make mistakes, and that to find divinity, we only needed to believe that no matter what, we were perfect in both our light and our darkness.

A door popped open behind me, but I couldn't turn my head to look at it. I knew who had walked through and I wasn't sure how I would react to stare into that face.

The shuffle of shoes against the floor was punctuated by the hard thump of a cane. It felt like hours before a fourth body sat down in the seat beside me. Taking a breath, I turned and faced a man who was identical to the one who'd abused me.

It wasn't fear that clogged my throat to look at him, it was something else.

The reporter conducting the interview cleared his throat and said, "Thank you, Jacob, for agreeing to be here. I wasn't positive you'd actually show."

Although he was being spoken to, Jacob didn't release my stare. He simply nodded his head and continued looking at me with some unspoken thought

372

rolling behind his blue eyes. I, too, was caught in a state of shock, having to fight to pull my face away and return my attention to the reporter.

I won't bore you with all the details of the interview. You know what happened by now, but what I will tell you is that something came to life inside me on that stage, something I doubted could ever exist again without driving a spike of pure panic through my battered heart.

We were questioned about how each of us had been affected by Jericho Hayle. Jacob answered the questions regarding Jericho's past, about the abuse he'd suffered at the hands of his father and other men, about his intention to bring down the Church through the use of that small rural parish. He also filled in the parts about what happened in the compound when he'd been saved. Barely surviving the wounds inflicting, Jacob had been pulled from the compound before it caught fire. But due to the nails that had been driven through his feet, he would never walk unassisted again. Tears burst in my eyes when he admitted how even when Elijah hammered the nails in his feet, Jacob had only repeated that he loved him. And my heart warmed toward a man who admitted that despite what his brother had done, he'd still found it in his heart to forgive him.

I filled in the parts about life inside a cult, about the daily activities and the sermons that had been used to confuse us all.

While Molly spoke about her experiences within the small town, I dared a peek at Jacob who sat at my side, his head turning my direction as if he could feel my eyes studying him.

Warmth burst inside me that I hadn't felt for a long time. It caused my hands to shake and my lips to part open as I struggled to drag in a deep breath. His eyebrows drew together in concern, but he didn't speak or say anything to me about my reaction.

I remembered him in that instant, remembered the time I'd spent with him in the parish believing that he was my husband. He had been kind to me in that week, but I was still left with so many questions.

The interview concluded after several hours and we all got up from our seats to go our separate ways. But before I could take a step toward the room where I knew my brother was waiting, I felt a hand touch my shoulder, and heard a familiar voice asking me to wait.

Turning, I stared back at Jacob, my face a blank mask because I didn't know what I was feeling.

His eyes searched mine before he finally admitted why he'd stopped me from leaving.

"I wanted to apologize," he said, his voice deep and soft. "For lying to you. For taking advantage when you didn't even know your own name."

"I forgive you," I answered, and I meant it.

His smile stretched his face. Even though he looked identical to Elijah, somehow I felt that he was different. I thought it would hurt to see him again, thought it would throw me back into the mindframe of a helpless victim. But, in truth, seeing him only made me feel stronger. I'd survived a man who was truly wicked – one who'd hidden behind a mask of religion to hurt the people around him.

Nodding his head, Jacob began to walk away, but I couldn't let him. It was my turn to reach out and stop him in his path. Twisting around, he used the cane to slowly spin his body back to face me.

"I have a question," I said, a smile lighting my face.

His eyebrow arched, his eyes sparkling beneath the overhead lighting. "You have my attention."

It was as if none of the past had happened, like we were two strangers meeting again for the first time.

"Did you ever go back to the priesthood? Have you given your life back to the Church?"

Sorrow filled his eyes, his mouth pulling taut as he dragged in a deep breath. Finally blowing it out, he laughed softly and answered, "No. There's too much darkness inside of me still. But that doesn't mean I've lost faith."

Laughing at his answer, I reached out to run my fingers down his cheek. "Perhaps we can explore that darkness together. Now that I'm healed."

His expression betrayed his shock, his eyebrows shooting up his forehead as his eyes widened and then narrowed again. "You can't be serious."

What can I say? In all the therapy through the year since I'd left the family, there was still a large part of me that hadn't changed. I wanted to explore that part regardless of what anybody would say about it.

"I'm serious," I whispered, laughing again to see his face.

A smile split his lips when he answered, "We should do this the proper way."

Keeping one hand on the cane while extending the other, he said, "It's nice to meet you, Sedra. My name is Jacob Hayle."

Taking his hand, I enjoyed the warmth of his skin where it touched me. "It's nice to meet you, too, Jacob."

Walking from the room together, we entered the room where Joshua waited. My brother's eyes darted between Jacob and me, his breath rushing over his lips on a loud huff. But eventually, he stood to shake the hand of the man who'd saved us both.

The three of us walked from the building together, all of us changed, but still the same. And as we made our way down the sidewalk to find a restaurant to have dinner, I let go of the past to look toward the future and a life where I would finally be safe.

THE END

LILY WHITE
BESTSELLING AUTHOR

If you are interested in reading additional books by Lily White or would like to know when new books are being released, Lily White can be found on:
Facebook, Instagram and
Twitter

Join the Mailing List!
If you are interested in receiving email updates regarding additional books by Lily White or would like to know when new books are announced or being released, join the mailing list via this link.
http://eepurl.com/Onoeb

Join the Facebook Fan Group!
If you are interested in receiving exclusive previews for upcoming novels, or to participate in giveaways, join the fan group for Lily White Books.
FAN GROUP LINK

Follow Lily on BookBub!
https://www.bookbub.com/profile/lily-white